END OF THE ROADIE

Elizabeth Flynn

LION FICTION

Published by Lion Fiction
an imprint of
Lion Hudson plc
Wilkinson House, Jordan Hill Road
Oxford OX2 8DR, England
www.lionhudson.com/fiction

ISBN 978 1 78264 205 3
e-ISBN 978 1 78264 206 0

First edition 2016

A catalogue record for this book is available from the British Library

Printed and bound in the UK, July 2016, LH26

Chapter One

A buzz of excited, anticipatory conversation spread beyond the area immediately in front of the theatre. The huge crowd milled and flowed, joked and laughed and ordinary passers-by found themselves weaving and bobbing just to get wherever they wanted to go. The October evening's unseasonal warmth helped the conviviality along and every time the traffic lights caused a lull in the constant stream of vehicles another batch of concert-goers poured across the road to join the party. Several yards away, the Hammersmith flyover's huge underbelly partially blocked the view of a very pleasant evening sky.

Detective Constable Gary Houseman, in his polo shirt, cords and casual jacket had found a relatively clear space just inside one of the glass-paned front doors. He scanned the street outside, waiting to see a familiar head of chestnut hair bouncing through the crowds. Madeleine hadn't been sure exactly what time she would arrive. Still on probation in her new job, she didn't want to try for time off until she'd become a bit more used to the office protocol. A warm glow spread through Gary as he thought of her, imagined her crossing the road underneath the flyover looking out for him in the place where they'd agreed he would wait. Relief mingled with his anticipation of Maddie's arrival. A new boy himself, still at everyone's beck and call, at one point his hopes of making this date had looked doubtful. He had booked the tickets months ago; but as the concert drew close, the new roster for the Homicide Assessment Team assigned him to duty. It turned out all right, though. Detective Inspector Angela

Costello, his line manager and Maddie's stepmother, told him she'd could get cover if necessary.

"Enjoy yourself; that's an order," she'd said.

He grinned as he remembered this and cast a look down at the programme in his hand. Tonight's show, the closing night of seven at this theatre, marked the culmination of a national tour by pop sensation, Brendan Phelan. He'd heard of him, of course; who hadn't? That charismatic personality, fine tenor voice and proven musical abilities had ensured a steady ascent in every music lover's consciousness to prestige as a huge star. Though Gary knew this, he still couldn't name a single one of his tracks. The tickets were meant as a special night out for Maddie.

"You'll like him, I promise," she'd assured him when they were originally deciding where they would go. "His music's amazing. He does this fantastic blend of pop-rock and classical and he uses gunshots and whip cracks on stage!"

Gary had tried unsuccessfully to imagine this bizarre blend of theatrical effects and music, but it sounded exciting. He felt open to giving the man a chance.

"What, *real* guns and whips?" he'd wanted to know.

"Oh yeah, not just sound effects." Then she'd qualified it. "Well, I suppose the guns are stage guns but they make a heck of a noise, and the whips are real. I've seen it a couple of times and it works with the music really well."

This I must see, Gary had thought, unconvinced but definitely intrigued. The photos on the programme gave the impression of a spectacular show, anyway. He looked out into the crowd again; any time now she'd be here. A raised voice diverted his attention suddenly away from the street in front of him to the area near the box office behind.

A well-dressed man in his forties with four girls of about sixteen in tow stood, rather red in the face, having some sort of altercation with one of the theatre staff. "What do you mean?" he was saying. Gary could hear the stress in his tone.

"I'm very sorry, sir," the staff member replied softly, clearly hoping to avoid an embarrassing scene, "but these are not authenticated tickets."

"Not authenticated?" His voice became closer to a shout now as anger took over. "I paid an absolute bundle for these! This is a birthday treat for my daughter and her friends." The girls with him looked at one another apprehensively as they could see the longed-for treat disappearing before their eyes.

As Gary watched, another man, dressed in an evening suit and an air of authority, moved close to the noise. Calm control oozed from every pore of his skin. Gary judged him to be from higher up the theatre management chain. "May I help you, sir?" he asked the father of the birthday girl.

"Yes, your assistant here says there's something wrong with my tickets and he's refusing to let us in."

The manager took the tickets and looked at them. He looked up at the theatregoer, his face full of regret. "I'm very sorry, sir. My assistant here is perfectly correct. You'll need to contact the agency where you bought them. I'm afraid I'm not able to help."

"But I paid for them with my credit card. There's a record, surely."

The mouth of the birthday girl began to wobble and tears sprang into her eyes. "Dad," she croaked. "Dad, let's just go. We can talk about it outside."

"Babes, there must be some mistake. I got them online from a reputable site." He turned back to the attendant and for a moment it looked as though he might square up to him, but his daughter's obvious distress stopped him and he started to move the party towards the street. "Scoundrels ought to be locked up," Gary could hear him muttering as he shepherded his young charges through the doors.

"Oh dear, what a shame; that happens a lot, I think," said a familiar voice in Gary's ear. He jumped and turned to smile into the face of Madeleine Costello. He leaned forward and kissed her.

"You do hear of it quite a bit," he agreed. "Those poor girls aren't going to get their special birthday outing now."

"Oh, I don't know," said Madeleine, looking out into the street. Gary followed the direction of her eyes. As the man and the girls stood irresolute on the pavement, they were being watched by a ponytailed, T-shirted man in his twenties with narrow tattoos of hawks swooping down each bare arm.

"Ah yes; do you reckon that's a tout?" he asked.

"Wouldn't be surprised; they can smell disappointed punters from a long way off."

Together they watched as the tattooed man sidled towards the group and moved slowly in a semicircle to its other side where their leader stood. The man's daughter was still dabbing at her eyes with a tissue. The tout leaned a little closer and said something to catch the man's attention. He gave some instruction to the girls and moved with the tout a short distance away from them.

"He didn't waste any time homing in on the situation, did he?" remarked Gary.

"They're haggling," said Madeleine, watching the transaction take place.

"I bet he'll pay up. He won't want to disappoint his daughter and her pals."

Madeleine nodded her agreement. "It's going to cost him a bomb; Brendan Phelan is a really hot ticket." She slipped an arm round his waist. "Come on, let's go and get our seats."

The atmosphere in the auditorium was electric. They could

feel the eager anticipation of a good night's entertainment in the air. Seeing himself surrounded by ardent fans, Gary suppressed his reservations about the evening ahead but remained sceptical as the lights dimmed. A hush fell over the packed auditorium. He sensed the audience waiting expectantly.

Silence.

Darkness.

Then everybody jumped at the resounding crack of a whip. At that exact moment a set of spotlights illuminated three backing singers dressed in black. Seconds later the same thing happened to bring the band into view. Each visible person on stage stood motionless, the darkness outside the pools of light, absolute. Gary sensed the audience holding its corporate breath. Again a loud whip cracked out across the stage, and a gunshot blasted from somewhere above as a bright single light illuminated Brendan Phelan standing stage right and solitary, his head bowed. He jerked his face up, spread his arms, smiling, and everybody in the place erupted to a thunderous applause. Brendan Phelan, megastar, knew how to wow the crowd.

Three numbers in, Gary's applause had become spontaneous; two hours later he admitted to himself that Madeleine was right. Brendan's charisma, his lyrics – sometimes poignant, often incisive – his melodious voice and his showmanship had drawn him in.

He had been especially impressed with the sound effects. "Those gunshots worked well with that song, didn't they?" he leaned across to say in her ear after one particularly astonishing number. Even so he'd felt some concern when two figures, again in black, appeared from either side of the stage and began shooting into the air, the shots ringing out in perfect timing with the beat of an instrumental break in the middle of a song. It was very effective but Gary still found it a bit worrying. A recent case he'd worked on had involved someone taking a potshot at D.I. Costello and the memory was still all too vivid. Maddie, even sitting right next to him had to listen intently to catch what he said.

"Oh yes," she nodded emphatically. "I'm amazed how he does it."

As the show drew towards its close, most of the audience rose to their feet. They calmed down from the clamour of appreciation greeting the previous number for no longer than it took to recognize the opening chords of Brendan's anthem. Then the foot stomping, clapping and cheering started all over again. In writing "Battle For Your Love", Brendan had incorporated elements from the 1812 overture. This was Maddie's all-time favourite.

"I hope he's not going to use real cannons," joked Gary. Before tonight he would have considered messing about with the 1812 not far short of sacrilege. But Maddie had turned to face the stage again and he couldn't be sure she heard him.

He shook his head to clear the image of real cannons on stage, and joined in with the clapping and the stomping, wholeheartedly this time. What a sensational night this had been.

Brendan gave them four encores, each more enthusiastically received than the previous one, but finally the show came to an end and they joined the massive crowd slowly feeding out along the aisles towards the exits.

Madeleine clung to Gary's arm as she felt herself pushed and pulled in the crowd. "Don't let go of me," she said.

Gary hugged her more tightly. "I've no intention of doing that," he answered. She smiled at the deeper meaning beneath the obvious one. They hadn't been going out together for very long but each could recognize something solid and deep forming in their relationship.

"I wonder if they'll make that announcement about Brendan having gone," said Gary after a few moments, shuffling patiently in step with the pack.

"What, like the old 'Elvis has left the building' line?"

"Yeah, so people don't waste their time going round to the stage door trying to get an autograph."

"You can't get to the stage door at this venue," replied Madeleine. "I've been to a couple of concerts here before. They've got it blocked off from the public."

"Fans must still try, though, surely?"

"I expect so but there are probably heavies guarding the place."

"Yes, I suppose – oh hello, I can feel night air on my face. I do believe we've nearly made it to the outside world."

Madeleine laughed as they pushed their way across the foyer and into the street.

"There's the flyover," he said, pointing. "OK, the tube's that way, then."

"Sure, but let's just have a quick peek at the stage door first," said Madeleine, pulling him along to the right.

"There's no point if it's blocked off and guarded," protested Gary. He stopped, surprised by the sheepish smile that suddenly appeared on Madeleine's face.

"We might just see him from a distance, you never know," she said.

He looked quizzically at her. "Are you a bit star-struck?" he asked

"Just a bit," she admitted.

He grinned and, accompanied by the noise of the traffic roaring round the Broadway, followed her to the corner just a short way along the street. A few other concertgoers had the same idea and they formed a small, untidy procession of people pulling away from the bulk of the crowd. A few yards brought them as far as they could go. Black iron gates to cut off access to the alley stood slightly ajar but, as predicted, a couple of tall, chunkily built men stood guarding the entrance. They moved to bar the way when Madeleine and Gary, at the front of the bunch, appeared, but relaxed a little as it became clear they had no intention of venturing further. The alley was barely visible, though Madeleine stood on tiptoe and Gary craned his neck for a better view. They could just see a white van parked some way along. A box of some sort sat on its roof with what looked like a black bin liner fluttering a little in the night air. A dark crate stood, half-hidden, behind it, ready to be loaded, but they could see no one moving around.

"Packing up already. They don't waste any time," said Gary.

"It seems not."

"I don't think you're going to see him," he said, looking at her regretfully. He turned towards the road, wanting to be on his way to the tube.

"No, you're –" Suddenly a resounding shot rang out, closely followed by the sound of a door banging within the enclosure. It seemed to come from beyond the van. Both the heavies started and their heads whipped round to face the alley, though neither man budged from his post. Gary noted the questioning look that passed between them then, and his police training kicked in immediately. He checked his watch: 23:05.

"What on earth was that?" cried Madeleine, stepping a little closer to Gary.

"A gunshot," he replied. "Wait here and have your phone ready." He fumbled for his police ID and started forward.

One of the bouncers moved to block him. "Sorry, mate, out of bounds."

"Police," he said, holding up his badge. "I heard a shot."

The other guard joined his colleague and put a hand up to prevent Gary passing. "S'all right officer," said the second man reassuringly, humouring him. "They use shots in this performance."

"The show's over," Gary retorted. He pushed past them, dashing towards the van, evading the hands reaching out to grab him, dodging the guard who cursed and ran in pursuit. He had every expectation of making a fool of himself. He'd find nothing more than backstage staff horsing around with the guns. A scene began to roll in his mind – himself backing off through the gates with a sheepish expression on his face; apologizing to the security guards, and to Madeleine; too embarrassed to reprimand the culprits for larking around with loaded weapons, fake or not.

But what met his eyes once he got past the van obliterated all thoughts of anybody playing around, or stage props filled with blanks.

Like an awful parody of the show, the bulkhead light above the stage door shone down on a man sprawled motionless on the ground where he had fallen. The light reflected on a spreading pool of blood seeping from the back of his neck. As the bouncer at his heels stopped in his tracks and let fly several expletives, Gary hurried to the fallen man and hunkered down, trying not to disturb anything. He took hold of the unresisting wrist – no discernible pulse. Ignoring the doorman now speaking urgently into his walkie-talkie ("Tango One to Foxtrot Four, Tango One to Foxtrot Four, dammit! Come in someone!"), Gary pulled his mobile phone out of his pocket and punched in the emergency number.

Only one other person was present, on the far side of the alley. As he spoke into the phone Gary's eyes travelled up from the feet. He saw the black trousers and shirt, unchanged since the performance had finished, the shiny, silvery waistcoat which had glinted and glistened under the spotlights just a short while earlier. Finally, Gary met the horrified, staring eyes of Brendan Phelan.

Chapter Two

Beyond recognizing that the star of the show seemed to be in deep shock, Gary busied himself with calling the emergency services. Behind the van he heard the stage door open and a man came hurrying into view round the end of the vehicle. He stopped abruptly at the sight of Gary bending down close to the body. "What the – ? Hey! What are you doing? Oh no – that's – is it – blood?"

"Yes. Police." With his free hand, Gary reached for his badge and held it aloft for the new arrival to see. He lowered his phone away from his mouth momentarily. "Deal with him," he barked, nodding towards the frozen Brendan Phelan.

The newcomer broke out of his appalled fixation to spare a thought for the traumatized performer. "Hey, come on, Brendan; it's all right, mate." He went towards the other man. "Let's get you inside."

"No!" said Gary, breaking off from giving instructions to the operator. "He's probably a significant witness. It's best we don't disturb the scene. Get him what he needs – a chair, a coat. A hot drink, if there's a machine handy. He needs to be kept warm; he's in shock, I think. When you come back, walk in a wide circle to get round to him, OK?"

The man gulped, nodded and moved quickly back through the stage door. Gary, relieved at the sensible way he took the instruction, finished the call and spoke to the singer. "Don't worry, Mr Phelan; you just stand right there and we'll soon get you sorted. Don't move around, or you might tread on something important."

15

Brendan, his eyes never leaving the dead man, gave an infinitesimal nod. Having finished the 999 call, Gary quickly scrolled through his contacts and found the number of his boss, Detective Inspector Angela Costello. She picked up the phone very quickly.

"Hi, Angie – what? Oh yes, it was great, thanks. Listen, there's been an incident here at the theatre; someone's been shot. I've made the official call, but as our lot are on the roster for tonight I'm giving you the heads-up." He broke off the conversation and stood up hastily as a small crowd of people erupted through the stage door with shouts of "What's going on?" and "Is it Oliver?"

"Stop!" called Gary. "Stay right there. Don't come any closer, please. You might contaminate a crime scene." Like a small flock of sheep kept at bay by a Border Collie, they came to an instant standstill, bunched close together in the alley. Gary could feel their shock and bewilderment. "I'm a police officer," he began, but another man, seemingly going about his normal business, pushed a second large crate through the door towards the one already there.

This wouldn't do. "Please! Stop that!" Gary ordered, aware of all eyes on him. The latest arrival straightened up in astonishment, taking in the tense atmosphere and strange silence from his colleagues.

A puzzled look stole over his face. "I'm only starting on the get-out for tomorrow," he protested. Then his jaw dropped as he noticed the murdered man. "What the – ? What happened?" He turned to the silent bunch of theatre staff. "What's going on?"

Gary didn't hear if anyone answered him. He felt himself gripped by a sudden, overwhelming sense of panic. A corpse – all these people – the bouncer looming – Madeleine waiting – Angela at the other end of the line… He was a small boy again. He didn't know what to do. He could feel himself beginning to hyperventilate.

Just at that moment, the first man came back. A lightweight folding chair and a warm-looking coat were tucked under one arm and he held a steaming polystyrene cup in his other hand. He stepped carefully in a wide circle around the body and reached Brendan Phelan; a sensible man doing as he'd been bidden. Gary felt comforted at the sight and calmed down a little. From somewhere he dredged up the instruction to take a deep, slow breath. It helped even more. A small part of his panicked brain allowed a chink of rational light to shine on the situation. So far, he had always arrived at a scene of crime in the company of a team of officers, in response to a summons. He took another deep breath and although his legs felt decidedly wobbly, the panic began to subside.

"Will everybody please go back into the building? This is a crime scene and it mustn't be disturbed," he called out, in the most authoritative tone he could muster. Aware that Angela, on the other end of the line, could hear him, he cursed the slight shake in his voice. "Nor should anything be added," he said, pointing towards the crate that had just arrived. "My colleagues are on their way."

The backstage crew began retreating cautiously and with some reluctance through the door. Gary could hear them telling the newcomer that he was from the police.

"Sorry, officer," said the latest arrival. "I'll sort it." He began pulling at the crate. Its castors rasped and grated on the uneven concrete, initially rolling the crate closer to the one already there. As he huffed and puffed with the effort, Gary turned away to shield himself from the noise, put his free hand to his ear and spoke into the phone.

"Got it, Angie? Great. Can you ask Patrick to ring Maddie and let her know? She's only up on the main road but I can't leave the scene until someone turns up, obviously. OK – thanks. See you soon." He looked around him. The bouncer who'd chased him down the alley had gone back to his colleague. He'd made contact with whomever he reported to and Gary had heard the crackly orders to wait there coming through the instrument.

Brendan, now seated and enveloped in the coat, sipped at the drink as he stared at nothing in particular. In spite of the coat, Gary could see him shivering. Even at this late hour, it was pleasantly warm, so he guessed he'd been right about the singer being in shock. The other man stood by him, a comforting hand on his shoulder.

"Are you all right, Mr Phelan?" asked Gary. He thought Brendan gave a slight nod but he couldn't be sure.

"OK, Bren," said the other man, in a soothing voice. "We'll soon have you inside in the warm; just got to wait a bit until the police get here." A more visible nod was the only response.

"What's your name?" asked Gary.

"Don Buckley. I'm the manager of the support act, Foursquare."

"Thanks for your help."

"No problem."

Brendan Phelan moved his head to look up at Gary. His eyes had lost a little of their glassiness and he was working his mouth, trying to speak.

"Do you want to say something, Mr Phelan?"

Brendan's mouth opened and shut a few times, but eventually a sound came out. "Why?"

"Why?" repeated Gary, and after a moment: "Why what, sir?"

"Why can't I move?"

The words came out on a sob.

He'd moved from his original standing position, but Gary didn't think it would be helpful to point this out. "You're in shock, Mr Phelan," he said, gently. "Don't worry, sir, help will be here any minute now." He looked towards the theatre to try to get an angle on what Brendan might have seen as the gun fired. The van blocked most of his view of the stage door. He could only assume the shot came from that direction. The stuff he'd already noticed piled on top of the vehicle could have shielded someone. He took note; it would all be properly looked at later. It seemed possible the sound he'd heard of a door banging had been the noise of the killer escaping back into the theatre.

A moment later he saw a shadow out of the corner of his eye. He turned and saw one of the bouncers inching the gate open to allow a man to come through. He carried himself with an air of authority. Relieved, Gary guessed he was a fellow policeman. "Local CID?" he asked.

The newcomer nodded and flashed his badge. "D.S. Hoskins," he replied. "I was nearby when I got the call; the operator said something about a detective constable phoning the incident in?"

"Yes. That was me." Gary moved away from Brendan and Don and lowered his voice. "I'm a D.C. with Homicide Assessment. I was in the audience here tonight. I've alerted my team as well, because…" Gary's voice tailed off as he realized he had no need to explain about the relationship of his girlfriend to his boss.

The other man, taking his comments on purely professional grounds, nodded and grinned in sympathy. "That makes sense. Your lot are probably going to get it anyway." He flicked his eyes briefly towards Brendan. "Rather you than us, if you ask me. This will be a high-profile case and we can do without the aggro."

Gary nodded. Now help had arrived he wanted to check on Madeleine. "I'd like to pop out to the main road, if you don't mind holding the fort."

"No problem; I'll protect the scene. The ambulance should be here any minute."

"Right, thanks. I'll alert those bouncers. We'll need access."

A crack appeared in the gates as Gary approached. "Thanks," he said to the nearest bouncer.

"All right, mate," replied the man, as he slipped through. He hoped Madeleine would still be there, but thought it likely that Patrick had now phoned her and she'd set off for her home on her own.

But no, Madeleine was waiting where he had left her. He hurried across. "Sorry," he said.

She smiled. "Don't worry, I'm fine." She nodded along the pavement and, turning his head, he saw a crowd of people hovering. He could hear a buzz of several speculative conversations "They're getting wind of something up," confirmed Madeleine. "Some of them are worrying something is wrong with Brendan."

He heard the slight anxiety in her own voice. "He's all right," he said, "but I can't say any more than that." She nodded her understanding and muttered her relief, but her voice was drowned out by the sound of a siren. Looking in the direction of the noise, they saw an ambulance closely followed by the Homicide Assessment Team car tearing around from the Broadway. Gary turned back to the gates.

"Here we go," he said to the bouncers.

"OK," came the reply and the gates began to move open.

"There's quite a crowd here," Gary called.

"It's all right, sir," said the larger of the two. "We'll keep everybody but the police out."

"Thanks," replied Gary. He turned back to Madeleine.

"This could turn into a long night," he said.

"Yes, I know." She smiled and at that moment a "beep-beep" attracted his attention. He looked in the direction of the sound to see Angela's car approaching. She waved at him from the driving seat, slowing down but making no attempt to turn in through the gates. Instead, Madeleine called out, "Night-night, Gary," blew him a kiss, swapped places with her stepmother, and pulled out into the traffic. Gary smiled at her retreating tail lights and waved. Her hand fluttered back momentarily through the half-open driver's window before the stream of vehicles swallowed her up.

So, he thought, *while I was guarding the scene, they got themselves organized, like a good team should.* He'd noticed their relationship seemed to be developing pleasantly. It had seemed to him that when Madeleine had moved back home to live, Angela had been apprehensive about it, probably wondering if she would find herself compared, unfavourably, to Madeleine's mother, who'd died while she'd still been a little girl. It looked as though her fears were proving groundless.

He beamed as Detective Inspector Angela Costello hurried to where he stood. Her dark brown waves bobbed around her head and a smart royal blue jacket, unbuttoned, flapped open as she moved. She held an "evening out" shoulder bag in her hand but he knew it would still contain her police notebook, an evidence bag and some rubber gloves. He recognized his relief at her presence. She could take over now.

"You got here quickly," he said, falling into step beside her.

"Evening, Gary – oh, hang on; is it?" She looked at her watch. "Ah yes, it's not midnight yet. I wasn't at home," she explained. "Patrick and I were having a meal, just on the other side of the river, as it happens. What have we got?"

"It looks like a fatality, and a deeply suspicious one."

"Did you try for a pulse?"

"Yes, I couldn't feel one."

"Shot, you said."

"It looks like it; in the back of the neck."

"Oh, my! It doesn't get much more suspicious than that." They were now through the gates. They'd walked a short distance along the alley when Angela stopped. "OK, Gary, give me a rundown."

"The dead man might be someone called Oliver," he said. "From the street I heard a shot and what sounded like a door banging and came running." Gary then went over the event as briefly as he could, finishing up with when he'd been on the phone to Angela. "I managed to make everyone go back inside. One of them even tried to bring out another crate but I got him to take it back again."

"Yes, I heard that bit through the phone. Let's hope he hasn't messed up any forensics."

"Sorry, he was bringing it through the door before I could stop him."

Angela realized that having been first on the scene, Gary was worried about how he'd handled everything. She remembered the nervous quality to his voice as he was speaking to her on the phone. "Not to worry, Gary. We all get caught on the hop now and again. You'd just gone out to see a concert and got lumbered."

As he'd guessed, she had rubber gloves in her bag. She took them out, put them on, approached the crate and lifted the lid. They found themselves gazing down on a sizeable collection of neatly coiled extension leads. Angela closed down the lid gently. She looked at the body. "I suppose there's a good chance that whoever fired the gun might have been standing by the van." She cast her eyes over the whole scene again. "They would have been shielded from view."

"Yes, you're right, they could have been," replied Gary.

"Yes, indeed," Angela nodded and looked back at the van. "I wonder what that stuff is doing on the top there; there's no rack for it to be attached to."

Gary looked with her. Now that he was able to look properly he could see that the box was actually a long, narrow crate; some kind of clear, coloured plastic in a frame leaned up against the end it. The bin bag flapped gently as if trying to break free from its moorings. "I noticed that from the street," he said.

Angela looked at him and raised her eyebrows. "What do you reckon?"

"I reckon a person could hide behind that and shoot someone in the alley here."

Angela nodded. "I think you might be right." She glanced up at the stage door. "Aha! Will this make our job easier, I wonder?"

Gary followed the direction of her eyes and found himself looking at a security camera mounted on the wall. He felt himself blush. "Oops, I hadn't noticed that. I should have clocked it before now."

"Stop beating yourself up, Gary. You've only got two eyes and they were fully occupied. This is why we work in teams."

Her attention was drawn to noise and movement in the stage doorway as more of the local CID and a forensics team arrived. They'd obviously made their way in through the theatre itself.

She nodded. "OK, we'd better get started." She nodded in the direction of the star of the show. "The man himself, I presume. I think I recognize him from the television."

Gary nodded.

Angela went over to Brendan Phelan, carefully avoiding the dead man. "Mr Phelan, I'm D.I. Angela Costello. We're going to try to get you inside as soon as we can, sir."

Brendan's eyes flickered but he didn't look up at her.

Angela decided to give it a try anyway. "Can you tell me what happened, Mr Phelan?" she asked.

This time Brendan blinked and seemed to engage with his surroundings but almost immediately a look of horror crossed his face. He worked his mouth again. "A bang," he whimpered eventually. "He looked really…" Words failed him, his face began to crumple and Angela realized it wouldn't be fair to press him. She looked up at the man beside him.

"This is Don Buckley, Angie," explained Gary. "The manager of the support act. He's been very helpful."

"Thanks, Don," said Angela. "Will you go inside with Mr Phelan? We'll have a police doctor here any minute, but – "

"That's OK," said Don. "There's a theatre doctor. I'm sure someone's called her by now." He leaned down to his charge. "OK, Bren, we're going inside now, going to get you sorted." He helped the singer to stand up and, carefully retracing his original circle, they disappeared into the theatre.

Angela watched as they disappeared from sight. "Has Brendan Phelan been out here all this time?"

"Yes," confirmed Gary. "Just where you saw him, but he was standing at first."

Right, well, I hope he's going to be all right." She turned to Gary. "You brief the scene of crime officers."

"OK, Angie."

"I'll see you when you're finished out here. I'm going inside. Whatever was going on must have started there." Angela made a wide circle round to the door and went in. She looked briefly into the deserted area where the stage doorman must normally sit. She moved on, pushing open a couple of doors where she came into a wider space. Several crates similar to the one outside stood in a neat stack against the wall. She lifted the lid and looked into one. Like the one outside it contained a jumble of electric cables and extension sockets. Heavy black curtains hung in front of her, but a slight chink showed a light through to a further dimly lit space, and she made for it. She passed three standing microphones, stopped between two keyboards and gazed at a drum kit set at the back of the area. *Ah, I've just come from the wings and I'm now on stage*, she realized, and allowed herself a moment's frisson of wonder. Rich, red drapes now hung before her. She guessed them to be the curtains separating the performers from the audience and allowed herself to imagine, for a brief moment, what it must be like to be a star, to have these curtains open onto your audience. She smiled and shook her head as another picture took over. Scenes from a variety of comedies flashed through her mind and she recalled images of hapless characters looking foolish as they got caught up in stage curtains in an attempt to reach the front. *I don't think so*, she thought.

She took her mobile phone out of her bag and called up one of her sergeants, Rick Driver. "Rick, it's me. I'm on the stage. Where are you? OK, I don't know how to get to the auditorium, will you…? Thanks."

After a few moments she heard the sound of a door opening to one side and footsteps approaching. Detective Sergeant Rick Driver appeared.

"We're round here, Angie. There's a pass door through to the auditorium and we've got everybody assembled there."

"Ah, good; just take me through and then go and bring Gary in as soon as he's finished what he's doing."

Angela came into the brightly lit auditorium, and as the hum of animated chatter rose to greet her, she took in the scene. About thirty people were sprawled out along the first few rows of the stalls. Some, from their uniforms, could be easily identified as front-of-house staff. Here and there a few small groups of people in ordinary working clothes had huddled together and looked as though they'd been practising card tricks with each other; she noted a couple of deft shuffling movements as the cards seemed to whizz through the air to be caught neatly into single blocks in the hand. *Not a sight you see often*, she thought. *It makes a change from having everyone huddled over smartphones.* Three women, one in a dressing gown and two in evening dress, she surmised to be part of the show, along with two men in sparkly waistcoats similar to the one Brendan had been wearing. She hadn't followed Brendan Phelan's career, but was sure she'd seen him performing on television accompanied by a band and trio of backing singers. The rest seemed to be in ordinary clothes and she assumed they were the behind-the-scenes staff. Somebody had to work the lights and sound. In spite of the chatter, their faces were grim and pale. A young girl in the middle of the front row was weeping audibly and being comforted by one of the men.

Angela moved forward. "Good evening, everybody; thank you for your patience. I'm Detective Inspector Angela Costello. I'm sorry, we're going to have to ask you all to stay a little longer." *You liar, Angie,* she thought to herself. *We'll all be here for a good while yet.* She recognized her own tiredness mirrored in the faces of everybody in front of her. She and Patrick had enjoyed a very pleasant evening in one of their favourite restaurants and were looking forward to going home to bed when the call had come through.

The thin young man with the hawk tattoos on his arms, backpack swung casually over one shoulder, watched the ambulance and police cars from a safe distance. He edged closer to the crowd gathering around the entrance to the side alley and listened to the excited rumours about the shooting. He heard someone say that Brendan Phelan had been gunned down – killed. This caused near-hysteria among some of the women bystanders, so that he could hear nothing coherent for several minutes. Then, over the heads of the crowd, the loud authoritative voice of someone who announced himself as Detective Sergeant Hoskins called out that Brendan had been taken into the theatre in a state of shock, there was nothing any of them could do, and they should all go home and learn about it from the news. The voice fell on deaf ears; nobody budged an inch, except to try to move closer.

His body tensed at this point and his eyes widened. He'd been aware of the conversation that was due to take place just after the show and knew everything had always gone very smoothly before. Once he'd spotted the first journalist on the scene, he retreated further and stood, irresolute. A few minutes later, the sight of a night bus heading in the right direction made up his mind.

The journey took very little time. A convenient connection to another bus got him across the river and forty minutes later he was forcing the lock on the door of a flat near the Elephant and Castle.

He moved swiftly over to the desk where the computer sat and pulled out the top drawer. Everything he needed was there. He emptied out the contents, hastily stuffing them into the backpack. He cast an appraising glance at the computer but left it there. He gave a last look round at the familiar room. The place was in chaos – a confused muddle of belongings flung randomly into every corner. He let himself out, with a quick glance around the empty street to make sure he was unobserved.

Chapter Three

Angela didn't get much beyond her initial introduction before she was interrupted. "Will you please tell us exactly what's going on?" The voice, a strange mix of nervousness and pomposity, came from a man in an evening suit, sitting with a group of uniformed people several rows back.

"May I have your name, sir?"

"I'm Barry Grieves. I'm the front-of-house manager. We were told there's been an 'incident' and that nobody is to leave the theatre." He took another breath to continue, but Angela moved in quickly.

"Yes, there's been what looks like a very serious incident outside the stage door; a suspected fatality." She remembered the blood oozing from the victim's head. A doctor would by now have pronounced life extinct; even so, she must be cautious, not pre-empt the news.

Her words stopped the front-of-house manager from making whatever comment he had prepared. "Oh – I – er – er..." He opened his mouth and shut it again a few times before contenting himself with a muttered, "Well, that's terrible, of course."

Angela didn't take a lot of notice because her attention – and that of everyone else in the place – was drawn to the low anguished moan coming from the young girl in the front row.

"Ohhhhh! It's not Bren, is it?" A sob escaped her. "Tell me it's not Bren!"

That's interesting, thought Angela. *Why do you think Brendan might be the victim?* "Although he's in shock," she said, "Brendan Phelan doesn't appear to be harmed in any way."

"Ohhhh! Thank God," breathed the girl. The depth of her relief caused fresh tears to overflow her eyes and pour down her cheeks. The man beside her folded her into a comforting embrace and muttered soft, soothing words. Angela watched the numerous small movements among the others, noting several people raising their eyebrows at this small drama, exchanging glances with each other. *Hmm*, she thought, *undercurrents to be explored here.* Almost immediately she picked up on a name, mouthed in some quarters and whispered audibly in others. Heads shook and nodded in covert exchanges, shoulders and hands were shrugged in discreet expressions of supposition and conjecture.

Angela remained silent, looking carefully around at them all. *Someone's going to just come right out and say it in a minute*, she thought.

She didn't have long to wait.

Just below her on the end of the front row sat a trio of men, two wearing the sparkly waistcoats, the third in black jeans and T-shirt. After a little more nodding and shaking of heads it seemed the assembled staff looked to this man as spokesperson.

With reluctance he accepted the unspoken but evident election that singled him out. He looked up at her. "So – is it Oliver, then?" he asked.

The atmosphere relaxed as the question came out into the open.

"We're not sure yet, but it's possible. You have a colleague called Oliver, I presume."

Again they all looked towards the unofficial spokesman. "We have," he answered. "Oliver Joplin, he's a roadie, of sorts." Angela detected a sneer in his tone.

"Is it possible this Oliver went home early, or just didn't hear the summons to gather here?"

The spokesman raised himself slightly in his seat and gazed all around. "He's the only one missing. Of course, we haven't looked under the chairs." His sneer became more pronounced. "Do you want us to do a search?"

Hello, Mr Angry, what's your problem? thought Angela. Even first thing in the morning when she felt full of energy she wasn't prepared to play games with witnesses; in the run-up to midnight the idea was a non-starter. "May I have your name please, sir?" she asked, in a carefully polite and formal tone.

"I'm Terry Dexter, musician/songwriter/lead guitarist."

"Thank you," she replied, not bothering to take up his challenge. "We're going to need statements from each of you. My officers will deal with that and we'll try not to keep you any longer than we have to."

"It's OK," returned the man, with an unmistakable undercurrent of sarcasm. "It's not like we wanted to get our things ready for a charity performance at the O2 tomorrow night, or anything."

Angela walked to the edge of the stage. She kept her manner relaxed and her face expressionless. "At the O2?"

The man who had been comforting the young woman further along the front row spoke up. "Yes, Inspector. Brendan is one of the acts in a gala for a children's charity. It's a big event. That's why I'd taken one of the flight cases outside and was bringing another one through when your bloke – er – one of your officers – said to take it back inside."

"Flight cases?"

"Yes, it's what we transport the equipment and stuff in. We're taking some over there for the show."

"Oh, you mean the big, black crate things by the van and at the back of the stage?"

"Wow! She's got it! 'Big, black crate thing', no: flight case, yes," said Terry Dexter.

Angela made a point of addressing herself to the second man. "That whole area is a crime scene at the moment and it won't be possible to do anything there until the forensic team have finished."

"I understand," he replied. Along the row, Angela's antagonist let out a huge sigh but said nothing.

"OK," she said, addressing the assembled company. "Can you tell me who's in charge here?"

The man comforting the girl gently disentangled himself and stood up. Another man, further back, got up and eased his way past the people in his row. "May I see you two gentlemen backstage, please?" She turned and went back through the pass door, preparing to feel her way through the gloom but, as she negotiated the wings, lights suddenly came on bathing the whole area in a harsh glare. She moved into centre stage. Gary appeared at the back as he came through from the alley where she'd left him. "Hi, Gary, stick with me. I'm going to try to get an angle of the way things work. How's the star of the show?"

"I think he's coming to a bit now, but he's still shocked. The doctor's taken him to his dressing room. One of the forensic guys came in and checked him for powder burns and went through his pockets; they found nothing and he's handed his clothes over for testing."

"So far, so good, then," replied Angela. "It would upset a whole army of fans if they knew, but we can't rule him out as a suspect."

"He's really knocked sideways, though, Angie."

"Nonetheless..."

Gary nodded. "Yes, you're right. The doc's going to give him a sedative. She said she wants him to go home to bed as soon as possible, though."

"I don't have a problem with that. We need him clear-headed when we interview him." She turned round at the sound of the two men from the front joining them on stage. "Did you turn the lights on?" she asked the one who had been sitting with the girl.

"Yes," he nodded.

"Thank you. I'll be right with you, gentlemen," she said, and turned back to Gary. "Where are Rick and Jim?"

"Here," called Rick. His voice came from the still-darkened wings at the other side of the stage from where Angela had entered. "Hey!" the curtains jerked and swung. Shapes were punched into them as Rick fought his way through – the pitfall Angela had avoided earlier.

She laughed. "Curtains one, Rick nil," she said as he finally emerged looking a little red in the face. "OK, we'll be here for a while. All those people sitting in the auditorium need to be questioned. Can you get started on that? Has anyone else arrived?"

"Leanne and Derek – and a couple of uniforms."

"That's good." She turned to the two men. "It about time we were introduced."

They moved towards her. The taller one of the two held out his hand. "I'm Doug Travers, Brendan Phelan's manager." Angela noted his crumpled linen suit and an open-necked shirt. The style aimed for nonchalance but the strain around his mouth and eyes told a different story. Angela would have been surprised if it had been otherwise. She shook his hand and looked towards the other man.

He moved a little closer. "I'm Jack Waring, the production manager."

"Does that mean you're responsible for all this?" asked Angela with a sweeping gesture.

"Only the equipment we bring in with us. Of course, what's already here belongs to the theatre."

"I see," she nodded. "We'll need two or three rooms where we can interview people. Is that going to be a problem?"

"Not at all," replied Doug. "I know there are a couple of dressing rooms not in use at the moment." He took out a mobile phone from his inside pocket. "Let me just make a call. There's bound to be somewhere front of house you can use as well."

"That would be very helpful, thank you." She looked at Jack. "If the dead man is this Oliver and he's a roadie, I presume you're his boss." Waring nodded his head. He thought for a moment and turned a shade paler. "I suppose you need someone to identify him."

"We do, I'm afraid."

Jack Waring hesitated a moment before nodding reluctantly.

"Thank you," said Angela. "Once we've established that it's him we'll need to know about his family."

"He's got someone, I think. They live in south London – Peckham, I believe. I know there's a sister, at least."

"OK," Angela nodded at Rick. "Go with the sergeant, here, and do the ID, and then will you give him the contact details of the family?"

"They're on my laptop in Bren's dressing room. Is it all right to go there?"

"I would think so, it's not part of the crime scene."

"Right," replied Waring. He moved smoothly through the stage equipment in the manner of one completely familiar with where everything is. Rick followed in his wake and they disappeared out of sight.

"Right, we'll need to talk to Don Buckley first, I think, Gary. Can you go and get him, please?"

Once Gary had gone, Angela smiled at Doug Travers, who had finished his call and joined her again.

"All sorted," he said. "There's a room near the ticket office. The front-of-house manager will show your officers where it is. Together with these dressing rooms back here, you're sorted."

"Thank you. Maybe we can get through the preliminaries fairly quickly, then. Right, Rick and Jim, we can take a room each. I'd like you to speak to Jack and Doug here, I'll take that girl from the front row and the support act manager – Gary's already gone for Don Buckley – the one who was looking after the singer."

"Sure thing, Angie," said Rick as he and Jim moved back towards the pass door. "We'll see to the others, as well."

"Thanks. Oh – I want to take Mr Angry."

Jim turned and looked quizzically at her. "Man in a black T-shirt sitting with some others in sparkly waistcoats," she explained. "He's a bit mouthy."

Jim gave her a thumbs-up as he disappeared out of sight.

Five minutes later, Rick texted her to confirm the doctor had pronounced life extinct and the dead man was, indeed, Oliver Joplin, and she was settling into one of the larger dressing rooms. She didn't bother to turn on the lights surrounding the huge mirror above the counter along one wall, contenting herself with the central light hanging from the ceiling. She and Gary shifted a jumble of stage make-up and sequinned masks from a table by the wall onto the counter, positioning the table under the light for interviewing. They took four of the five chairs ranged to face the mirror, and set them two either side of the table.

"OK, we're ready," she said, finally. "I don't suppose there's a person in this building who doesn't want to go home to bed right now, so let's just get started and get through as best we can." She looked at Gary. "Don Buckley?"

"Outside, waiting to be called in."

Don Buckley stood about five feet ten, slim, with dark blond hair and a pleasant face.

As Angela welcomed him in and invited him to take a seat across the table from herself and Gary, she noted that he seemed quite composed and alert. Perhaps he was a night-time person, she surmised. She wasn't.

"Well," she began. "This isn't how you thought the evening would end, is it?"

"You've got that right. We're all knocked sideways."

"How did Oliver get on with the rest of you?"

"Um, I don't know that I can answer that, really."

"But you all worked together backstage, didn't you?" Angela thought back to the evening when Madeleine had first talked about going to this concert. She was quite a fan of Brendan Phelan. She remembered – yes, that was it – Maddie had talked about it being the final show of a national tour. "You've all been together for some weeks now, haven't you?" she asked, glad she could dredge up that detail from her memory.

"Yes, we've been on tour for some months, but you've got to know how it is. We're the support act, right?"

"Yes, I get it."

"So, like, we're really made up about being on tour with these guys; Brendan being who he is, of course; it's a big opportunity for us but we make sure we mind our p's and q's. Don't get me wrong, we all get on all right and there's a good vibe backstage. We go to the pub together and all that stuff but, well, Brendan's crew are Brendan's crew, and we wouldn't necessarily know all their business. You know what I mean?"

"I think so; you're talking about company politics."

Don hesitated for a fraction of a second. "Yes."

Hmm, interesting, thought Angela, as she made a note. *I might need to come back to this point but I'd better stick to the straight and narrow first.*

"So what can you tell me about what happened tonight?"

Don shrugged. "Not a lot. I was with my group, Foursquare, in our room, just chilling after the show, when I heard a shot. Our room is near the back of the theatre. It made me jump but none of them seemed to be bothered. I said, 'Did anybody hear that shot?' and Luke, one of the band, said he'd stopped noticing gunshots."

"He said what?"

"Well, you know – actually, why should you know? Brendan uses guns in the show, and whips. Not my thing, really, but I have to admit they're very effective."

Angela turned to Gary with an enquiring glance. He nodded. "That's right. I wouldn't have expected it to work, but it does."

"So what happened after you heard the shot?"

"I came down and went out the back and that's when I saw Oliver on the ground and him – er – your officer there." Don dipped his head in Gary's direction.

"That's right," confirmed Gary.

"And then I tried to sort Brendan out because it was obvious that he was shaken up."

Gary spoke. "I asked him to get something to keep Brendan Phelan warm. Once he'd gone off, loads of the other backstage people crowded out through the door. It reminded me – " Gary broke off. "Never mind," he said. "I told them all to go back inside."

"It strikes me as being a bit extreme, using guns in a pop-rock show," remarked Angela. "I mean, as part of the act."

"Apparently Brendan's always been into guns," replied Don. "In a gun club even when he was at school. Some of the crew also shoot, even one or two who didn't before. They got interested through working with Brendan."

"They use real guns?"

"Oh no! They're starting pistols. Jack – you know, the bloke looking after the equipment – is someone Brendan knows from his gun club. He's very particular about making sure everything is done properly."

"Is he related in some way to the girl who was sitting next to him, the very distressed girl?"

"That's Carla. No, they're not related. She's – " Don stopped.

"She's what?"

He ran a tongue round his lips. "She's the runner."

"I see." Angela let a pause elapse. *I'm sure you were going to say something else just then*, she thought. She let the silence lengthen and after a moment Don spoke again.

"Jack got Carla the job. I thought he was her dad at first but he's not. He looks out for her, though."

"Comes from the gun club as well, does she?" asked Angela, with a smile. She said it as an amusing aside but the answer surprised her.

"Yes. I think she was junior champion or something. A very good shot by all accounts."

Chapter Four

That should teach me not to be so sexist, thought Angela. "So how many people working on this show are familiar with guns?" she asked.

Don grinned, his eyes full of sympathy. "At least five that I know of," he said. "Won't make life easy for you, will it?"

Angela nodded, her heart sinking. "We'll have to wait and see how all the statements and alibis hold up," she said. "So you heard the shot and came down to see what had happened. After that you helped out a bit with trying to calm Brendan Phelan."

"Yes."

Angela looked up from her notebook and smiled at him. "Thank you for your help. We might need to speak to you again."

Don smiled as he rose. "Not a problem. I'm not going anywhere."

Once he'd left the room, Angela turned to Gary. "During that interview you were about to say something and then stopped."

Gary raised his eyebrows. "Was I? Oh yes," he grinned. "It was nothing."

"Still, something struck you."

"It doesn't have any bearing on this case, Angie. I think it was to do with one of the blokes who came out to see what was going on. He stood by one of those flight cases and for some reason the sight took me right back to being a little boy of nine or ten at home with my dad watching some magic act together. I think it's the cases, they're like magician's boxes, aren't they? I'd started to panic a bit, to be honest, at that point; felt a bit like a helpless kid."

Angela smiled. "Never mind, the cavalry soon turned up, didn't we?"

Gary laughed. "Yes, thank God."

"OK, let's see this young girl next. Carla, is it? She looked like she could do with going home to bed."

"Does she need an appropriate adult sitting in?"

"We'll check it out before we begin."

A short while later, Carla, waiflike and still tear-stained, stood facing them on the other side of the table like a schoolgirl called before the headmistress, frightened of what punishment awaited her. Angela hastened to put her at her ease. "Take a seat, Carla, don't look so scared."

Carla didn't look much comforted by this advice, but she sat down as directed, gave her full name as Carla Paterson and astonished Angela and Gary by revealing her age as twenty-two.

"We need to know where everybody was when the shooting occurred," said Angela.

Carla sniffed as a fresh tear rolled down her cheek. "I don't know," she replied, picking at a brightly coloured fingernail. "When was it?"

"So you didn't hear the gun go off?"

"No."

"OK, so where were you between 10:45 and 11:05 this evening?"

Carla shrugged and her expression became even more scared. "All over the place. I'm the runner."

"How did you become aware of what had happened?"

"I'd just taken some dresses to the wardrobe and I popped into the loo. While I was in there I heard a couple of the blokes going past in the corridor. They were full of it. They were, like, 'Have you heard what's happened? It's unbelievable, man.' So

I guessed something was up. Then I came downstairs and we were all being asked to go and sit in the auditorium because there'd been an incident outside the stage door and the police were on their way." More tears rolled down her cheeks.

"I'm sorry to distress you, Carla, but these questions have to be asked."

Carla gave a sniff, wiped her eyes and nodded. "S'all right, I know they do."

"Were you particularly fond of Oliver Joplin?"

Carla looked at Angela with an astonished gaze. "Oliver? Fond? You must be joking. I'm upset about Brendan!"

Angela and Gary exchanged glances. Angela gave an infinitesimal nod towards Gary to indicate that he should take over the questioning. Gary moved forward a little and rested his notebook on the table.

"Why would you be upset about Brendan?" he asked.

Carla widened her eyes as if she thought the question silly. "Well, he'll be worried, won't he? Frightened; it's horrible, him being the target of this sort of thing."

Gary and Angela were careful not to look at each other but both, at that moment, took a well-educated guess at the other's thoughts. Gary spoke again. "I understand that having one of his crew shot is very distressing, and will be a matter of concern for Brendan, but why would he be frightened? It was Oliver that was shot."

"Yeah, but the bullet must have been meant for Brendan, mustn't it?" argued Carla.

Angela took over. "Why do you say that, Carla?"

Carla's eyes shone. "Well, he's great, isn't he? He's fantastic. The best. There must be jealous people out there who've got it in for him. And in any case, who'd want to shoot Oliver? He was horrible. I'm glad he's dead. He was nothing but trouble." Carla shut her mouth tightly as if afraid of saying more. Angela and Gary, while recoiling from her questionable logic, focused on the gem lying among all the silt.

"Why do you say he was trouble?" asked Angela.

Carla's face gave the impression that she thought she'd said too much. She shrugged. "Don't know." She looked up from under lowered eyelids and her glance travelled from one to the other.

You don't seriously think I'm going to let that pass, do you? thought Angela. "You must have some reason for thinking he was trouble," she said.

Carla gave another shrug but didn't look up at them this time. "I really don't know. I think he was up to something. I heard whispers here and there but nobody tells me anything."

"What kind of whispers?" asked Gary.

"I don't know. They don't tell me, do they?" she replied. "Look at me. I'm small. I look young for my age. I'm just regarded as some sort of kid around here – the runner – right? Nobody tells me anything. I think I deserve more respect than I get."

Angela wasn't prepared to be diverted. "But you must have some idea about what these 'whispers' mean."

Carla gave a sigh, as if she resented the information being dragged out of her. "Look, I don't really know but I think he was up to something, that's why – " she stopped abruptly, stealing another upward glance.

Realizing that Carla was playing this interview according to some agenda of her own, Angela felt her patience wearing thin. "You can't leave it there," she said, dropping the calm, formal tone and injecting a harsher note into her voice. The look Carla flashed her showed she understood.

"You'll have to ask the others," she replied. "I really *don't* know, but Oliver had been on the crew longer than anybody else and he gave the impression he had some sort of 'in' with Brendan."

"What do you think, Angie?" asked Gary as the door closed behind Carla.

"I can't make her out. There's this gamine thing going on. Then when she spoke about Brendan the first time she sounded like an adoring fan. She put up a big signpost about some undercurrent, though, didn't she?"

"Yes, and I got that a bit with Don. He hesitated when you mentioned company politics."

"Indeed; just for a nanosecond. Look, forget what I said earlier; let's just see this Terry Dexter next and then we can have a quick meeting with the rest of the team. We'll make sure we've got everybody's names and addresses and allocate who's going to speak to whom. And once the SOCOs have finished with the crime scene we'll call it a day. I don't know about you, but I'm not much of a night owl and I don't do my best work when I'm shattered."

The smile on Gary's face showed his relief at the decision. "Woohoo!" He stood up "I was hoping you'd say that. Thank you, Angie. I'll go and get Terry, then. Wonder what he's got to say for himself?"

"He seemed to be trying to give the impression that he knows everything about everything, didn't he?"

His energy renewed at the thought of going home, Gary disappeared from the room. A few moments later the door was thrust open and Terry the musician/songwriter/lead guitarist stood on the threshold. "At last!" he said, coming fully into the room, allowing Gary to slip in behind him.

The slight smugness in his face did not escape Angela. *No doubt he thinks it's only right he's one of the first interviewed*, she thought. "Take a seat, Mr Dexter," she began.

"Before you ask," he said, sitting down, "yes, I'm the person who co-wrote Bren's biggest hit, the one that kick-started his whole career."

Angela thought it diplomatic to make a note of this unexpected information. The most surprising things might later become relevant. In any case, she could gain nothing by antagonizing a man who'd already demonstrated his readiness to become irritated by small matters. "Right, got that," she said, lifting her pen from the page. "Now, about this terrible business tonight."

"We go back absolutely years. We were at school together."

"You were at school with Oliver Joplin?" verified Angela, as Gary made a note of the fact. She wondered if it would have a bearing on things.

A look of irritation passed across Terry Dexter's face. "Olly Jop…? No, I'm talking about Brendan Phelan."

Angela felt so glad she'd made the decision to go home after this interview. "Mr Dexter, how well did you know the dead man?"

A look of annoyance settled into his face as Angela bypassed his claim to fame. "As well as anyone else working with Bren, I suppose. He'd been on the crew for – well, a long time, unfortunately."

"Unfortunately? Why do you say that?"

"Because he did naff all," said Terry. "If I'd been in charge I'd have let him go a long time ago. But there you go; Brendan's a soft touch. He needs protecting from himself sometimes."

"Really, in what way?" asked Angela, and watched as a guarded look came down on his face.

"Oh, just that, really," replied Terry, making a creditable stab at airy nonchalance. "He likes to give everybody the benefit of the doubt."

Angela wrote, "*backstage politics*", "*undercurrents*" and "*soft touch*" in her notebook and got back on track. "Did you hear the gunshot?"

"No."

"Where were you at eleven o'clock?"

"As it happens, I can be fairly exact. I was hovering in the wings. Nobody else was around so I suppose I can't prove that."

"Why were you there?"

"You know we're due to do a set tomorrow – well, tonight now – at the O2? I like to make sure I'm around when my instruments are packed away, so I was waiting till the team got to my stuff. I remember being so deep in thought that I didn't register the shot. I think the door from the back of the stage must have been opened by someone and I heard one of the crew saying, 'What was that?' and I saw others moving in the same direction. So I followed." He shook his head. "Of course, I should have known. I should have stuck closer to Bren."

"Why do you say that?" asked Angela.

"It's not good for Brendan to be associated with this kind of incident," replied Terry. "Like I said, he needs looking after. He's very gifted, he's rich, he has an enormous number of fans; that sort of life brings its own burdens and pitfalls."

"But," Angela kept her tone carefully neutral, "it isn't Brendan who's been shot."

Terry seemed not to register what she said. "A rich and successful person will attract leeches, Inspector; you know what I'm saying? And sometimes they can seep through into the closest of inner circles round a celebrity."

"Was Oliver Joplin a leech, do you think?"

For the first time in the interview, Terry looked guarded. "Who knows?" he said. "All I can tell you is that his technical skills weren't of the highest order, which is a shame in a techie. If it had been up to me, I'd have sacked him long since."

Everyone's an expert, thought Angela, hiding a smile. Every industry had its share of people who thought they could run it better if only they were in charge. It seemed that show business was no different. "Were you aware of any tension between Oliver and other members of the backstage staff?" she asked.

Terry's gaze slewed off to the right and he brought his hand up to tap his mouth as if considering the question. But the actions were slightly out of sync, and the pause a shade too long. "There are all sorts of tensions that arise in a crew like this, it's only to be expected, mostly little niggles which are forgotten the next day. Olly was involved in his fair share of them."

You haven't really answered the question, said Angela to herself, making yet another note.

"Of course, the motive might be somewhere in the man's history," continued Terry.

Angela looked up to find herself staring into a very direct gaze. "In the history?" she queried.

"Yes, back in the mists of time, so to speak," answered Terry, doing better with the nonchalance, this time. "Don Buckley, for instance, knew him years ago, and there's no love lost between them, from what I can see."

"Are we talking about open animosity?"

"Not really; they mostly avoided each other."

"Wouldn't that be difficult on a tour?"

"Not for someone as antisocial as Olly."

"Do you know the reason for the bad feeling?"

Terry shrugged. "Search me; it must stem from way back."

Angela made a note. *I'm sure you've got more to tell me*, she thought. *But I'll let it rest for now. You've got a verifiable alibi for the time of the shooting, so I'll just pick your brains.* "Tell me how things work backstage on a show like this," she said.

Terry sat up straighter in his chair and became much more animated. She could see he was more comfortable with this line of enquiry. She could imagine him holding court in pubs and cafés near whatever venue Brendan was appearing in. *"Ooooh, do you actually know, Brendan Phelan?" "What's he really like?" "Can you get me in backstage?" "Can you get me his autograph?"* They would recognize him, of course. Brendan was often photographed with his backing singers and band. Angela wouldn't be surprised at all to discover that Terry had, over the years, become very used to basking in Brendan's reflected glory. She wondered how that made him feel, deep down inside.

"It's quite a simple set-up, really," he said. "Most theatres have their own staff to deal with any equipment belonging to the venue. Besides that, we bring quite a bit of our own stuff – catering, wardrobe, lighting rig and sound deck; as well as our own instruments, of course. We fit into the venue as a self-contained unit, but we're free to use, in addition, whatever of their staff or gear we require."

"How many of you are there?"

"OK, let me see…" Terry started counting on his fingers. "Five in the band; a drummer, a keyboard player and three guitarists. I play lead guitar but I can step in on keyboards if necessary. We've got three women on backing vocals. Then there's the crew. Three on lighting – well, obviously we're a man down after tonight's event – and a couple more on sound. We've got Jack overseeing everything, Doug managing us all and Carla running errands. I make that sixteen."

Angela nodded. "Your maths match mine. So, Oliver worked on the lighting?"

"Yes. And this show was the last in a national tour. It's been pretty hectic but very successful, I'm happy to say. There's been a great atmosphere and the audiences have loved us."

"That's good. And several of you are interested in firearms, I gather."

A flash of mild pique flitted across his face and Terry looked at Angela from under his eyebrows. She felt a little puzzled by the reaction but immediately realized that she interrupted his exposition on 'My Life on the Road with Brendan Phelan'; a subject she presumed was normally of great interest to his listeners. He didn't like to be deflected from it.

He recovered his poise quickly enough. "Brendan and I joined a gun club when we were still at school. In fact, we knew Jack from those days; he worked there. And right from the early days we experimented in tying up the sounds of guns and whips with the music. Jack used to laugh at us, he didn't think such a thing could work, so we invited him to one or two rehearsals. The timing was fortuitous because the owner of the club retired and wanted to close it down just as we were looking to gather a team around us, so we offered him the job of production manager."

"Quite a career change for him."

"Actually no; he'd started off as a runner himself, back in the day. Not in the music industry, more Variety. Seaside entertainment, I think, jugglers, high-wire acts, all that kind of thing. We knew he'd run a very efficient club so we felt comfortable about inviting him onto the team."

We? Thought Angela. *When did you and Brendan become a double act?* Terry went on: "It's also handy having someone on board who's up on firearms regulations and careful about making sure the guns are locked up properly, even though they're only stage props."

"I'm sure. Er – about guns. Do you and Brendan have your own? Real ones, I mean."

"Oh yes!" Terry nodded in affirmation. "We're both very proficient marksmen – as is Jack."

"So there are several people on the crew who wouldn't have any difficulty in shooting Brendan?"

"Shooting *Brendan*?"

"Yes. It's been suggested that the killer might actually have aimed for Brendan."

A stillness came over Terry. He blinked slowly once or twice. "Inspector, that thought is seriously scary."

Chapter Five

"So, what's he like, then?" asked Madeleine at breakfast the following morning.

Angela smiled at her over the steam rising from her coffee. "I didn't get a chance to find out," she replied. "The doctor hustled him away to give him a sedative and put him to bed. I'm going to interview him later today."

"Couldn't you borrow a uniform for me and take me along as your notebook holder?" suggested Madeleine. Angela laughed. Madeleine turned her attention back to the newspaper spread out by her plate on the table and read the caption under a picture: *Police officers leaving the theatre in early hours of this morning.* "I can tell that's you holding your arm up in front of your face, but only because I know you."

"I wasn't being camera-shy. I was just defending myself against all the flashes. A small army of media people had gathered by the time we left, and facing them was the last thing I felt like doing at two o'clock this morning. Uniform had set up a barrier and had the fans contained behind it, but they were making a huge noise. The press were corralled just in front of them. So what with the fans calling out to know if Brendan was all right, the journalists shooting off their questions and all those lights, it felt like minor chaos. I said that so far as I was aware, Mr Phelan was perfectly fine under the circumstances. Then, just as I got into the car, a microphone was thrust under my nose and a voice asked what those circumstances were, exactly."

"Yes, I can see that here. It says, 'When questioned, the officer replied that she had nothing more to say at this juncture.'" Madeleine looked up at Angela with a quizzical expression. "Juncture?"

"I know; I've got this tendency to be really formal at times."

Madeleine smiled. "The headlines are huge but there's not a lot of information. Just that there was a fatal shooting after the concert. I was worried something had happened to Brendan at first, but when Gary pushed by the bouncers I managed to get a quick look before they shut the gates again and I could see him standing in the alley. In spite of everything, I was thrilled. I've never been that close to him before."

"Yes, apart from the fact that Gary had arranged a chair for him and something to keep him warm, I don't think he'd moved from that spot by the time I arrived. The doctor treated him for shock."

"As I drove away I saw people beginning to realize something serious had happened. They were talking in groups and then asking others. I was tempted to park up somewhere and hang around. But it would only have been worth it if I could have got another look at Brendan and I didn't think it likely."

"You made a wise choice. I think his manager hurried him away in a car with tinted windows – well, as far as you can hurry someone who's been sedated and is more or less out of it."

"It doesn't say who got shot."

"That's because we haven't released the name."

Madeleine looked up at Angela and studied her for a moment.

"What?" asked Angela.

"You've got that same look on your face that Dad used to have when he was in the police and I asked him about a case."

"Oh, really? And what look is that?"

"Inscrutable."

"We do special training to achieve that look."

Madeleine laughed. "Seriously, you've no idea how frustrating it is that you're going to be rubbing shoulders with my absolutely most favourite singer and I can't even ask you about him."

"You can ask."

Madeleine grimaced. "Yeah, and a fat lot of good that will do me!"

"Actually…" began Angela, and stopped.

"What?"

"We could have a very unfair exchange of information."

"Er, like, I tell you everything I know about Brendan Phelan and you tell me absolutely nothing about your meeting with him."

"That's the sort of thing I mean."

"That's just the sort of line Dad would take! OK, then."

"You're a star, Mads," said Angela, taking her notebook out of her bag. "So what do you know about his private life?"

"He's got a girlfriend but I read somewhere that they don't live together."

"How long have they been dating?"

"A year or so, maybe."

"Do you know her name?"

"Tilly Townsend. She's an interior designer. Very successful she is, too. He commissioned her to do his decor; that's how they met."

"Ah! Yes, I do know of her and now that you've mentioned her I realize I've heard them spoken of as a couple. Do you have to go?" asked Angela as she saw Madeleine looking at her watch.

"Sorry, Step-ma. I can answer more questions tonight, if you have any."

"Thanks, this is great to be going on with."

Madeleine closed the newspaper and got up. "*Pas du tout.*"

"You seem to be settling in well to this job."

"Mm, nice crowd, the work's not too arduous and I get to use my French."

"That's good. You've taken after Patrick there. I didn't even know he spoke the language until we were on honeymoon."

Madeleine moved around the kitchen, gathering her bag and keys together. Angela, watching her, suddenly said: "I'm sorry, I forgot to ask how the concert went! Gary and I only had the briefest of words about it last night, and then we were launched into this investigation."

Madeleine smiled. "Oh, it was great. Fab. Mind you, I've never been to a bad Brendan Phelan gig. Gary wasn't at all sure about him at first, but I think he felt a bit differently by the end of the evening." She went into the hall and took her jacket from its hook.

"That's good. And how are things going there? You and Gary, I mean."

Madeleine smiled as she opened the front door. "I'm sorry, I have nothing more to say at this juncture. See you tonight."

"Now who's being inscrutable?" laughed Angela as the door closed behind her. The telephone rang – her husband, Patrick. A coroner's officer, he'd been at work an hour by now, and was calling from there. She picked up the phone. "Morning, darling."

"Morning, sweetheart. What time did you finally get home?"

"Two-thirty to three, I think; I'm glad I didn't wake you. I was totally zonked."

"Yes! You didn't even stir when I left this morning. I wanted to make sure you were up. A forensic post-mortem will begin in about five minutes and D.C.I. Stanway is already here."

"And I suppose after that he's going straight to the incident room and expects to see me there?"

"Hey! You took the words right out of my mouth."

Angela laughed. "Thanks for the heads-up, Pads. I'll be on my way in about five minutes."

"Good-oh. Stanway'd already run the gauntlet of the press when he arrived at the public mortuary. He's a bit twitched by it all from what I could see."

"He would be; he's not comfortable dealing with the media. You just watch. He's the senior investigating officer, but he'll put me in the firing line."

Patrick laughed. "A wise child knows its own parent; ditto worker and boss."

"You can count on it. How exactly was Stanway in front of the press this morning?"

"Awkward, but then, how many different ways are there to say that you've got nothing to say? And, of course, they were all asking about Brendan Phelan and whether or not he's involved. It's like the dead man is an afterthought."

"Are you surprised?"

"Not really. Turns out Stanway's daughter is a keen fan."

"As is yours."

"You speak truth, O queen. Well, I quite like a lot of his stuff myself. When are you going to interview him?"

"As soon as it can be set up after this morning's briefing in the incident room."

"OK, well see you this evening."

"Cheers, Paddy – love you." Angela drained her coffee and left the house.

Angela slipped into the incident room three minutes ahead of D.C.I. Stanway. Her eye went straight to the big whiteboard on the far wall. The totally pristine surface she might have expected at this stage would have been understandable, but she took in with relief the pictures of Brendan, his band and the three women backing singers already stuck to it – evidence for Stanway of a team already hard at work. She beamed and turned to the only other two people in the room, Detective Sergeants Rick Driver and Jim Wainwright, lounging on chairs, waiting for the briefing to start. She noted Jim's redrimmed eyes and Rick's stifled yawn. "Mm," she said. "I feel a bit like that too. It was one of those nights. Who did this?" she asked, cocking her head towards the photographs.

"Who do you think?" said Jim. "Our keen young Girl Guide and Boy Scout." Jim, never at his best in the mornings, didn't take well to only getting a few hours' sleep.

With the reflex of long habit, his partner moved to smooth whatever feathers Jim might ruffle. "Leanne and Derek got here first, Angie," he said. "They've been printing off photographs from the Internet."

"Very enterprising of them," remarked Angela, ignoring Jim. The door opened and Detective Constable Derek Palmer came in carefully carrying a tray of coffees. He was closely followed by D.C. Leanne Dabrowska and Gary.

"Brilliant! Coffee," said Angela swooping on one of the cups. She noted that even if he was too tired to be polite, Jim could wake up enough to grab a cup of coffee.

A moment or so later, D.C.I. Stanway breezed in. "Morning all," he called, with all the cheerfulness and energy of a man who'd had a full night's sleep. A chorus of greetings in varying degrees of enthusiasm met his. "Ah, good, the gang's all here," he said, looking around the room. He cast a brief glance up at the photographs. "Well done, whoever got started on these."

"Thanks, Leanne and Derek," said Angela. She believed in credit going where it was due.

"Right, I don't need to tell any of you this is going to be a very high-profile case," continued Stanway. "Brendan Phelan is so famous even *I've* heard of him." The polite laughter in response to this weak quip was a testament to the restorative effects of caffeine. "So, there's going to be a lot of media interest. Angie, you come out here."

Angie rose and joined him in front of the board. *Here it comes*, she thought, *no wonder he looks so cheerful, he's about to offload his most hated job*. Stanway looked around at them, his face serious. "*All* press contact will be dealt with through Angela," he said. "And I'll liaise with her about what gets said and what doesn't." He looked slowly around at them all. "I don't want anybody talking about this case in public; understood?"

They all nodded and murmured their acquiescence.

"Right." He smiled around at them. "I've been to the scene this morning and I attended the PM, so let's get started."

"Cause of death, sir?" asked Angela.

"What? Oh, yes! No surprises, gunshot wound to the back of the head. Death was instantaneous. Even though the production manager told us yesterday, the dead man's sister formally identified him this morning. I'll give you her details, Angie."

"Yes, sir. I'll make contact."

Stanway nodded. "How did the preliminary interviews go?"

"Much as you'd expect. We managed to get a few done, but they were all shocked and very tired, so I called it quits at about two this morning. We'll get going on them again now."

"Good, good. Right, I'll leave you to get on. I'll be keeping a close eye," said Stanway, making for the door.

"Yes, sir," replied Angela. The door closed behind him. She looked around at her team. "OK, Leanne and Derek, get hold of those uniformed officers who were helping out at the theatre, and go back to where we left off in the wee small hours." They got up and began moving towards the door.

"Don't you want us to go with them, Angie?" asked Rick.

"Yes, I do, but I also want you to find out about the security situation at the theatre. I saw a camera over the stage door and we'll need to know what's on the tape."

"It'll be too much to hope the whole thing was filmed," said Jim, getting up and moving across the room. "Unless the murderer's a complete idiot."

"I should think so, but we've got to check," replied Angie. "Another thing for you and Rick to deal with is a search of Oliver Joplin's home."

"No problem, Angie," said Rick. "We'll get uniform to seal the place and get there as soon as we can."

"Good-oh," replied Angela. "Yes, we've got quite a long list with this one."

"Guv?" Leanne hesitated and looked back, her hand already on the door handle. She seemed slightly embarrassed.

"Yes, Leanne?"

"If you're going up to Brendan Phelan's place later, will you need someone to carry your notebook?"

Angela smiled and looked at her. "You too?"

"'Fraid so."

Angela laughed. "Sorry, I think you'd better stick to the jobs you've already got. If I let you hobnob with the star, it'll only upset Derek."

Brendan Phelan lived in a gated property close to the street known as "Millionaires' Row" in Hampstead. Two distinct groups, fans and media, had established themselves in the vicinity to get a good view of the gates. The media team had gone a step further, actually blocking the entrance with one of their vans. Gary slowed down as they approached. "Shall I go and find who's in charge, to get this moved?" he asked.

Before Angela could reply, they both heard a loud humming noise from overhead. They looked up and saw a helicopter appear. "They're going all the way on coverage, aren't they?" said Angela. "The roof of our car will be on the news later. I don't think you need to go anywhere to find the boss," she added, looking through the side window. Gary looked in the same direction. A pack of avid journalists and photographers now surrounded the car. Some of the fans also peeled away from their party and reinvented themselves as press rearguard. She lowered the window and stared into a variety of camera lenses, trying to distinguish between a babble of shouted comments and questions.

"Can-you-give-us-any-information?-Is-Brendan-a-suspect-are-you-close-to-an-arrest?-How-is-Brendan?-Tell-him-we're-here-for-him!"

"Move that van, please."

"We'd-just-like-a-word-for-our-viewers/listeners/readers.-Is-it-true-that-the-Mob-have-infiltrated-Brendan's-team?-How-many-times-was-the-victim-shot?-I-love-him!-Can-you-tell-him-that?"

"Move that van, please."

"We just – "

"The only comment I'm prepared to make is that I'm planning to arrest your driver for obstructing a police enquiry." She turned to Gary. "Gary, drive up close to that van."

Gary edged them forward, stopping inches from the other vehicle. The driver had his head turned away from them. "The horn, Gary; I'm not playing games."

Gary sounded the horn.

Then he sounded it again, louder.

The van moved.

Ignoring the camera flashes and continued attempts to extract information, Angela rolled the window back up. She and Gary now had clear access to the shiny, black wrought-iron gates, which slid smoothly open to admit them once they had paused at the intercom to identify themselves. Gary drove them slowly along the short, impeccably maintained gravelled approach to a palatial entrance concealed from the road. Wide, red double doors were set into a vast porch bordered by two imposing columns.

"Wow! Nice pad! Maybe I should have stuck to my piano lessons," remarked Gary.

"Who knows where they would have led," agreed Angela, getting out of the car and coming round to the driver's side, where Gary had the window wound down.

Gary, still absorbed by the house, hadn't really heard her. "Those are Doric-style columns, aren't they?"

"Yes, I believe you're right. I wonder what happens now. Do we just go and ring the bell, or will someone come out? They know we've arrived, after all." Looking uncertainly towards the grandiose entrance, she saw the left door open; a man emerged. In his mid-forties, dressed in understatedly elegant casual clothes, he came across the gravel to them with a smile on his face. Angela thought he looked familiar and couldn't think where she might have met him. His first words told her.

"Detective Inspector Costello and Detective Constable Houseman? Hi, I'm Desmond Phelan, Brendan's brother. I was watching your arrival on our CCTV. It didn't take you long to get through that horde. I'm impressed."

"I had enough of their questions as I was leaving the Apollo at far too early an hour this morning," replied Angela. "They'll get their next statement when I'm good and ready."

Desmond nodded. "Just leave the car there," he said to

Gary. "It will be brought round for you when you leave." He looked from one to the other as Gary left the vehicle to the house staff and joined Angela on the gravel. "OK, this way." He turned and preceded them through the door. Angela and Gary exchanged one brief, expressive glance, then they obeyed.

Desmond led them into a spacious bright, round hallway. An expanse of deep green carpet covered the floor and pale apple-green walls rose the full height of the house to a domed glass ceiling, through which sunlight streamed down on them. The effect was stunning.

Tilly Townsend did him proud, thought Angela.

Desmond closed the front door. "Please come this way," he said, setting off across the sea of green carpet to a circular staircase which began to their right and continued up, as far as she could tell, nearly to the dome. Silently they followed him up the stairs and along the galleried landing into a large, airy living room on the upper floor. Desmond stood back, indicating they should go in before turning away and heading back down the stairs. Here a different colour scheme reigned, peach (carpet) and cream (wallpaper). Light poured in through a magnificent floor-to-ceiling window taking up one entire wall.

As she took in her surroundings Angela quickly realized that it was half-living room, half-music room. At one end stood a baby grand piano covered in loose pages of sheet music paper, and she counted two guitars on stands, a flute, a small drum kit and a keyboard.

A figure sat very still at the piano. Angela's eyes, moving from the drum kit, saw his bare feet first and travelled up past his jogging bottoms and sweatshirt to find his watching eyes fixed on hers.

Brendan Phelan.

As she met his gaze, the vulnerability she sensed affected her sharply. He seemed somehow smaller than the previous evening when she had seen him resplendent in his concert clothes.

"Mr Phelan."

The vulnerable look vanished immediately, replaced by his gracious and assured public persona. "Please – call me Brendan." He stood up and came to meet her, hand outstretched, emanating confidence. This talented, superbly successful man had become accustomed to pre-eminence. "Detective Inspector Costello," he greeted, shaking her hand. "And this must be D.C. Houseman," he added, turning courteously to Gary. "Can I get you some coffee?" He led them to the other end of the room.

"That would be lovely," said Angela, sinking into the depths of the cream armchair he indicated, while Gary took the sofa. She could see why he had so many women fans. His manner was totally unselfconsciously charming.

Brendan picked up a phone and spoke into it. "Any chance of some coffee, please, Des?" and after a few seconds, "Thanks, bro." Replacing the receiver, he smiled at them. "It won't be long. Des runs things around here. He had his own building company, but just as my career was taking off he injured his back and had to find something else to do."

"Sounds like a good arrangement," said Gary.

Brendan flashed a disarming smile. "It keeps my mum happy at any rate, having big brother on guard. She's heard some terrible things about the wicked world of rock music and she thinks every one of them could apply to me." Angela and Gary laughed politely. "Thanks for coming here to see me," he continued. "I was expecting to be summoned to a police station."

"It depends on the circumstances," replied Angela. "In

your case, we weren't sure if you'd fully recovered. Late last night you seemed to be in quite some distress."

A shadow of horror flitted across behind his eyes and he shuddered. He glanced out of the wide window at the beautifully tended shrubs and trees in his garden. "I was stunned."

That's a bit of an understatement in my view, thought Angela, but she remained silent, waiting for him to say more. He turned back to the room and looked at her. "This is going to sound extraordinarily naive, Inspector, but I've only ever associated guns with sport; boys and their toys, eh?"

At that moment Desmond entered with the coffee, a fresh pot, and three cups on a tray. "I mean," Brendan continued, "of course I understand they're dangerous and must be handled with care. But always in sport. And, to be candid, it's one I excel at. There's a thrill in hitting the bullseye. It's just good fun."

"Ah."

"Yes." He nodded soberly. "It wasn't fun last night, was it?" He sat down on the other cream armchair. "I never imagined it could lead to… that brutality." She watched his stricken face as he relived the sight of Oliver Joplin lying motionless and bleeding on the ground.

When Desmond had left the room, Angela got out her notebook and asked, "Would you like to tell us exactly what happened? Everything you can remember."

Brendan turned a distracted gaze upon her. He seemed not to have heard her. "This should solve the problem," he said.

Chapter Six

Gary put his coffee cup down and slid his notebook and pen from his pocket.

"Which problem would that be, Brendan?" Angela asked.

He flicked his eyes to Gary, back to her, and gave her a rueful smile. "I must think before I speak. There isn't one, now. And even when it existed, nobody would kill over it."

"Now you've got me completely intrigued."

A short laugh escaped him. "Yes, if I carry on like this I could dig myself into a very deep hole, and all for nothing."

All for nothing? thought Angela. "Nonetheless?" she said.

"Yes, of course, you're looking for motives for his murder. I can't give you one. Olly and I were having a conversation outside the theatre, in the alley."

Angela nodded. "I became very familiar with the layout last night. What was this conversation about?"

Brendan leaned back in his chair. "There was an issue with Olly and I wanted to talk to him about it, to check it out myself."

Angela took her time writing this down and noted that Gary did the same. She looked up from her notebook into Brendan's attractive face and was suddenly struck by something she should have noticed before. He had the look of Patrick about him, the same Irish type, intelligent, charming, a similar smile. Brendan's eyes didn't yet crinkle as Patrick's did; he was still too young. She pulled her mind back to the job.

"Tell me about this issue."

Brendan took a sip of his coffee. "There'd been whispers for a while about him not pulling his weight. He was a bit too fond of checking out the nearest pub at any venue we were playing, and he'd be in there when he should have been working. The other techies covered for him, but things had got a bit worse lately and he nearly missed a couple of cues. I can't have that. The lights work in conjunction with the sounds – well, they do on most shows."

"Yes," nodded Gary. Both Angela and Brendan turned towards him. "I've seen the show," he explained, addressing Brendan. "I was there last night."

"Ah! Did you enjoy it?"

"Very much," replied Gary, with enthusiasm. "The sound and lighting effects were tremendous. Those whip cracks are *something else.*"

Brendan looked pleased. "Thank you. We've worked hard on it."

Yes, definitely a Paddy-type smile, thought Angela. "Is it normal for you to deal with your staff like this – yourself, I mean?"

Brendan turned his attention to her. "I know what you're thinking and you're right. I've got a production manager to handle that sort of thing."

"It does sound like having a dog and doing the barking yourself."

"Yep; normally Jack would deal with it but I've known Olly – I *had* known him – a long time, and I like to think there's a good team spirit in my crew."

"I see," replied Angela as she made a note. She didn't really feel her question had been answered but couldn't find an argument against Brendan's explanation. Brendan must have sensed this because he spoke again.

"When you're a megastar you tend to get a lot of things done for you that you'd do yourself if you were an ordinary bloke. Every now and then, I go through this thing where

I tell myself I need to *man up* and take responsibility. This was one of those occasions." He produced another disarming smile. "It won't last."

Angela laughed, noted the comment in her book and placed a large question mark after it. "So, you were talking to Oliver about his attitude to work."

Brendan nodded.

"Why out in the alley?"

"I knew we wouldn't be disturbed out there. You can go right to the other end of it and be private."

"Surely you'd get the same privacy in your dressing room?"

"I could ask for it, but there's a lot goes on after the show. A whole host of people appear backstage and you're either pleased to see them or you've got to glad-hand them. I'd be forever answering knocks on the door and asking people to wait. You know how it is?"

Angela didn't really, but she could imagine.

"Can you take me through the sequence of events?"

A look of distress she had no doubt was genuine clouded his features. "I think I'm still traumatized. We were talking."

"Right."

"So I'm trying to gee him up without it turning into something aggressive. You know, just a bloke-to-bloke thing. 'People are talking, Ol,' I said. 'You need to smarten your act up.' I didn't want to get too heavy and I thought Jack might, if I left it to him."

"That makes sense," said Angela. She could see Brendan relaxing, but she added another question mark to the page. "And then what?"

Brendan steadied himself with a couple of deep breaths. "I can't remember exactly what I'd been saying. We walked to the other end of the alley and back and I think we'd stopped. No, I'd stopped. Olly had been moving, walking to and fro and suddenly his face appeared in front of mine. He said, 'OK, Bren, I get it,' or something of that sort. Then there was this colossal noise echoing all around us. I immediately thought of a gunshot but didn't see how it could be. Then I thought, maybe a car had backfired. The next thing, Olly's eyes went wide. He kind of stared like he was really puzzled by something. I think I wondered for a moment if I had dirt on my face. Then he staggered towards me, just a step, and fell. I think he might have reached out to me but I'm not sure now." Brendan's cheeks had become red and his breath came in short gasps. Clearly the shock was still with him. "I didn't see any blood at first."

"What were you aware of?"

Brendan calmed a little. "Not much. I think I might have heard a door bang."

"Yes," said Gary. Both Angela and Brendan looked at him. "I heard a shot and what I thought was a door banging while I was standing in the street."

"You said so last night," remarked Angela.

"I think I remember you," said Brendan, looking closely at Gary. "And Don; did he bring me a coat and a chair?"

"Yes," Gary confirmed.

Brendan nodded. "I hadn't been aware of feeling cold but I do recall suddenly feeling better with the coat round my shoulders." He looked at Angela. "I'm sorry, that's all I can remember."

"You've done very well," replied Angela. "Your account is helpful. Please let us know if any other memories of the event come back to you."

"I will, of course."

"At any point in the conversation were you conscious of anybody behind Oliver?"

"No... I..."

"What?"

"It's nothing."

"I think I should be the judge of that, Brendan."

Brendan flicked a glance at her as if recognizing her authority for the first time.

"I don't see… oh, OK. A van was parked outside the stage door, right?"

"Yes, I remember seeing it."

"It was to take some things to the O2 for tonight. I was due to sing a set at a charity gig, but I've cancelled. I mean, it's a matter or respect, but the doctor also advised me to."

"Very wise, I'm sure. What was odd about this van?"

"Not the van itself. There was a long, narrow flight case on top of it and a gel leaning up against that at an odd angle. And, I can't be sure but there might have been a black bin bag up there at well."

"A gel?"

"A gel is a square of, like, transparent coloured Perspex or acetate that you put in front of a spotlight to produce the different colours."

"Oh I get it."

"Yes, so a gel isn't just stuck in front of a light, of course. It goes into a frame and is fitted on the front of the spotlight. You can have a few gels fitted onto a spot at the same time and you bring each colour on as and when needed."

"Oh yes," said Gary. "There was a moment last night when the whole stage seemed to be bathed in this red light and then it went to blue and back to red all in time to some whip cracks."

"That's it."

"It was a stunning effect."

Brendan smiled. "Yes, I like that moment. You can always sense the audience going, 'Wow!'"

"So," continued Angela. She remembered the items on the top of the van very well, but wanted to know why Brendan had mentioned them. "There was a narrow flight case, a gel and possibly a bin bag lying on top of the van. Should they have been there?"

Brendan had fully recovered now. He smiled. "No."

"Why not?"

"Jack's very particular about the packing. Someone drove off once leaving a very valuable piece of equipment stuck on top of the van. It fell off, needless to say, and it's been a no-no ever since."

Ah! thought Angela, and suddenly remembered looking closely at the roof of the vehicle the previous evening. "I noticed there was no roof rack on the van."

Brendan shot her a sharp glance, as if impressed that she'd noticed. "Possibly not, though we sometimes use one with a rack. Even so, I wasn't planning to take the whole show to the O2, just a couple of bits and pieces. I'm certain what we needed would all fit inside."

Angela saw that Brendan had become completely relaxed, almost relieved, about something. She wondered what internal process had brought this about. "Are you saying somebody could have hidden behind these things on top of the van to shoot at…?"

"Either one of us," confirmed Brendan. His voice was low and the tone sombre but he had no fear in his eyes.

"Do you think you might have been the intended target?" she asked.

He flicked a glance towards his windows, took in Gary and settled back on Angela. "No, I don't. It's in the interest of everybody I work with to keep me hale and hearty, Inspector."

Hmm, thought Angela. She made a decision. She wanted to think a few things through before she went much further with him. She closed her notebook and stood up. "Thank you so much for your time, Brendan, I think that's all for the moment. I need to liaise with my team, get an overall picture of the events and see what other interviews have turned up. I probably will need to speak to you again, though."

Brendan rose with them. "No problem, Inspector. I'm just staying around the house for the next few days, taking things quietly. Let me see you out." He moved to the circular staircase and led the way downstairs. He came to the door with them himself and stood on the step as they drove away. Angela, behind the wheel, could see him in the rear-view mirror. He watched until they turned the corner of the drive.

The proportion of the two groups in the street outside seemed to have changed slightly – more fans, fewer journalists. The fans faithfully called out their enquiries about Brendan, but the journalists seemed to have decided she and Gary weren't worth the copy.

They'd left Hampstead behind before Angela spoke.

"What did you make of that, Gary?" she asked.

"Did you cut it a bit short?"

"Yes, I did." Angela turned this comment over in her mind. "Didn't seem too abrupt, did I?"

"No, not that. I just had the feeling you had more to ask then changed your mind. I don't think he would have noticed."

"That's good. OK, I've got a couple of thoughts. Remember Terry Dexter talking about the dead man being a less than ideal technician? Well, surely the others must have noticed, don't you think? Besides which, if Terry knew, I'd have thought the rest of the world would hear all about it in short order. So why, when Brendan decides to tackle him about it, does he make such a thing of having privacy?"

"Er… just common decency, I'd have thought. Plus, it's an employment protocol thing, isn't it? If D.C.I. Stanway had to tell me off over something everyone knew about, he'd still do it in private."

"Yes, but that begs another question. The D.C.I. would probably assign me the job of dealing out the reprimand in the first place."

"True," agreed Gary. "What was the other thought?" he asked, as they emerged into the traffic that roared around Swiss Cottage as their journey took them closer to central London.

"Well, it arises from what that runner, Carla, said. I didn't want to mention it when we were with him just now, even though he acknowledged that either one of them could have been hit. But she seemed to think Brendan must have been the target."

"She struck me as a bit of a loose cannon; mouthy little piece, as well. She would have run that interview if you'd have given her the chance. It hadn't occurred to Terry Dexter until you mentioned it and he must know if Brendan's got any enemies."

"You're right. OK, scrub that idea for now. Let's wait and see if it comes up in other interviews. We mustn't lose sight of the salient points."

"Which are?"

"There were still just the two of them talking outside in the alley and we've established that Oliver's slapdash ways couldn't have been much of a secret."

"Perhaps Brendan really did want to take this one on."

"Possibly. I could be mistaken, but I don't really buy this *man up* business. A star of Brendan's calibre doesn't talk to his staff about their work. His manager does it, no matter how much of a team spirit he likes to think they have."

"So what were they really talking about?"

"Exactly, that's the question. But it beats me how we're going to get the answer."

"You don't suppose...?"

"What?"

"Is it possible that Oliver initiated the conversation, not Brendan?"

Angela considered the matter. "It's possible, I suppose. I would have thought the same protocol must apply in the other direction, surely. If Oliver wanted a word with Brendan, he'd have to go through Jack Waring or Doug Travers. But I'm not au fait with show business circles."

"It was just a thought."

"And a good one; keep 'em coming."

"Actually, I've got a thought which might be totally ridiculous but I'd like to air it."

"Air away."

"Don't laugh, but could Brendan have done it?"

"I'm not laughing. Let's consider it. From what you told me last night you got to the stage door very quickly. How much time are we talking about?"

"I was in the street with Madeleine and we'd been trying to see into the alley. I heard the shot and went to the gates where those bouncers tried to stop me entering. I flashed my ID at them and pushed past. I was by the body in about – oh – no more than a minute, probably a bit less, from when the gun went off."

"And Brendan stood there looking very shocked with a smoking gun in his hand?"

"No gun, obviously, and the SOCOs didn't find one in the alley, but I've been thinking about that."

"OK, take me through the possible scenario."

"Brendan is talking to Oliver. Oliver's not static, he's

turning this way and that, just as Brendan told us. When he's not looking, Brendan pulls the gun out of his pocket. When Oliver's back is to him, he shoots him. Oliver falls down. An accomplice takes the gun and dashes into the theatre."

"Thus making that door banging sound. Right, with you so far."

"Depending on which way he fell, Brendan nips round to make it look like he had been facing Oliver when the shot was fired and just at that moment I show up."

Angela considered the possibility. "Hmm. I'm not sure about this."

Eventually Gary spoke. "Are you laughing quietly?"

"Not at all, Gary. I was only thinking it through. It's very tight for time and you'd need the most amazing confidence to pull it off. So many things could go wrong – unexpected coppers appearing in the alley, for one thing."

"OK, stupid idea, let's forget it."

"No, no, we won't forget it. After all, he is a man of great confidence – not least in handling guns. We'll put it into the mix with everything else we find. Who knows? Maybe that's exactly what happened."

A mile further on Gary let out a huge sigh.

"Oh my goodness, you sound like the weight of the world descended on your shoulders!" Angela remarked.

"I've just had a thought."

"Oh – the butler did it after all?" She looked across at him and grinned.

He laughed. "No, if the murderer turns out to be Brendan and I'm on the arresting team, will Maddie ever forgive me?"

Angela let out a kindly bark of laughter. Every now and again Gary said something that reminded her he was still a very young man.

Chapter Seven

They bought sandwiches at a shop near the office and joined their team for what turned out to be a working lunch.

"It looks as though everybody had a busy morning," remarked Angela, looking up at the whiteboard. The names of everybody backstage the previous evening had now been written up, and several proper photographs had taken the place of the hastily printed pictures. Somebody had drawn a crude map of the area from the gates to the stage door. "Who's the budding artist?" she asked. She pointed at the drawing of a stick figure just inside the gate area waving a police ID card; the name "Gary" appeared just underneath. Brendan Phelan and the prone Oliver Joplin were also represented as stick figures.

D.S. Jim Wainwright guffawed and his colleague, D.S. Rick Driver, grinned and held up a hand. "I do my best," he said.

Angela laughed. "It's helpful, but I'd advise you not to give up the day job. OK, everybody. What have we got?"

"We've spoken to the band, and we're going to take on the backing singers and the crew who travel with Brendan Phelan," began Jim. "Then there's another crew of permanent theatre staff, involved in all productions – including Brendan Phelan's."

"We're doing those," said Leanne. "We've talked to the front-of-house staff already and we're going for the backstage lot this afternoon. Most of them weren't there this morning."

"What about a stage-door person?" asked Angela. "Wouldn't there normally be someone sitting in that little cubbyhole near the stage door?"

"Yes, there's a bloke who does that job. He's part of the permanent theatre staff, so we'll be talking to him when we go back," said Derek.

"OK. So what have we got from this morning, then?"

"Some heard the shot and some didn't. Of those that did, they didn't immediately clock it as anything strange because they're so used to hearing shots in the performance. So, not a lot, really," answered Jim.

"Except…" added Rick.

"Yes?"

"Our deceased doesn't seem to have been a very popular person."

"What makes you say that?"

"That's just it," Jim cut in. "We couldn't really get an angle on it. Most of them had worked with him for years, so they knew him well; but when we asked if he had any enemies, or if they knew of anybody with a grudge, it was like a wall of silence suddenly went up. Mostly they looked at each other and said he did his own thing."

"Which is?"

"That's the catch-22 line," said Rick. "We asked that. But because it *is* his own thing, nobody else was in on it."

"Oh, how neat," said Angela, thinking back over her interview with Brendan Phelan and the questions he'd raised in her mind.

"That's what we thought," agreed Jim.

"Leanne, write: 'What was Oliver up to?' on the board, please. It can't be left like that; we've got to pursue it."

"OK, guv," said Leanne getting up from her chair.

"What about the scene of crime?" Angela asked of the room in general.

"I don't think it's going to get us very far," said Derek, picking up a sheet and reading from it.

"Really? Why not?" asked Angela.

"There's just so many people coming and going through that stage door in the course of a concert."

"And Gary and I had a look in that crate – sorry; flight case – left standing by the van."

"Yes, full of heavy-duty electric cables," said Derek. "And on top of the van that – " Derek looked up at her with a puzzled frown – "gel? Is that right?"

"Yes, it's OK, I know what a gel is now," said Angela.

"Not something you put on your hair, then?" surmised Derek. The bafflement hadn't completely disappeared from his face.

Angela laughed. "When you go back to the Apollo, get someone to show you what a lighting gel is. It's to do with colouring stage illumination. But you haven't yet mentioned the thing I'm waiting to hear about," she said to him.

"No sign of a gun anywhere, guv."

"Hmm. OK. Blind alley. Gary and the bouncers at the gates. Then it looks like the perp dashed straight into the theatre with it."

"That must have been the door-banging sound you heard, Gary," said Jim.

"Must be," replied Gary.

"Which means," said Angela, "he or she could be among the group of people who came out of the stage door right after Gary arrived by the body."

"Were they all searched?"

"Yes, guv," said Derek. "The uniformed officers got them to go through their pockets and once the auditorium was empty we all had a good search under the seats, but we didn't turn up anything unusual."

"It's probably in the Thames by now," suggested Jim.

"Not far to go to chuck it in, is it?" added Rick.

"Well done, Derek and Leanne, for hanging on to check under the seats in the wee small hours," said Angela. "Rick, Jim, make sure the dressing rooms get searched, OK? I'm sure you're right, it's much more likely to have disappeared by now. The river is the best bet, but we've got to tick all the boxes." The room stirred into life as everyone scrunched and dumped their sandwich wrappings and gulped down the dregs of their drinks.

"OK, everybody, so what do we do now?" she asked.

"We dig deeper," came back the chorus.

"Yep," she agreed. "Don't forget the security cameras," she reminded Rick.

"They're on the list. As soon as we've finished the interviews," he assured her. "Where are you off to, Angie?"

"I'm going to talk to Brendan's manager," she answered, finishing the last of her coffee, crushing the polystyrene cup before tossing it into the bin.

Angela and Gary found Doug Travers in his office in the heart of London's theatre district. Glossy publicity photographs of Brendan Phelan adorned the walls in a cramped reception area and gave way to more personal ones as they entered his office. Doug and Brendan, in evening dress, smiled at her over champagne glasses. From a frame behind the desk, Brendan – looking every inch a country gentleman, in Barbour and gumboots – beamed proudly, a mean beast of a rifle slung over his shoulder as he leaned back on the bonnet of a 4x4. Angela's eyes travelled from the photograph to the man sitting in front of it. She found him watching her, a small smile playing around his mouth. "It looks like Brendan Phelan's got into the hunting, shooting and fishing set," she remarked. "Or was he always?"

The smile on the manager's face widened. "No, it's Terry

who's set himself up as landed gentry. Brendan's a townie through and through, but he likes to go out to Terry's place – just beyond Amersham, it is. They take a pot at clay pigeons from time to time."

"Ah yes, Terry Dexter," replied Angela, and without thinking began the self-applied description she remembered from interviewing him, "musician/songwriter – "

" – lead guitar," finished Doug Travers. Angela glanced at him and caught an unmistakably ironic smile on his face.

OK, I might as well start here as anywhere, she thought. "He told me he'd co-written Brendan's first hit."

The sense of irony in Doug's expression deepened into scepticism. "Hmm. He did the riff. It fitted in well so Brendan saved himself the effort of writing one."

"What did his co-writing amount to? Fifty per cent of each song, would you say?"

Doug shook his head gently. "More like twenty. He bigs himself up, does our Terence; but he's loyal. And to be fair to him, he's a competent musician. Reliable, too. And they do go back a long way."

Angela nodded and looked more intently at the photographs filling every available space on the walls. She could see more scenes, casual and formal, beach, bar and boardroom, and in each one Doug featured, either to one side or just behind Brendan.

"I've got a good gig and I know it," he said following the direction of her eyes. "Fifteen years ago I was running a stable of third-rate acts who, frankly, would never get a better booking than their local pub. I was on the point of chucking it all in when a certain London-Irish teenager strolled through the door of my office with a second-hand guitar slung over his shoulder. That was then, this is now. Neither of us look back much, except to be grateful."

Angela nodded and sat on the chair in front of his desk. Gary found a stool in a corner. "How did you know he wasn't just another third-rate act?"

"I didn't, not immediately. But he had a kind of presence about him, it's unmistakable and that's always a good start. Then he sat just there, where you're sitting now, and sang me one of his songs and completely blew me away. That voice – you must have heard him sing." Angela thought she might have done, but Gary nodded with enthusiasm. "And the stuff he writes; he's way ahead of the field."

"That's no guarantee of making it," objected Angela. "There are any number of talented people out there who can't afford to give up the day job."

"That's true. I couldn't have known for sure. I still took a risk but, with Brendan's talent and charisma, a lesser one. I'd been front of house," he continued, as if he'd been asked the question. "I'd been to see someone. I got back to the stage door area just when it all kicked off."

Angela passed to the reason for her visit with equal smoothness. "Did you hear the shot?"

"I did. My immediate thought was that someone had had a bit of an accident putting the guns away."

"So then what happened?"

"Don came past me. He looked really agitated, which is unusual in a normally placid man like him. I was just about to ask him if anything was up when he said someone had shot Olly and it looked like Brendan had turned to stone. Anyone else and I might not have believed him, but Don doesn't mess around. I think I said, 'What?' but he just said he needed a coat and went off somewhere. I was still standing there trying to take it in and figuring my next move when Jack went past pushing a flight case."

"Yes," remarked Angela, remembering what Gary had told

her of the moments immediately after he'd arrived at the stage door.

"He would have been getting stuff out for tonight. There's a big charity gala on in aid of abused kids. It's an annual thing. Brendan's done it about four years in a row. Well, he's not doing tonight's now, the doctor advised against it."

"So I understand."

"The next thing I remember was that we were all being asked to congregate in the stalls and wait there. As I joined them I could hear some people whispering about Brendan and I felt worried about him because I didn't know what Don meant by being turned to stone. Then I saw Don going through to the back with a chair and a coat. And I think he had a drink as well. He said Brendan was all right but a bit shocked and that a doctor was on the way. That calmed me down, although I would much prefer to have been able to go out to him."

"What do you make of it all?"

Doug let out a noisy breath. "I didn't know what to think; I still don't, to be honest. It was a real shock. I know show business can have some dodgy connections, believe me I've met one or two in my time, but I've never come across anything like this."

"Were you aware there's been a suggestion that Brendan was the intended target?"

"Who said that?" he asked. Angela remained silent. "Doesn't seem very likely to me."

"You don't believe it?"

Doug scratched his temple. "Not really. I mean, I know there are some crazy people around and it's always possible that Bren's got an enemy, or someone who thinks he's an enemy, but then I'd expect it to be someone lurking on the outside – you know – like it happened with John Lennon. No members of the public can get into that area." He shook his head. "I don't see that somehow."

"How well did you know the dead man?"

"That's an interesting question. When it comes to the crew, Jack does the actual hiring and firing, so I don't have to be really involved with them. And some you get to know better than others, as you'd expect."

Angela nodded. "Yes, I can imagine. So, Oliver Joplin…?"

"Olly – well – his case is a bit different because Brendan dealt with Olly directly. I think he felt comfortable with him, being the longest-serving crew member, and Olly had known him from just as he began to get really famous. And I seem to remember Brendan once saying he felt sorry for Olly because he had a sister to support."

"How did you get on with Oliver?"

Doug shrugged. "There was no animosity. We said hello and how are you and that sort of stuff; but that's not really knowing someone, is it? He was a fairly quiet bloke, usually on the edge."

"The edge?"

"The edge of any little circle. I never saw him at the centre of the conversation, but on the other hand he wasn't outside of it, either. But you need to talk to Jack, really. He was a lot closer to him – to them all, in fact. My contact with the crew is through Jack. Maybe I should be a bit more involved 'cause it does seem strange."

"What seems strange?"

"When I talked to Brendan he passed it off as 'manning up' and 'taking responsibility' but I don't buy it. A star of Brendan's calibre doesn't talk to his staff about their work… Jack deals with the crew; it's what he's paid for. But it apparently doesn't seem odd to anyone else that Brendan was outside the stage door talking to Oliver Joplin."

Chapter Eight

Rick Driver noted beads of perspiration on the front-of-house manager's reddening face, wondered briefly what he was nervous about, then realized he hadn't listened to a word the man had said. His attention had been elsewhere. Apart from last night, he'd only ever been in a theatre as a member of an audience and being here at this time of the day was an intriguing novelty.

"I'm sorry, Mr – er – " Now it was Rick's turn to blush. He hadn't even caught the man's name and he should have checked his notes anyway.

"Grieves. Barry Grieves." Evidently Rick's distraction supplied a small measure of relief from his discomfiture. "We're still looking into what's happened."

Rick nodded, considering the other man's words. What's happened? Ah yes! He and Jim had asked to see the footage from the CCTV camera that covered the stage door. He dragged his mind back to the job, but almost immediately became distracted by the sight of a very famous woman moving gracefully across the space to his left. Forgetting all about Barry Grieves, he tracked her progress across the bar area. The singer, a country star, known almost as much for her feminine allure as for her deep, throaty voice, stopped and turned to face the two policemen. He saw Jim pull his shoulders back. Rick automatically straightened his tie and smoothed his jacket. The lady looked at them and Rick felt himself go very hot. She smiled at her reflection in a large wall mirror behind them and passed out of their eyeline, a small posse of minders and assistants following in her wake. Rick turned back to find Jim staring, mouth open, after the now-invisible apparition. "It was her, wasn't it?" he asked.

Jim, apparently still contemplating the image in his head, smiled beatifically. "Sure was. She's a cracker, isn't she?" He glanced at Rick and seemed to come back to earth. "Seems a bit smaller in real life; well, the hair's just as big as on the telly, of course."

Rick turned his attention once more, and fully this time, to the theatre manager. "That was Georgia Pensay, wasn't it?"

"Yes," Barry Grieves confirmed, manifestly grateful for the distraction she had fortuitously provided. "Yes, it is. She's doing a series of concerts here and she's in for the sound check this afternoon." He shook out a spotlessly clean handkerchief and mopped the trickle of perspiration from his brow, his equilibrium now fully recovered. "Completely sold out, I'm afraid," he added, as if worried that Rick and Jim might push for tickets.

Rick, mistaking his meaning, smiled at the incongruity of a theatre manager being "afraid" of the idea of a full house. "I love the play of words in her name," he remarked.

"I beg your pardon? Play on words?" Barry Grieves knew he still had to face the embarrassing matter temporarily in abeyance, but Rick wondered if the prospect felt less alarming by the minute as he realized these policemen were fans, not just officers of the law.

"Yes," said Rick. "You know – Georgia *Pensay*. Her name. 'Pensay' is – I read it in an interview in the *Metro* – from the French *pensée* which means a 'thought'. She chose it because of the song 'Georgia On My Mind'. Get it? Pensay – a thought – on her mind?"

"Ah – yes," Barry Grieves's face broke into a smile. He clearly hadn't heard this before. And then, irrelevantly: "I'm rather fond of the sound of a brass band myself, to be honest."

Rick decided they'd better get back to the business in hand. "You were explaining about the CCTV footage," he said.

"Yes," Barry was equal to the occasion now. Any sense of dread under interrogation had apparently been dispelled when the officer of the law turned out to be just one more man whose mouth dropped open at the sight of a celebrity in close proximity. "There isn't any, unfortunately. Our IT person is coming in later to check things over, because I think we've been hacked."

"Hacked?"

"That's what it looks like. We've got a camera covering the stage door itself, one at either end of the back alley and one trained over the security gates. We've checked thoroughly, and there's nothing wrong with the cameras themselves – not as far as we can tell, anyway. The problem seems to be in the computer program. Those particular cameras were all controlled as part of one group in the system, so if one went out they all did."

"Blast!" Rick gasped in frustration.

"Quite," agreed the manager. "They seem to have gone wrong just as we came down."

"Came down from where?" queried Rick.

"Sorry – theatre jargon. When the show ended."

"Just at the crucial time," added Jim. "Which means either it's an amazing coincidence, or – "

"Yes. Or it was planned and someone went to a lot of trouble to set this murder up," said Rick. He looked at Barry Grieves. "We'll need that IT report the minute it comes in."

"Oh yes, no problem. I'll send it through straight away."

Rick frowned in thought, recollecting the details Gary had described of last night's crime scene.

"Most of us entered through the front door," he said, "but my D.I. and another colleague came in through the stage door and they told us this morning there was nobody sitting in that little place where – "

"Oh yes, where the stage doorman normally sits. Yes, that's true. Trevor's the man you mean. He's our stage doorman. The monitors for those cameras are there and he keeps his eye on them, so when he noticed the screens had gone blank he naturally tried to find out what was going on."

"How would he have done that?" asked Jim.

"In the first place he'd have called through to the front, to my office; but by then both my assistant and I were standing more or less where I am now, waiting for the audience to start piling out. So that's when he left his post to come and try to find one of us."

"And did he find you?"

"No, by the time he got round to the front the place would have been heaving with people. But as it happens he tripped over something left lying about in the corridor. It gave him a nasty bruise and a cut to the shin, so he took himself into the toilets to administer a bit of first aid."

"So when did you hear about the cameras?"

"Sitting in the auditorium with everybody else waiting for the police to come and talk to us. Trevor came to find me. He mentioned it then."

"Have you any idea who might have hacked the system? And why do you assume it was hacked? Couldn't it just have broken? Has it happened before?"

"Never. I actually thought it must have been a simple computer glitch at first, but I got to thinking while we were sitting waiting in the stalls. It seemed very suspicious that the cameras in just the right place should have gone down at just the moment somebody got murdered. That's why I came to the conclusion we must have been hacked. But, who did it? I can't help you there, officer. As you can imagine, I've given that a great deal of thought."

Rick could see he'd gone as far as he could with this line

of questioning. "OK. Just as soon as your IT people have got back to you, then – let me know."

Barry Grieves nodded. "I will."

"We'd still like to speak to – Trevor, you said his name is?"

"I can give you his address."

"Oh. He's not working today?"

"He wouldn't be in at this time of the day in any case but, as it happens, we're dark now until Georgia Pensay opens at the end of the week."

"Dark?" asked Jim.

"Sorry – I mean we haven't got a show in at the moment."

Rick made a note of this snippet of theatre jargon. He thought it might come in handy for another interview.

"Is there anybody here who was here last night?" asked Jim.

"Oh, certainly. The theatre technicians and some front-of-house staff, plus the cleaning and maintenance still have to go on. Would you like to speak to whoever I can find?"

"Yes please, Mr Grieves," replied Rick. They followed him across the crimson carpet of the foyer.

Angela and Gary heard Jack Waring before they saw him. As they approached through an industrial unit in north-west London, they could hear somebody whistling, a rich, cheerful sound.

"Ooh, that's familiar but I just can't place it," remarked Angela, after listening for a moment.

"Me neither," agreed Gary, "but I know I've heard it before."

The whistling stopped just before they reached him. Seated on a stool in the open doorway of a small warehouse, sipping from a very large mug, he looked up at their approach. Inside they glimpsed various items of lighting equipment and several of the flight cases they'd seen the previous evening. A couple of these had the lids open. Everything else seemed to be stored very neatly. "Good afternoon, Mr Waring. Sorry to disturb your tea break," began Angela.

"Oh – please! 'Jack'! Not a problem." He stood up. "I knew you'd be along for a word at some point. There's a café round the corner, there," he said, pointing.

"We won't bother," replied Angela.

Jack sat down again. "I think I'm going to disappoint you."

"Really, why is that?"

Jack moved his head from side to side. "Saw nothing, heard nothing, did nothing." He grinned.

"When did you become aware of what had happened?" asked Angela.

Jack screwed up his eyes and thought for a moment. "I'd agreed with the lads that we'd do the get-out as soon as we could. You know, we had to load up our van with some things for the O2 tonight. I was able to put some things in a case while Bren did the encores, and I got that one out to the van."

"Ah, yes," said Gary. "The one already outside when the shot was fired."

"That's right. After I took it out, I went to the stage to wait for Bren to come off. I wanted to greet him – congratulate him, that sort of thing. There's a nice feeling backstage at a moment like that, everyone's pretty much on a high."

"I can imagine," said Gary.

"I thought I must have missed him – thought Bren must have already gone to his dressing room, because there was no sign of him, and the band and singers had left the stage; so I got started on another case. The rest of the crew took a breather at that point – they probably stopped for a cuppa in the crew room before dismantling the bigger bits of equipment. I was just stashing the easy stuff."

"Did you hear the shot?"

"No, I didn't hear a thing. As I say, I got this second case ready and wheeled it through and that's when I found them all standing outside the stage door looking at Olly, dead on the ground. And Bren – well, you know what he was like." Jack addressed this last comment towards Gary.

"Yes, I remember your arrival," said Gary.

"Yes. So I took the case back in, like you said, 'cause I was disturbing a crime scene. Phew!" He looked at Gary with sympathy. "You expect scenes in a theatre but not outside, and not like that, eh?"

"No," said Gary. "It reminded me of a magic act. I suppose it was these black flight cases." He pointed into the open space behind Jack.

Jack half-turned. "I suppose they can seem a bit like the boxes magicians use." He turned back and smiled at Gary. "That takes me back. That's how I started off in the business."

"What, show business? Working for a magician, you mean?"

"Yes, on a seaside show. Looking back I can see I got the job because I was cute – just a little kid, you know – and in reality we were quite a tacky outfit, but I was so thrilled. I was a magician's assistant and I had to dress up in Eastern clothes with a turban on my head; thought I'd arrived at the big-time, I did. And I got to see all the tricks of the trade. I had to help the lady get into the box – "

" – who was then cut in half! That's it!" said Gary, gleeful at the memory. "Yes, one of those acts. It's all come back to me now."

"I thought you ran a gun club," said Angela, deciding that if they were going to take a trip down memory lane they might as well keep it relevant.

"That was later," said Jack. "I did the seaside show for a couple of years until I got too tall to be the magician's lad."

"And I expect you grew out of your 'cute' phase," remarked Angela.

"Oh yes. The stage manager gave me a job backstage. By then we had a Wild West act in the show, a marksman dressed up as Wyatt Earp picking off cardboard coyotes and plugging the symbols in playing cards while some pretty girl held them up close to her face – you know the sort of thing. There's not much call for it nowadays, but that's when I became interested in guns and it stayed with me – which was useful."

"Useful?" asked Gary.

"Yes, I had a few lean years when I couldn't seem to get theatre work at all, but I was a member of a gun club – just as a hobby – so when the owner needed a new manager he offered me the job. I settled for that, but it's funny how things work out, isn't it? Because that's where I met Brendan and Terry; still schoolboys, they were then. And, lo and behold, at the time Brendan began to become well known he'd started using guns in the act and needed someone he could trust to handle them properly. So here I am, back in show business again."

"I think you're employed for more than just experience of guns," suggested Angela, admiring the clean, neat interior of the garage.

"Yes, I like to keep things tidy. You know where you are then. And you have to keep track. Some of the equipment's our own, but some is hired in. Sorting out what's what is down to me."

"You said you thought Brendan had gone back to his dressing room?"

Jack flicked a quick glance up at Angela from under his eyebrows. "I did. I was wrong, obviously. He must have gone outside with Olly for one of their little talks."

"'Little talks'? What were those all about?"

Jack shrugged. "Search me. I don't know what their relationship was, but every now and again some sort of hush-hush conversation went on between them. If we saw the two of them with their heads together we generally steered clear of the area. And sometimes they'd phone each other, too. No – hang on – I think it was usually Olly phoning Bren."

"Do you think," said Angela carefully, "Oliver could have been supplying Brendan with drugs of some sort?"

Jack lifted his shoulders and let them fall again. "I wondered about that at first, but I don't think the idea's a goer. Brendan did a bit of pot here and there in his younger days, but drugs aren't really his thing – unlike certain members of his band."

Angela resisted the lure. She thought back over her interview with Brendan and his explanation of the conversation in the alley; manning-up, taking responsibility. *I knew you were spinning me a yarn*, she thought. *I shall be visiting you again, Mr Phelan.*

"Tell us about Oliver Joplin," said Angela.

A shadow crossed Jack's features and he looked at her with a mirthless smile. "What is there to say? You get all sorts in a crew."

This non-answer intrigued Angela. "What was he like?" she persisted.

Jack grimaced as he thought. "All right, I suppose. Not the best techie I've ever had. He was usually a bit late when there was any lifting and carrying to be done. In the concerts he worked the lighting console and was there when he needed to be, so I can't complain."

Yet I think you'd like to, thought Angela. "How did he get on with the other crew members?"

Another grimace. "I'm not sure that he did, really. I think

he thought himself a cut above the others, being a bit closer to Brendan, so he kept a bit apart."

Angela nodded, thinking of Doug Travers's perception of the dead man as being "on the edge".

"I believe he'd been with you for a long time, but if he wasn't the best techie you'd ever employed, why – ?"

"– did I keep him on? Good question. I wouldn't mind knowing the answer to that myself." Angela's eyebrows went up into her forehead. "See, it's like this," continued Jack. "Crew members, they're not on a retainer, so at the end of a tour they get laid off, right?"

"Yes, I get it."

"Well, they can't hang around waiting for the next tour. They need to live. So when we're getting another tour together, we cast about for a crew. The ones we like working with, we call them up, see if they're available. A lot of them will have got other jobs by then."

"Yes?"

"By the same token, if there's one we don't particularly want on the road with us again, it's the easiest thing in the world to not call him."

"And?" Angela sensed there was more to come.

"Every bloomin' tour we've done for the past nine years, he's been there. I haven't put his name down. I haven't called him. But I hand a list over to Doug and when I get it back, whose name has been added every time?"

"Oliver Joplin."

"That's right."

"Why do you suppose that is?"

Jack shrugged. "Beats me," he said. "But at the end of the day, our little outfit is not different from any multinational corporation."

"Meaning?"

"You know where the decisions come from?"

"From the top?" ventured Angela.

"Exactly," said the production manager.

Chapter Nine

"That was useful, wasn't it?" opined Angela, as they headed towards home a short while later.

"I'll say," agreed Gary. "There's definitely something in the relationship between Brendan and Oliver that needs another look."

"Absolutely. OK, let's qualify that. There's no reason on earth why a rock star can't be friends with someone on his road crew; but..." She looked across at him. "What's the 'but'?"

"It wouldn't be a hole-in-the-corner sort of thing that everybody knows about but nobody mentions."

"Got it in one, young Houseman; you may have a merit mark."

"Cor! Does this make me teacher's pet?"

"Steady on, let's not go mad!"

Gary laughed. "So it's another trip up to Hampstead for us, isn't it? Brendan Phelan said he'd be chilling around the house for a few days."

"Yes, he did, but I don't want to go straight back to him. I'd like to see what else we can find out about this first. We'll gather the troops and see what they've managed to come up with today. Rick and Jim and Derek and Leanne have already spoken to the two crews, and – "

"Two crews?"

"Yes, the road crew that travel with Brendan and the permanent theatre crew."

"Oh yes, of course. And the band and backing singers, don't forget."

91

"No, I wasn't forgetting. They've covered everyone, including the front-of-house staff but that was just the normal, *where-were-you-when-the-gun-went-off-and-did-you-see-anything-suspicious* routine. Now we can focus."

It was clear to Angela, when she got back to the incident room, that a heavy day coming on top of a short night was taking its toll on her team. She noted the stifled yawns and sluggish movements, and had to admit she felt almost too weary to think as well. But they still had a job to do, so she crossed the room and stood in front of the whiteboard. "OK, everybody, what have we got?"

"Nothing much," said Rick, on behalf of them all.

"Nobody saw anything," added Leanne.

"Not even the cameras," Jim put in with a grin.

"What, did you question the cameras?"

A tired laugh burst out from everybody present. "We spoke to the front-of-house manager, Barry Grieves," explained Rick. "By the way, we saw Georgia Pensay when we were there."

"Georgia Pensay! No way! I love her," gasped Derek, all tiredness forgotten. "Did you know her name is a – "

" – play on words; yes, we did know that," said Jim. "Mind you, the manager didn't," he added, as if he thought that meant he had one over on Barry Grieves.

"OK, everybody, let's concentrate," admonished Angela. "What's this about the cameras, Rick?"

"Mr Grieves thought they'd been nobbled, Angie."

"Nobbled? You mean…?"

"Yes, they were out of action at the relevant time. As far as he could tell, there was nothing wrong with the cameras themselves. He thought the computer system had been hacked and he was waiting for his IT man to turn up and take a look. We've asked him to send us a report."

"OK, good. Well, just before we all knock off for the day, Gary and I have picked up on some information that looks interesting and will mean you going back to the band, the singers and the crew."

They all made a passable attempt at looking lively. "What's that, then?" asked Rick.

"We've been talking to the manager, Doug Travers and the production manager, Jack Waring."

"Roadie," muttered Jim.

"If you like," acknowledged Angela. "But head honcho roadie, in that case. Both these men talked about the relationship between Brendan Phelan and Oliver Joplin as something they found puzzling. Every now and then they'd notice some sort of conversation going on which nobody else was party to. Oliver didn't mix that much with the other crew members, apparently, and didn't seem to be that good a technician. And yet, it seems the dead man was receiving preferential treatment from Brendan."

"So is Brendan gay?" asked Jim.

"Oh, no!" They all turned towards Leanne and the horrified look on her face drew a laugh from them all. She hesitated before adding, "He's got a girlfriend."

"That's no guarantee of anything," said Jim.

"Well, he's not," protested Leanne, putting her hands on her hips.

"OK," said Angela in a soothing voice. "I think we'd have picked up on it before now if Brendan was gay, Jim."

"So we need to check this out," said Rick.

"Absolutely; your first task for tomorrow, team. Nail down this the situation between Brendan Phelan and Oliver Joplin. All his crew seem to have noticed it so they must have opinions about it."

"It could even be something everyone else was in on but

not discussed in front of the management," Rick suggested.

"It's just possible," replied Angela, "but I'd be surprised. "I think they're a tightly knit bunch."

"We'll dig it out whatever's there," said Rick.

"Good," Angela answered. "Gary and I'll take the support act's manager, Terry Dexter, and the runner, Carla Paterson, because we've already spoken to them. I'd also like to see the next of kin. Doug Travers seemed to think Oliver supported his sister. He said Brendan was mindful of this and kept him in employment for that reason. Leanne, will you text me the address before we leave here tonight, please?" She cast a sympathetic glance around her sagging team. "OK; let's wrap it up for today, then."

Within five minutes the room was deserted.

Since Gary's status as the boyfriend of Angela's stepdaughter, Madeleine, had become established over the past couple of months, he was very relaxed about visiting the home of his boss. About half an hour later he sank into the cushions of the sofa in Angela and Patrick's living room with no sign of a blush or the awkwardness that had been present at the beginning of the courtship. He cheerfully accepted the invitation to stay for dinner, even though he didn't actually have a date with Madeleine that evening.

"What's Maddie got on tonight that you're not a part of?" asked Patrick, as he poured a tot of whisky into a couple of glasses, handed one to Gary and the other to Angela.

"Her class reunion," said Gary. "It's the first time they've met up in about five or six years, I think."

"Oh, I expect you're glad not to be invited, then. It'll be a very intense trip down memory lane, won't it? 'Do you remember this, do you remember that?' Who had a crush on whom and the tricks they played on the French mistress."

"Oh yes, I expect it'll be a nostalgia-filled evening," agreed

Gary. "I've said I'll drop her off, then go home and get an early night."

"Exactly what I'd do in the same circumstances," replied Patrick.

"I bet she's quite cross that the reunion's tonight," said Angela. "I know she's been looking forward to it but she must feel quite torn." She grinned as her husband and colleague turned puzzled faces towards her.

"Why?" asked Patrick.

"I think she'll be itching to corner Gary and wring out of him every little detail he knows about Brendan Phelan."

"She can ask you the same things as me," objected Gary.

"Yes, but she wouldn't have nearly so much fun pinning me into a corner," explained Angela.

They all laughed at this and were still chuckling when they heard Madeleine's footsteps coming down the stairs.

"Evening, peeps," she said, standing in the doorway. She looked round at them and burst into laughter at the astonished silence she had produced. "You should see your faces," she added, her eyes twinkling with mischief.

"Where on earth did you get that?" asked Gary, when he found his voice.

Madeleine came fully into the room and gave a twirl. "It's my old school uniform," she said, fingering the two pigtails she'd made of her hair. "I'm rather chuffed it still fits."

"White socks, even," remarked Gary. He looked a little horrified. "You're not going like that, are you?"

"Good grief, no," Madeleine reassured him. "It's just that we've agreed to bring something from our schooldays, if we have anything – you know, photographs, exercise books, that sort of thing. When I was searching I came across this uniform. I had no idea I still had it, to be honest." She smiled at him. "You don't like me in this, do you, Gary?"

"Not really. You look about twelve and, I dunno, I prefer you as you are now."

"Don't worry; it's all going in the recycling tomorrow. Now, what were you all laughing about just before I came downstairs?"

"You pumping me for information about Brendan Phelan," explained Gary.

Madeleine smiled. "I haven't… yet. But I'm going to. You'd better be forthcoming or I'll get the thumbscrews out."

"Told you," said Angela.

"The thing is," answered Gary, "whenever I think about this case, the first thing that comes to mind isn't Brendan at all."

Madeleine turned a disbelieving expression towards him. "How can it not be?" she said, accepting a glass of whisky from her father.

"Not everyone's a mad keen fan like you, remember," said Patrick.

Madeleine smiled and waggled her finger at Gary. "You're just not normal, that's your trouble." He made a face at her. "So, come on," she continued. "Let me pretend I'm not obsessed for a minute. What *is* the first thing that comes to your mind, then?"

"Well, the whole thing has expanded since yesterday," began Gary. "At first, it was this memory of me watching telly with my dad when I was about nine. We were watching some magician. Since then, I realized that it was, in a small way, one of those rite-of-passage sort of things."

"Ooh, is this going to get heavy?" asked Angela. "Shall I cue some meaningful music?"

"*Da, da, da, daaaa,*" voiced Patrick in what was recognizable as something dramatic from Beethoven.

"They make a good double act, don't they," remarked

Madeleine. "Never mind them. You just carry on."

"It was these flight cases they use in theatre to transport equipment around that reminded me in the first place. And today we went and spoke to the production manager. When we were talking he said he started off in show business as a magician's assistant and that brought even more of it back. I remember sitting in our living room and the magician brought this young girl on and had her get into a box. I'd seen that sort of thing before, and knew he would let us think he was sawing her in half. I was old enough to know it was just a trick, but I hadn't figured out how it was done. In this particular act, the magician sawed the girl in half lengthways, then separated the two halves as if he now had two boxes; you with me?"

"Yes," said Angela. "There was now, apparently, half a girl in each box."

"That's it, and I'm sitting there saying, 'That's really brilliant, Dad. I'd love to know how they do that.' And then, just to show how clever he was, the magician told the audience he was going to prove there was half a girl in each box and he knocked on one of them and told the girl to put a hand through a hole in the side of it. A hand came out and he shook it. Then, obviously, to prove his point, he went to the other box and said, 'OK, darling, put out your other hand now.' And blow me down, the same hand came out and shook his."

A silence greeted the end of Gary's tale. "I'm not quite sure I get that," said Patrick.

"Oh, hang on," said Angela. "The first girl put out her, say, left hand, and the, supposedly other half of the same girl, also put out a left hand."

"Exactly," said Gary. "I got so excited to have seen through the trick I was bouncing up and down on our sofa, saying,

'Look, Dad! Look! She's got two left hands!' or it might have been the right, but you get the point."

"Of course," said Patrick. "I see what you mean. He hadn't coordinated his assistants well enough."

"And you noticed!" said Angela with admiration. "You see, you were a budding policeman, even at the age of nine."

"I must have been," agreed Gary.

Madeleine took an anglepoise lamp from a shelf and pointed it at Gary. "OK, buster, that's enough tripping down memory lane. Talk time; gimme the lowdown about Brendan Phelan."

Angela and Patrick exchanged smiles and headed for the door. "Yes, definitely, she's going to have much more fun getting the information out of you than me, Gary," said Angela as they disappeared in the direction of the kitchen.

They worked in pleasant harmony for a while. They said little as Angela prepared a salad and Patrick cooked some vegetables to go with a casserole already in the oven. The silence allowed them to hear occasional questions from Madeleine, mostly on the lines of, "So what's the room like?" and a more frustrated, "Oh, Gary, didn't you take *any* notice?" They both stopped what they were doing and grinned when they heard Madeleine say, "I hef vays of mekking you talk," followed by a burst of laughter from Gary. Patrick had lifted the dish onto the work surface, taken the lid off and filled the kitchen with a delicious aroma of rich gravy before he spoke.

"Just out of curiosity – " he began.

"He reminds me of you, Pads," answered Angela. "The same sort of Irishness, and his eyes crinkle like yours do when he smiles, or they will when he's a bit older." She stopped and thought for a moment, remembering Brendan in his room and noting the similarity. She realized now, there was more to it than that. "His expression is more guarded, though."

"What can you expect? He's a major celebrity. Pulling up the drawbridge, so to speak, is probably one of the first lessons he learned on becoming famous."

"I expect you're right, but there was something strange about his relationship with the dead man."

"Really, in what way?"

"Too early to say at the moment, but it seems they had private conversations here and there which everybody else around them had learned to ignore. And he, Oliver Joplin, was still employed even though he wasn't the first choice of the one who does the hiring and firing."

"Ah, got preferential treatment from the star, did he?"

"That's what it looks like."

"Perhaps Brendan Phelan liked working with him."

"That would be the simplest answer to that question, but if so, he's the only one who did, from the sound of things. Everybody else we've spoken to seems to regard him as a bit of an outsider. Actually, it could be as simple as that. They were outside the stage door having one of these conversations when he was shot. Brendan reckons he was telling him to pull his socks up. Perhaps they got on well and Brendan tried to help him out, you know, workwise, but also wanted to be discreet."

"Doesn't he have a dressing room to be discreet in?"

"We asked Brendan about that but he said it wasn't convenient, too much coming and going. So they were seen here and there in conversation, but not very often. Oh – and Jack overheard the occasional phone call coming through from Oliver. In any case, Brendan's the star and he calls the shots. If he wants to talk to someone he can, it's nobody's business but theirs."

"So it's a perfectly innocent relationship and there's no can of worms for you to open?"

"Er… possibly."

Patrick looked at Angela. "You don't buy that, do you?"

Angela gave a rueful grin. "No, not really," she said.

Chapter Ten

Angela intended to interview the dead man's sister when the following morning's briefing concluded, but a call from the front desk derailed her plans. Someone had come into reception wanting to see her. She asked for the person to be shown to an interview room, and appeared there with Gary a few minutes later to find a very attractive blonde woman pacing back and forth across the small space. Her movement displayed more a desire for exercise than agitation. Dressed in a smart jacket and jeans with a wrap thrown around her shoulders, she presented a picture of casual elegance. Angela thought she looked familiar but couldn't think where she'd seen her before. The question was answered as soon as they'd all sat down.

"Thank you for agreeing to see me, when I know you must be so busy. But I wanted to have a word about Brendan."

Ah, thought Angela. *That's where I've seen you. On Brendan's arm at some premier, photographed for a glossy magazine.* "You're Tilly –"

" – Townsend. Yes. I'm Brendan's girlfriend."

"How may I help you, Miss Townsend?"

"I think I'm probably being very silly. I might even be wasting your time. I'm partly looking for reassurance and partly hoping to help the investigation in a small way."

"OK, let's start with point one; you don't strike me as a silly person. We all need reassurance from time to time and all leads we get in any investigation are gratefully received."

Tilly smiled and relaxed. "I didn't think it would be like this. You're quite human really." Angela and Gary both laughed. "The thing is, I talked to Brendan early yesterday but he was still out of it on whatever the doctor had given him, and I've been rushed off my feet with business meetings since then. A couple of the newspapers I've seen are speculating that the bullet might have been intended for Brendan."

"That's probably just those papers trying to boost circulation," said Angela. She thought of what the runner, Carla, had said. "Of course the possibility has to be on our radar," she added in a guarded voice.

"You can ditch that theory, no problem," said Tilly, pushing a thick swathe of hair back behind her ear.

"Really? Why is that?" asked Gary.

Tilly looked at him through narrowed eyes. "Haven't you discovered yet that they're all crack shots on that team? If Oliver got shot, then Oliver was the target *quod erat demonstrandum*."

Angela thought for a moment before speaking. "Er..." she said, eventually, "the assumption I'd jumped to is that you wanted reassurance about Brendan as the intended victim."

"No, I want reassurance that he's not in the frame for the murder."

"Oh! How much do you know about the event?"

"Not much," admitted the other woman. "I couldn't get any sense out of Bren, as I said, and when I tried talking to the others they all went a bit cagey and said they shouldn't speak about it really, as the matter is under police investigation."

"All very true, of course," agreed Angela. "But I can tell you with certainty we are quite satisfied it was not Brendan who pulled the trigger."

Tilly narrowed her eyes again as she considered this. "Hmm. I'm still not reassured. That sounds as though you haven't ruled out a conspiracy."

"Conspiracy?" Angela was intrigued. "Is this where your

hope of helping our investigation comes in?"

"Yes. Although, of course, I might just be muddying the waters." She sat up straight in her chair. "There's no way Brendan is responsible for Olly's death. He just hasn't got it in him, no matter how great the provocation."

"There's provocation?" asked Angela.

"Oh, I'm probably being melodramatic."

"All the same, a man has been killed."

"Yes. The thing is, there's definitely something going on with that tour."

"Can you be more specific?" asked Angela.

Tilly frowned. "I'm not sure I can. It's just how Brendan's been. I'm picking up the vibe from him, as you'd expect."

"The vibe?"

The frown deepened. "Sorry, this is going to sound daft. A change would come over Brendan on a regular basis; I don't know, about once a month, once every six weeks, something like that."

"What sort of change?"

"He'd be, like… haunted, in some way. And then it would pass, but not quite go away, if you see what I mean." Angela didn't, really, but she didn't want to interrupt the flow. "It… kind of… holds him back. Take us, for instance. I'm not saying we should be married by now, but we've been dating for about a year and, in my view, our relationship should be in a different place. We go out and we're seen around, but – I don't know how to explain it – we're not moving forward. When I ask Brendan if anything's wrong, he pulls himself together for a while; he tells me he loves me and smothers me in kisses, but I feel…" Her voice broke and her eyes suddenly misted over.

"Fobbed off?" suggested Angela.

Tilly brought her hand up to her mouth and nodded

through her tears. "I know he's not trying to be cruel or secretive. It feels more like he *can't* tell me."

"You've no idea what?"

She shook her head. "No, but whatever it is, I think this *thing* was wearing him down." She looked Angela full in the face. "It was affecting his music."

Gary's eyebrows went up into his hairline. "You could have fooled me. I was at that concert at the Apollo; he was marvellous. He's won over a new fan."

Tilly smiled, gratified on behalf of her boyfriend. "That's good, and you're right. He's enormously talented." She paused. "However, you're probably not aware of this, but he hasn't written anything new in a long while."

"Didn't he release a new album about six months ago? It was very successful from what my girlfriend tells me."

Tilly nodded. "He did, but the songs were all written in his early days. Fortunately he was so prolific when he started out he's got a lot of material he can draw on, so nobody's noticed anything. From what I can gather, all he does is tweak old stuff. But he wants to get away from this theme of gunshots and whip cracks. It's great and it works very well, but he's growing up and so is his audience. He really needs to move on and develop his style and that's just not happening."

"And you think this tension you sense in him now and again and the lack of output are linked?"

Tilly wiped away a tear that was trailing downwards across her cheek. "He's got some sort of monkey on his back and it's putting the whole of his life on hold."

"My goodness."

"Yes, and what's more, I think things were getting worse."

Angela and Gary discussed their meeting with Tilly Townsend all the way to the south London address where they had arranged to meet Kay, Oliver Joplin's sister. Though her concerns intrigued them and they could see it all tied in with the sense of mystery they'd already picked up on, they realized they could get no further without more information, so they reluctantly called a halt to the speculation as they approached the terraced house fronted by a tiny garden. In spite of the shabbiness of the street, gloss paint glistened on the window frames and door and snowy lace curtains shielded the front room from prying eyes. A few shrubs in the garden battled bravely against London pollution.

The roar of traffic from the nearby A2 could be heard, a steady stream of cargo and ferry passengers making their way to London from the Kent coast. Angela and Gary's appearance at the gate brought a curious Asian lady out from the adjoining house. She gave them a quick glance, adjusted a brightly covered shawl over her sari and disappeared back inside.

Kay greeted them at her door, a slightly built woman, not unlike Carla Paterson in type. They saw a pale face with large, round blue eyes, the lids of which were, at this moment, pink and swollen. She had a crumpled tissue in one hand.

When Angela introduced herself and Gary, she turned and led the way down a narrow passage to a room at the back of the house. They found themselves in an airy, cheerful kitchen. It looked as though the breakfast hadn't been completely cleared away; two bowls of cornflakes and a plastic beaker with what looked like the dregs of some fruit juice stood on a counter running along one wall. The fridge door was a riot of activity. Magnets clustered across most of its upper half, each one pinning some piece of paper to the surface. A shopping list and a cake recipe half-obscured a couple of child's drawings, and further over, Angela and Gary could see pictures of Oliver and Kay smiling at the camera at what seemed to be a party.

Another scene from what looked like the same party showed Oliver, a pint of beer in one hand, with an arm round the neck of another man. The picture oozed camaraderie.

Through the back door they could see two little children, with large dark eyes and halos of curly hair, peering in to see who the strangers were. The boy, about five, played on a bright red tricycle, and a smaller girl constructed something from plastic bricks. A baby girl of about four months was dozing in a stroller just inside the room.

"I can see you've got your hands full," began Angela. "I'm sorry to have to disturb you."

"S'all right," said the woman, sniffing and raising the tissue briefly to her nose. "I knew you'd be here at some point. This is as good a time as any. Take a seat."

Angela and Gary sat down at the plastic-topped table and Kay seated herself opposite them.

"We're very sorry to intrude on your grief for your brother," said Angela, "but we need to get as clear a picture of him as we can."

"Yeah, I understand."

"First and foremost, I have to ask, do you know if he had any enemies?"

The sleeping baby stirred slightly. Kay turned towards her, reached out a hand to the pushchair handle and jogged it gently up and down. "Shouldn't think so. Why would he have enemies?" she asked.

Angela blinked. *Because somebody killed him*, she thought. "It's a question we have to address," she said.

Kay turned a mournful face towards Angela. "Yeah, sorry, I know. I think I'm in shock, still."

"That's understandable," replied Angela.

Kay dropped her gaze to the table. "Don't think so anyway," she said. "Not that I know of."

"No enemies," said Gary, writing in his notebook. He looked up at her. "What about his friends?"

Kay gave a mirthless smile. "He was a bit of a loner, Olly. He liked to go his own way."

"But he must surely have had one or two friends," persisted Gary, his pen poised.

Kay shrugged. "I suppose; but I didn't really know them."

"What about the people he worked with?" asked Angela.

"What about them?"

"How did he get on with them?"

Kay took her hand off the pushchair handle. "I think he got on all right with them. He didn't really talk about work much." She brought her eyes up to Angela's. Fresh tears formed and began to roll down her cheeks.

"What about Brendan Phelan? Did he speak about him much?"

"Not recently. Brendan was just on the way up when Olly got taken on. You couldn't shut him up about it then 'cause it was really exciting. You know – a big star, all those fans. Sometimes, if they saw him in the street or the pub and recognized him from the crew, they used to beg him to introduce them to Brendan. But the novelty wore off. He hasn't talked about it for a long time now. Not to me, anyway."

"But he did get on with Brendan?"

"I suppose so. He'd been working for him a long time. Brendan must have felt comfortable around him. He didn't have to keep him on."

Angela felt frustrated. *These answers are trailing off into nothingness*, she thought, *and I can't figure out why.* She tried a different tack. "How about *your* relationship with your brother, Kay? Did you see much of him?"

Kay's eyes brightened; the first sign of animation they'd seen lit up her face. "He was very good to me, a really good brother. He looked after me. If I needed something I only had to ask. And he was good to the kids."

This raised a question Angela couldn't let pass. "How about your – er – the children's father?"

"What about him?"

Frustration rose in Angela. This was heavy going. "Well – did Oliver and he get along? Did they see much of one another? Is he around at the moment?"

"Sometimes. He's around sometimes. You know how it is."

Angela didn't, but she could guess.

"He got on all right with Olly," continued Kay. "They had a beer together now and again." Just at that moment a catchy ringtone sounded and Kay pulled a mobile phone out of her pocket, livened up a little more as she read the name on the screen, and lifted it to her ear.

"Yeah?" she asked, looking at the two officers.

They could hear a distant voice saying what sounded like: "You OK, Kadey?"

"Yeah," she answered. "The police are here, right? They're asking about Olly… Yeah, see you later." She finished the call and put the phone back into her pocket. "That's their dad," she said, casting her head around to take in all three children. "He's coming over later," she said, her brief animation departing once more.

"He uses a different name for you," said Angela.

Kay smiled. "That's just his pet name for me. He calls me Kadey; sometimes Kadey-Wadey; silly really, but – you know. My name's actually Kayleigh."

Angela smiled and nodded, resigning herself to the reality that this conversation had driven into another dead end. She looked across at Gary, raising her eyebrows, expecting to see confirmation of frustration equalling her own, but to her surprise he persisted, asking: "What about Oliver's friend in that picture?" He pointed to the cheerful photograph attached to the fridge door, showing Oliver at the party, his arm around his friend.

A flash of irritation appeared on Kay's face, as if the sight of it annoyed her. "Oh, that was ages ago. He hasn't been around for a long time."

Gary would not be fobbed off. "They look very friendly, though."

"Nah – Olly was probably just drunk, or well on the way to it, when that was taken. He could get sentimental when he'd had a few."

"What's the other man's name?" asked Angela.

"Couldn't tell you; don't know if I ever knew in the first place," replied Kay, dismissively.

"Could we take this photo, please?" Gary asked.

Angela was puzzled by the request but took care not to show it.

"Why?" asked Kay, suspiciously.

Gary looked at Angela's impassive expression. "It's such a good one of your brother – exceptionally clear. That sort of thing is a very valuable aid to focusing our thoughts and discussions in the incident room."

Reluctance showed in every part of Kay's face. "I don't have many of him," she replied, after a moment. "I'd rather keep it."

Gary gave a cheerful smile and nodded. "Not to worry," he said.

Angela waited for a moment in case Gary had anything to add, but he said no more.

"Thank you for sparing us some time," she said, briskly. "We might have some more questions at some point as the investigation proceeds. We'll let you know." She took a card out of her bag and handed it to Kay. "If anything occurs to you that you think is relevant – anything at all – will you contact me on that number?"

"Yeah, 'course," said Kay, looking briefly at the card before putting it down on the table and moving forward to see them out.

"Phew, that was hard work," said Gary, as they buckled up their seat belts in the car. "Where to now, boss-lady?"

"Back north to the river and then east. We're off to see Don Buckley in Wanstead. You're not kidding about it being an uphill climb, back there. It was an altogether odd interview. What did you make of her?"

"I couldn't figure out if she was spaced-out, stupid or hiding something."

"I was thinking spaced-out or not too bright. What makes you say 'hiding something'?"

"Well, that bloke at the party with Oliver."

"The one in the photo on the fridge door? Yes, I wondered why you wanted that. What about him?"

"I've seen him recently."

"Oh, really?"

"Yep. The night of the murder. I was waiting for Maddie to arrive when I saw him in the street in front of the Apollo."

"Are you sure?"

"Oh, yes. I got a good look at his face, as it happened, but those hawk tattoos on his arms were what really caught my eye. They're unusual. The kind of thing you'd remember anywhere – they really stood out." He threw a glance in her direction. "He was touting tickets."

"Ah." Angela relaxed back in her seat. "That's very interesting. Well, we've got quite a drive, so you've got time to tell me all about it."

Chapter Eleven

An hour later found them standing in a street looking at another terraced house across a modest-sized front garden, but a different atmosphere pervaded here in suburban east London. Away from the arterial route to the docks, the air felt cleaner and the surroundings altogether less drab.

Their ring at this bell was answered by a cheerful-looking woman who greeted them pleasantly, and stood back to let them in once she'd seen their ID.

"I'm Fay, Don's wife," she explained as they entered. "He's in the shed. First room on the right – that's it. Make yourselves at home, take a seat. I'll just go and call him." She hurried away in search of her husband, to be replaced a few moments later by Don, wiping his hands on an old towel.

"Hello again," he said, sitting down on the sofa opposite the two armchairs they had taken. "More questions?"

Angela wanted to probe what Terry Dexter had said about Don knowing Oliver some years before, but she decided to ease into the interview by a different route. "We'd like to ask you about the relationship between Oliver and Brendan," she said.

He looked puzzled. "I'm not sure I'm qualified to answer that. The beginning of the tour was the first time I'd met Brendan."

"Oh, I see. Had you ever met Oliver before?"

"Several years ago. He was trying to make it as a guitarist." Don had an open, honest face; but right now Angela read cageyness, even duplicity, in his expression. *Why do you want to gloss over your previous association?* she thought, making a note. She avoided turning her head to look at Gary, to evade alerting Don to her suspicion. *OK, definitely some depths to be plumbed here before I continue with the planned questions.*

"I suppose he couldn't have been much good as a guitarist, if he ended up as a roadie."

"He wasn't much of a roadie, either." Don's mouth formed a thin, hard line.

Ooh! What's going on here? Angela leaned forward, not bothering to conceal the intrigue on her face and exchanging an open glance with Gary, who raised his eyebrows.

A third voice broke into the scene. "You'd better tell them, Don. It'll be better coming from you and they'll find out anyway." Angela and Gary turned round to see Fay standing in the doorway. They looked back at Don, who gazed at his wife in silence. Fay came fully into the room and sat down. "It's best to get it out; you're no good at concealment, love, it just makes you look guilty when you're not."

Don grinned suddenly. "She's right," he said. "Olly and I had a history, but it's definitely ancient and at no point during the tour did it revive."

"Can you give us some more detail about that?"

"He turned up back in the day, when Foursquare were just starting out. I'd got involved because Andy and I – he's the singer – were best friends, from school. Just like Brendan and Terry, in fact. Anyway, they didn't have much of a clue, though they had enthusiasm by the bucketload. I didn't know much about the pop world in those days, but I asked in our local pub about doing a gig and we got a result. The landlord gave them a try-out. It went down very well, as it happens; they were offered a regular spot. Because I'd set it up, they – kind of – looked to me after that. To make the bookings, you know, and generally look after things. I – well – I suppose I drifted into being their manager. We bagged a few more gigs in pubs in the area. Things began to take off – it was really going great. We knew we'd got a toehold in the industry when Oliver came up to me in the pub one night after the show, to ask if we were looking for another guitarist. At that point none of us had turned professional. We hadn't thought of giving up the day jobs back then. Our bassist had just got accepted into the Civil Service and left us, so, yes we were. Looking for a guitarist, I mean."

"How did it work out?" Angela prompted.

"It all went fine at first, but then Olly began to disappear during the breaks. He only ever just made it back in time for the next set. He made the lads nervous and he was… kind of… not open."

"Not open?" Angela looked at him enquiringly.

"Yeah, you know. Any of us might pop out now and again – maybe we'd seen a girl we fancied in the audience, or we had a friend in to the show; that sort of thing. But with Olly, it was always 'seeing a mate about something'. Mysterious. Played his cards close to his chest."

"Ah."

Don nodded towards Angela, acknowledging her knowing tone. "That's right. To cut a long story short, it turned out he was peddling drugs and using our gigs as a base. We were more naive in those days, just cruising happily on. OK, we'd all tried the odd spliff, but none of us were into the drugs scene – a couple of pints each and we were happy. Then came the day we thought our big break had arrived; we actually managed to get a talent scout from one of the big labels down to see us, and we were over the moon. But that was the night we found out about Olly's little sideline."

"What happened?" asked Gary.

"The Old Bill turned up and raided the place. The landlord was *not* a happy bunny."

"I can imagine!"

"Yes. Olly couldn't be seen for dust – wouldn't you know it – and we only escaped prosecution by the skin of our teeth. Not only did we lose all our gigs but we became toxic. Every door we tried after that was slammed shut in our faces, just as we'd thought it was really going to fly. It looked like the dream was over. We gave up, thanked the good Lord we hadn't chucked in the day jobs, and we got on with our lives. But I was totally gutted for the boys."

"You came back, though? The dream didn't really die," suggested Angela.

Don smiled. "We thought it was dead but it wouldn't lie down. Within a couple of years we got the band back together. We started rehearsing again and I went round all the pubs and explained the whole situation. We started the climb back to where we were, until we reached the point where I thought I'd try that talent scout again. He'd left the label by then but he had a mate with contacts in Brendan's record company. He knew they were looking for a support act."

"So what did you think when it brought you face to face with Oliver again?"

Don smiled at his own naivety. "To be honest, I assumed he must have mended his ways. It didn't occur to me that a big star like Brendan Phelan would have someone dodgy on his crew."

"You gave him the benefit of the doubt."

"I couldn't think of any other explanation. But it didn't take long to see he hadn't changed. He still had his little game going on the sidelines. Although… well… I don't think it was drugs any more. He was into other stuff now."

"Do you know what sort of 'stuff' he did?"

Don shook his head. "To be honest, I kept out of his way. He came up to us at the first rehearsal and shook our hands.

We all said 'no hard feelings' and all that, but… well, it was a bit of a diplomatic gesture on our part. We knew we'd landed a good gig and we didn't want to blow it. As Andy said at the time, if he's up to no good, it's Brendan's problem."

"But you're sure he had something going on?" ventured Gary.

"Yes, he was doing the same disappearing act at odd times. I recognized the pattern from before."

Angela thought for a moment. She wondered if Don realized he'd admitted to having a very good motive for committing murder – revenge being a dish best served cold, as it was said. "How long ago did Oliver play in your band?" she asked.

"About ten years ago."

Angela nodded. Yes, a dish could get very cold in ten years. She thought she had enough on that subject but the direction the conversation had taken eased it back into her original question. She remembered hearing how Don had come out of the stage door and dealt promptly and practically with Brendan in shock. Evidently he was a coping person and, she thought, probably a noticing one as well. Brushing aside the possibility of what he may have been doing just before his arrival, she moved ahead. "Did you get any impression of the relationship between Oliver and Brendan?"

Don linked his hands, staring down at them for a moment. "I'm an outsider, really. Six months ago my band was a fixture on the pub circuit and the boys were glad of whatever we could get. Now they're in the limelight, an overnight sensation. It's what we all dreamed of, but this – the big league – is a completely different animal. I'm still feeling my way. I don't really know how to interpret everything I see." He looked up and met their eyes.

"Even so," Angela pushed him.

"OK; from a show business point of view, I didn't understand it at all. However, if I reframe it as a gang of lads at the local comprehensive, I'd have no problem telling you Oliver wanted to build his stock by being seen to hobnob with the most powerful boy in the class."

"And how did that work?" asked Angela.

Don thought for a moment. "Olly would approach him now and again to engage him in conversation. Brendan always listened."

"Do you know what they talked about?"

"That's the curious thing. He didn't ever come up and speak to Brendan within earshot of any of us. He managed to approach whenever Brendan was, you know, standing or sitting by himself. There'd be this snippet of conversation we could all see but none of us could hear. Then Brendan would just nod – and Olly would go back to what he was doing before."

"So you think Oliver was asserting for everyone to see that he was a long-standing member of the crew – that he had a special relationship with the star?"

"That's what I took to be the point of it."

"Did you form any impression of what Brendan thought – how he felt about this?"

Don gave this some consideration. "He put up with it. He was never rude to Olly, never cold-shouldered him. But on one occasion I managed to get a look at his face when he saw Olly coming towards him. And I would say he didn't like it. Not one little bit."

Here's somebody who, by contrast, doesn't see himself as an outsider whatsoever; very much the opposite, thought Angela as she and Gary scrunched across a gravel driveway to the imposing Buckinghamshire mansion that Terry Dexter called home. The musician was waiting on the porch, holding a lord-of-the-manor stance as he allowed them to approach him. The open front door behind him revealed a comfortable-looking hall carpeted in beige. "Inspector – welcome!" He held out his arm to usher them in, and followed them into the house. "Can I get you anything? A cup of coffee? Something to eat?"

Angela and Gary had stopped for a pub lunch on the A40, but only a hurried meal; they gratefully accepted the offer of a cup of coffee. Terry took them through to a roomy kitchen where a large wooden table occupied most of the central space. The designer had clearly been instructed to create an old-fashioned farmhouse kitchen, but this was strictly stylistic. State-of-the-art equipment ranged around the walls and on every work surface contrasted sharply with the self-consciously cosy ambience. They sat down, one each side of the table, while their host poured coffee from a percolator.

"I owe you an apology," said Terry, bringing a cup for each of them to the table, and sitting at their head.

"Oh?" Angela waited for what he would say.

"Yes. On the night of the murder, I behaved badly. I was boorish and objectionable. The whole thing shocked and upset me more than I realized at the time. I'm afraid I took it out on you. I'm sorry."

"Oh, don't worry," replied Angela. A marked contrast existed between Mr Angry and this person with the pleasant manner. "I didn't take offence," she added.

He smiled and Angela realized he did "charming" nearly as well as Brendan. "So, what now? More questions, I presume."

Angela took a sip and put her cup down in the saucer. "We're trying to understand the relationship between Oliver and Brendan."

"Ah! I expect you've been hearing about Oliver sidling up

to Brendan, drawing him into a tête-à-tête conversation in a corner – or trying to."

"Trying to?" queried Angela. "From what we've heard elsewhere, he quite often succeeded."

Terry shook his head. "Not when you see it for what it is. Oliver wanted to be seen having an 'in' with the star. You can understand it, really; as the longest-serving member of the crew he probably thought that gave him some extra kudos; but it didn't. Brendan would acknowledge him, just enough to be polite, then move on as quickly as he decently could. I never once saw him in Brendan's dressing room, where those of us who really are in the inner circle would hang out."

In spite of the apology, Angela remembered Terry's self-aggrandizement from the night of the murder, his recounting of their history as schoolboys together and his assertion that he was partly responsible for Brendan's biggest hit. "Yes, I've heard from Doug that he'd been on the crew for longer than anyone else. But can you enlighten me – how did that happen? From what you said the other night, he was less than adequate at the job. Why did Brendan keep him on?"

Terry spread his hands, shrugging. "Your guess is as good as mine. I did wonder about it from time to time, but it wasn't my department. I presume Jack Waring hired him. You'd need to ask him about that."

Angela thought for a moment. She had the distinct feeling she was being headed off at the pass. *You know more than you're letting on, Terry,* she thought. *But I haven't got enough to push for whatever it is.* She nodded at Gary and they both stood up. "Thank you for your help, Mr Dexter. We'll be in touch if we have any more questions."

Ten minutes later they were heading back along the A40 to the Perivale address they had for Carla Paterson.

"I had the feeling he was holding something back," remarked Gary.

"You and me both," said Angela. "There's definitely some sort of mystery surrounding these 'conversations'." She sketched quotation marks in the air. "I've got a feeling the matter will finally be resolved when we speak to Brendan next. But I'll be interested to see if little Carla has a take on that dynamic."

As they were about to discover; Carla provided them with the most interesting insight of all.

Chapter Twelve

They approached London from the west, got off the main road and meandered through leafy suburbs to the house Carla shared with two other people. She opened the door to them, and Angela was struck afresh by her waiflike appearance. She was wearing short white socks, cut-off trousers and a baggy pink T-shirt. Her hair was tied in two bunches, one poking out from behind each ear. Only the finest suggestion of a skein of wrinkles beginning around her large dark eyes showed that Carla was a woman. Her tiny frame and the pathos of her gaze belonged to childhood. Evidently bewildered, she looked from one to the other.

"Good afternoon, Carla. Do you remember us?" began Gary.

Her brow cleared, she smiled and stepped aside for them to enter. "Oh, yes! You're the police from the other night." Her soft voice carried an ingénue quality, which matched her general appearance. Angela, puzzled, followed Gary into the house. Though she herself might wear crops and a T-shirt to relax at home, she formed the distinct impression that Carla wanted to present herself as a little girl. Since she was only twenty-two, she had hardly enough years behind her to worry about her age. It struck Angela as odd.

They all moved into the living room, a bright, cheery space containing a television, a sound system, a sofa and a couple of armchairs. The clutter of objects on the shelf above the empty fireplace represented the debris of an entirely feminine household; odds and ends of make-up, tissues, tweezers, a manicure set and several photographs – mostly of Carla and two other women at a variety of social gatherings. On the chimney breast, a huge photograph of Brendan Phelan in concert dominated the room; a striking image, it showed Brendan highlighted by a spotlight, gazing down with intensity as he played his guitar. In the dimness behind him, Angela could make out Terry Dexter concentrating with similar focus on the keyboard he was playing, and remembered him saying that he could step in on the keyboard when required. A collage of images of Brendan hung in one of the alcoves to the side of the fireplace. Angela gazed at the photographs. She turned to Carla. "We've got a couple more questions for you. Do you have time to chat now?"

Carla curled herself onto one end of the sofa and drew her feet up under her. "Of course," she said. "Sit down." She sprang up again. "Oops! I should offer you something to drink, shouldn't I?" Her smile was self-deprecating, that of a pupil who's very nearly forgotten an important part of a lesson.

"We're fine, thank you," answered Angela on behalf of them both as they sat down. Carla curled herself up again and waited expectantly.

Angela looked once more at the pictures of Brendan. "I see you're quite an admirer of Brendan Phelan."

Carla raised her shoulders in a blasé manner. "Those belong to my housemates. They're so jealous that I'm working with him. Mad keen, they are, go to every concert they can. You should hear them pumping me for information whenever I come back from work. 'What was he wearing tonight? Did you speak to him? What did he say? Was *she* there?'" She gave a small laugh. "Gets on my nerves, it does."

Her whole demeanour belied her words. Angela would have been willing to bet money that Carla loved every minute of the attention she generated, and the apparent power which her position as the crew's runner gave her.

"She?" she asked.

"Yes, Tilly Townsend; Brendan's girlfriend. They've been going out for nearly a year now; but she won't last." This statement was delivered with the nonchalance of one with inside information and, no doubt, when she said it to her housemates, they were wide-eyed, and pressed her for more details. Her interview with Tilly Townsend remained fresh in Angela's mind and now triggered the memory of some details about Brendan's love-life culled from the media. He'd squired a small procession of women through a considerable variety of headlines. The end of these relationships, as far as she could remember, all seemed to have been identical. "Holly/Scarlett/ whoever is a lovely lady. It's not her fault – it's me," had been Brendan's claim. "He's got a problem with commitment" was the corresponding cry each time; statements skimming over the deeper truths of the matter.

"You think it'll fizzle out?" she asked now, keeping a conversational tone in her voice.

"He needs someone who understands," Carla asserted.

"Understands?" queried Angela.

"Yeah, you know, the pressure he's under; being a big star and all that. All the girls want him but they're, like, out there." Carla stretched out her arm to its maximum length to illustrate her point. "On the other side of the footlights," she continued. "Brendan, well, I work with him, so I know. He needs someone who... well, who's on the inside... a professional colleague, you know?"

Angela and Gary nodded. Angela began to have an inkling as to where this conversation could go and she was sure Gary had picked up on it. She thought it time to get back on track. "We're actually not here to talk about Brendan, as you can imagine," she said.

For an instant Carla looked surprised. "No? Oh, of course,

I suppose not. You're investigating Olly's death, aren't you?" She made it sound like a secondary issue. "You're not – " she stopped.

"We're not what?" asked Angela, always ready to be deflected in case the byway led to somewhere interesting.

"Well, you know…" A grimace appeared, belonging to the teenage persona Carla clearly clung to. "It's just… as I said before. I was worried in case the real target was Brendan. That's why I was so upset at the time. It still bothers me, to be honest."

"We've got that possibility on our radar," replied Angela, deciding that path was going nowhere and she'd better get back to the main drag. "When we spoke to you the other night, you said that Olly had something going on – though you didn't say what, specifically. Is there any chance you can enlarge on this?"

Carla brought a hand up to her mouth and began chewing at a fingernail. Again Angela was struck by the studied youthfulness of the action. Almost as if to underline this Carla suddenly grinned and put her hand away from her mouth. "Oops, I keep forgetting I've got false nails on." She giggled briefly. "I don't think I can tell you much. He kept himself to himself. Like, he'd arrive just in time for the show so he wasn't hanging around talking and joking with everyone else. Thought himself a cut above us all, if you ask me."

Angela decided to go with the flow. "Why would that be, do you think?"

"Well he obviously had some sort of special 'in' with Brendan."

Ah, thought Angela, and was aware of Gary's interest quickening as well. They had arrived where they wanted to be by a circuitous route. "We've heard about this from a couple of other quarters. What can you tell us?"

Carla took her time answering. She smoothed down one of her hair bunches, checked the state of the false fingernail and shifted a little in her seat. *OK, we get it*, thought Angela. *You think you know more than anybody else about this.* She was careful to keep her face expressionless as she waited for the young woman to speak.

"The thing is," began Carla, "Brendan's got his likes and dislikes, just as we all have." She widened her large eyes, looking with meaning first at Angela then Gary. "He's got needs, right? He's a regular bloke."

"Yes?" replied Gary, his tone inviting.

"Well, for those of us on the inside, those in the inner circle – " *Which I'm sure you're not*, thought Angela, " – well, some of us know that his girlfriends might not be – er – enough for him, if you get what I mean."

"I'm not sure that I do," hazarded Angela. She didn't want to break the flow, but given that Carla liked to dwell on all things "Brendan" suspected she could take a long time getting to the point.

Angela got the big wide eyes again. "Well, the girlfriends are all right. They look just right at first nights and parties, just the job, but Brendan needs a little something else to satisfy him." Angela looked enquiringly at Carla. Carla smiled in an enigmatic fashion and ran her hands over her bunches again. "He likes something a bit more... fresh?" Her intonation rose into a question at the end, in the current popular manner.

Angela studied her for a moment. The penny dropped; Carla's image, quasi-teenager, and young teen at that. Her heart sank. "Do you mean underage girls?" she said.

Carla looked horrified. "Oh no! Brendan wouldn't do anything illegal! He wouldn't! He just likes them *looking* young." Her hand went unconsciously to her hair again and both officers realized in an instant where her plans lay with the youthful manner and the gamine appearance.

A wave of pity for her rose up in Angela. "And what did Oliver have to do with this?" she asked.

Carla paused for an instant to give effect to her words. "Olly supplied him with the girls."

A brief silence reigned in the room. Whatever Angela had been expecting, it wasn't this. The information disturbed her in a way she couldn't have explained.

"How do you know this?" she asked, expecting more "those-of-us-on-the-inside" behaviour, but she was surprised.

"It's a big secret. I don't think anybody else knows," replied Carla. "I only found out by accident. I was in the pub before a show at the beginning of the tour and I saw Olly in there. He and a mate of his were sitting on bar stools and talking. I went over and stood beside him to say 'hello' – just to be, like, friendly – but he carried on talking with this bloke. So, after a minute or two I got bored. I mean, he hadn't even realized I was there. So I made a point of going in front of him, and when he saw me he jumped and said, 'How long have you been there?' He was a bit sharp, to be honest. I thought, *Oh, thanks very much, this is what you get for being polite!* So anyway, I said I'd only just arrived and Olly said to his mate, 'This is the new runner.' His friend went all mysterious. He stared at me, then he nudged Olly and whispered, like it was a secret, and said, 'Looks young; just right for Brendan' and they both looked at each other and burst out laughing."

"So his friend was in on the secret, was he?" asked Gary.

"Suppose so," answered Carla. "I was a bit worried at that point because I didn't want anyone to know that I'm a – that I live with a couple of fans. You have to keep a professional attitude when you're working in show business."

"Yes, I'm sure," said Angela.

"But at the same time, if there was a chance of getting off with Brendan... well... I could hardly believe my luck. It'd be the thing I want most in all the world. I mean, who wouldn't?"

Angela treated the question as a rhetorical one. "So how did you find out that Oliver supplied Brendan with suitable women?"

Carla couldn't disguise a look of pride. "He let me into the secret. It was time to go back for the sound check then, so we walked back together and that's when he told me."

"So how did it work, this demand and supply situation?"

"Every now and again there'd be this little conversation; it didn't take much, just a nod sometimes. But Olly always got the message and he'd deal with it. They had this arrangement, see? Olly was the only one he trusted, which makes sense; he'd been working for him longer than any of the other crew. He said every now and then, when Brendan had the urge on him, he gave the nod and Olly went and sorted something out. He explained that's why I'd see them having a bit of a talk now and again."

"And what about yourself, your own hopes?"

A strange mixture of pent-up excitement and anguish mingled on Carla's face, with an undercurrent of anger she could not conceal.

"I tried to keep it casual. I asked where he got the girls from but he just tapped his nose with his finger and said that was his business. So then I said, 'I've always been told I look young for my age' and he stopped and looked at me, all over, like. Then he said, 'You do, don't you? And you're quite small.' He looked as though he was seriously considering me as a possibility and my stomach turned right over. I could have died from the excitement but I knew I had to play it cool, so I made out like I thought it'd be a laugh. I said, 'I'd be up for it if you're stuck, the next time he asks.' I made sure he couldn't tell how keen I really was."

Hmm, right, thought Angela. She cast a brief glance across at Gary and guessed from his deadpan expression that he was concealing similar thoughts to her own. "What did he say to that?" she asked.

"He said he'd see what he could do the next time Brendan was *that way*, you know?" A tear rolled down her cheek. "But it never happened, and now the tour's over and I don't know when I'm going to get my chance."

"Yes, I do see," answered Angela. *More than you think*, she added to herself.

Carla looked at them as though considering her next move and decided to take them into her confidence. "It's the only reason I kept in with him," she admitted.

"Oh, really?" Angela was at her most inviting.

"Yeah, well, I didn't want to miss my chance, did I? But lately Olly had started to say that if I was prepared to 'oblige' him, you know, he'd definitely put my name forward as soon as Brendan tipped him the wink again."

"And have you done that?" asked Angela.

Carla, shrugging, studied her fingernails. "Well, yeah. I mean, for the sake of getting together with Brendan, why wouldn't I? I didn't like the idea of it, but I really fancy Brendan, so it's, like, worth it to me. I mean, I know if I got the chance I could really make Brendan happy. I feel like I could be his soulmate, you know? His girlfriends aren't doing much for him; they can't give him what he really needs."

I have serious doubts you could do any better, Carla, thought Angela. "Can you remember when the meeting happened, with Oliver and the man in the pub?" she asked.

Carla screwed up her face and concentrated like a

schoolgirl, still playing the teenage ticket. "A few months ago," she said eventually.

"Ah yes, you said, at the beginning of the tour." *So,* thought Angela, *you've spent most of the past few months trying to get noticed by Brendan. And you've been so remarkably unsuccessful you were reduced to entering into some unsavoury liaison with Oliver Joplin on the dubious grounds that he might present you with a window of opportunity.* Angela had heard and seen some very unpleasant things in her career as a policewoman and had become acclimatized to much of it, but she was always struck afresh by genuine naivety. Carla felt herself truly in love with Brendan and the combination of working on his tour and the opportunity Oliver seemed to offer clouded her judgment, a situation destined to end in tears. She felt pity for the young woman but had to move the conversation on. "Can you describe this friend of Oliver's, the man in the pub?"

Carla thought for a moment. "It was just a bloke," she said, eventually.

"Dark? Fair? Tall? Short? Fat? Thin?"

"Definitely not fat but he was sitting down so I couldn't tell how tall he was. And I can't remember the colour of his hair."

Angela felt her energy level depleting. She rose. "You've been very helpful, Carla. We might need to speak to you again but you've given us some food for thought."

"Not a problem," answered Carla, jumping up from the sofa and going ahead of them to the door. "Glad I was able to help. It's horrible for Brendan to have this upset going on around him. He needs to have it cleared up as soon as possible."

Gary must have been flagging as much as Angela because neither of them said anything in the car until they were nearly home again. Then: "What did you make of that, Gary?" asked Angela.

"I found it cloying; she's so focused on Brendan. I've never come across that before. I mean, I know Maddie really likes Brendan Phelan and plays his music a lot, but she's – well – she's got a life. It doesn't occupy her every waking hour. And the trouble Carla's taking to get to sleep with him. That's bizarre."

"It's not bizarre to Carla, Gary. The love she feels for Brendan is very real to her. But you're right; there are fans and there are *fans*. OK, fan considerations aside. What do you make of the premise that Oliver 'supplied' Brendan with women – well, girl-like women, at least?"

Gary shook his head as if to clear it of some confusion. "That makes him sound like a bit of a kiddie fiddler and I can't really compute that."

"Me neither. From what I've read in the papers, and now having met him, Brendan strikes me as an intelligent, normal man whose romantic taste runs strictly to his female contemporaries, and I'm sure he didn't need Oliver Joplin to provide them for him."

"Rhetorical question?"

"Yes?"

"Carla thinks otherwise, which means…?"

"Oliver obviously recognized Carla's not-so-well-hidden agenda and came out with this line about supplying women. Maybe he saw it from the start as a way to string Carla along and have her for himself."

"Which is what happened."

"Indeed, and she's swallowed the story whole because she desperately wants to be one of the 'women'."

"I have no trouble buying that explanation. But it still leaves us with the fact that an odd relationship *did* seem to exist between Oliver and Brendan."

"Yes." Angela sighed. "And if we don't think it was to supply underage-looking women we need to find out its true nature. But not tonight; I'm whacked. I'll get Leanne to set up another interview with Brendan. She'll love doing that."

Chapter Thirteen

Most of the crowd keeping watch across the street from Brendan's property had disappeared by the time Angela and Gary arrived the following morning. Just a few stalwarts hung on, staring with curiosity as their car drove through and disappeared out of sight of the road. As before, Desmond Phelan opened the door. "Ah, he's out the back," he said by way of greeting. "Follow me."

"Out the back" in Angela's experience meant a garden with a shed at the end, or possibly a small yard. "Out the back" in Brendan Phelan's house involved a walk past a very inviting-looking swimming pool and across a vast velvety lawn to a structure the size of a small house in the shade of some trees. Even then Angela wasn't sure they'd arrived at the end of the garden. Desmond led them into a tiny vestibule and opened a further door to a loud blast of music from within. As he went in ahead of them, Angela and Gary could see a very impressive sound recording console. Brendan, Terry Dexter and the other members of the band leaned over this, involved in some sort of discussion. Desmond went over and shouted in his brother's ear and Brendan looked towards the door. He smiled, nodded and addressed those present. "OK, everyone, cop-time for me. Carry on; I'll be back soon." He joined Angela and Gary. "Good morning, Inspector Costello and – er – not inspector," he smiled.

"Detective Constable," grinned Gary, as Brendan led them back to the house.

"Ah yes, Houseman, wasn't it? Any relation?"

"I don't think so," replied Gary. He looked, impressed, at

the other man. "My name has an 'e' in it. I don't often get asked that question."

"One of my teachers at school had a thing about the First World War poets. Housman and Kipling struck a particular chord with me."

"Sorry to interrupt your – er – jam session," said Angela. "I hate to disturb the creative flow." They'd reached the kitchen now, a sumptuously appointed room. They skirted round a central island top with glistening marble, arriving at the hall they'd first entered on their previous visit.

"It's not a jam session," answered Brendan, mounting the stairs. "More editing. We're redoing the arrangements to stuff I wrote a few years ago and haven't used yet." Angela turned her head and glanced at Gary, remembering Tilly Townsend's frustration about the lack of recent output from Brendan.

Once in the living room, Brendan sank into the cream sofa, indicating the empty space beside him and the chair opposite. Angela sat down next to him. Gary took the other seat. "Have you come to arrest me?" His eyes twinkled and a smiled played around his mouth, but it contained the merest hint of uncertainty. Smiling back at him, with what she hoped was a reassuring expression, gave Angela the opportunity to look more closely at his face. She took in the lines of strain and the dark shadows under his eyes. She decided to pick up the gauntlet he'd thrown down.

"Why would I arrest you?" she asked.

Brendan tried for nonchalance with a shrug but the burst of laughter that came out at the same time held a faint note of hysteria. "Oh, you know – I was conveniently placed, after all."

"Not for shooting Oliver Joplin in the back of the head," replied Angela. Brendan's response intrigued her. She made a note to go through every possible sequence of the event with

Gary, later. Her words had the desired effect; she saw Brendan relax.

"So, what's it to be today, then?"

"I want to ask you more about the conversation you were having with Oliver just before the shot," she said, smiling into his eyes; strongly reminded, once again, of Patrick.

The tension returned immediately. Angela could almost feel his mouth go dry. As if in confirmation his tongue came out and he moistened his lips. "It's just what I said before," he said. He attempted a cheery smile but it didn't go with the slight crack in his voice.

"We've been speaking to a few people and it seems that several of your team are puzzled by the relationship between you and Oliver."

"Relationship? You must be mistaken! They must be mistaken!" His voice had gone up a whole octave. He coughed as if to cover the rise in tone.

Angela felt sorry for him. She could see his natural inclination went towards honesty. He would never cut it as a liar. "Several of the people who work with you spoke of Oliver engaging you in conversation from time to time – separately and specifically. And by your own admission you and he were talking together outside the theatre when the shooting took place."

Brendan gave an uncertain smile. "I told you about that already."

"Yes." Angela flipped back the pages in her notebook. "You were taking him to task about his attitude, something you'd normally leave to your production manager but you said you'd decided to man up." Angela smiled at him. She didn't want him to think she was being sarcastic.

Brenda waited a moment before speaking. Angela sensed he wanted his voice to come out at its normal pitch. "That's it," he said eventually.

Angela decided to let him have the benefit of the doubt for the moment. "So what were these other occasions all about, when you and he were seen having these little chats?"

Brendan, relaxed, gave a tentative smile and emitted a small "Pah!" The nonchalance returned with greater strength. "Oh, you know, Inspector. Olly was the longest-serving member of the crew. He liked to do a bit of the old pals act in front of the others, give them the impression that he was 'in' with me in a way they weren't. There's a hierarchy backstage just as there is in any other organization."

"But he didn't have any special relationship with you?"

"Not at all – he was just a crew member, and not, as I think I've indicated, one of the most valuable ones."

Angela prepared a fresh page in her notebook. "If that's the case," she asked in a matter-of-fact voice, "why did you continue to employ him?"

The hands lying along Brendan's thighs balled into fists and the knuckles whitened. He flicked a glance to her, saw that she had noticed, and tried to straighten them out, but they refused to cooperate. "Oh, you know how it is," he said, making a very good attempt at keeping his voice normal. It nearly worked. "You get used to someone. It can be easier than breaking in new crew."

Angela looked at him. She was very gentle but firm. "I don't think that's quite how things were, is it?"

Brendan shot up and all but hopped across the room. He came to a stop before the tall window looking out towards the Heath. He swivelled round to face them then, his eyes darting from one to the other, the fear unmistakable. "I didn't kill him!" he shouted, his voice up again. He moved from one foot to the other, agitation showing in every sinew.

Angela remained very calm. "We're not accusing you of murdering him," she said. "But there's something here you're not telling us. It would be helpful if we could eliminate it from the enquiry."

Brendan took a couple of deep breaths to steady himself. "It's not relevant," he said finally, in a near-normal voice.

"I think I should be the judge of that," replied Angela.

Tears started in Brendan's eyes. "I'll be ruined," he croaked, barely able to get the words out.

"Brendan, we're investigating a murder. If this has nothing to do with the case it won't be mentioned again, but we do need to eliminate it."

Brendan's whole body sagged. He nodded in defeat. He came back and sat down next to her on the sofa. "Brother Xavier was right. When I was at school I thought a monk must be naive, not a clue what the real world's like; but I was wrong. He had the right of it then and he's still right."

"Did this, whatever it is, begin when you were at school?"

Brendan shook his head. "No, years after I'd left. It's been even worse since it all came out about the late Jimmy Savile and what he was really up to. And now there are all these other cases, some of them total nonsense, as you know. And that man, Oliver Joplin, was the monkey on my back for the past eight years."

Angela nodded, getting an idea of where this was leading. "Why don't you start at the beginning?"

"In the beginning – yes." Brendan steadied himself with a deep breath. "In the beginning there was a young pop star. He was doing very well, his songs were very popular and he had thousands of fans, most of them young women, many of them imagining themselves in love with him."

"Yes, I remember your meteoric rise to fame."

Brendan's worried expression softened for a moment. "Yes. It sounds like a cliché but that is how it happened." He looked at her. "The trouble is, my fame outstripped me. I got left behind."

Angela was puzzled. "I'm not sure I understand."

"I could fill a theatre with thousands of girls – but could I hold one in my arms?"

"Ah!" said Angela, then remembered. "But you have a girlfriend, surely?"

Brendan gave a bleak grin. "And a model of patience she is, I can assure you. I'm talking about eight years ago. Fame was still a new thing and a bit scary, if the truth be told. But I had my impulses and my energy, just like any other young man. The trouble was, I didn't feel comfortable with the women who made themselves available, you get me?"

"You're talking about groupies."

"Yes. Olly was someone who watched people. He could tell you all about the weaknesses of the entire crew and the band. I mean, I know this now; I didn't then. He came up to me this one time. I thought he was genuinely sympathetic. We were at a party, the end of the first major tour. It had gone way better than we could have hoped and I think we were all on a high. The drink flowed and the air had a slight tinge of wacky backy, and you could barely move for well-wishers. I think that's when it first struck me. Everybody either had a partner on their arm or was busy chatting someone up – and there's me in the corner doing a lonesome man act. The truth is, I suddenly realized I felt very, very frustrated and quite fed up."

"I see," said Angela, who was beginning to, very clearly.

"The next thing I knew, Olly is at my side wanting to know if 'there's anything he can get me'. He said it in a very particular voice. I knew exactly what he meant immediately. I trusted him; I didn't have any reason not to. I just said, 'I don't like the groupie scene' and he assured me he knew a respectable, clean young woman who knew how to be discreet, and he could vouch for the fact that she was no groupie. My goodness, that man knew when to choose his moment. I barely hesitated. The party was in a private room of a hotel. He led me upstairs to one of the bedrooms and there she was. I was so desperate, I didn't even stop to think at the time that he must have planned it all. She looked about nineteen or so, a sweet face, nicely dressed, make-up not garish and she was neither gobby nor gushing. Olly went out and closed the door and we didn't waste much time."

"What was her name?"

"Kay."

Angela's head shot up from her notebook. She and Gary looked at each other. "Kay?"

Brendan had been watching them. "Yep. Kay. You might have met her in the course of your investigation so far."

"Kay? You don't mean Kay, Oliver's sister?"

"Yep. The very same. She mentioned it later that evening. That's what brought me to my senses, but it was too late by then. We'd already done it twice."

"So how did Oliver become the monkey on your back?"

"Ah yes, Inspector, you'll like this. Talk about a honeytrap. Two days later he turned up at my house with a little girl. She was wearing a school uniform, short white socks, a boater, and her hair was in two neat plaits. Beyond thinking she looked a bit familiar, I barely recognized her."

"Oh yes!" responded Angela, realizing what was coming next.

"You've got it. This was the same girl, *sans* make-up and a slinky grown-up woman's dress."

"How old was she really?"

Brendan shuddered. "Fourteen."

"Oh my goodness."

A sob escaped him. "I just wouldn't, not if I'd known, I've got sisters myself. I… I… I *swear*, Inspector, I thought she was of age."

"I'm sure you did," said Angela. "Let's try another tack. When you went with her, you thought she was of age because she seemed to be. When you next met, how do you know she was actually a schoolgirl, just because she dressed like one? I mean, anyone can put on their old school uniform and look demure." She looked at Gary and could tell that he, like her, was remembering Madeleine prancing about the living room in her old school clothes.

Brendan gave a mirthless smile. "There's no mistaking it. At the time I had sex with that girl, she was fourteen."

It wasn't a proper answer but Angela decided to leave it for the moment. "I see what you mean about the monkey on your back." She looked across at Gary to bring him in and move the interview along.

"So, these conversations the others witnessed here and there?" he began.

Brendan nodded. "Oh yes, he was a clever one, Olly. He managed not to be too greedy. A thousand, or fifteen hundred – never more. Every now and again he'd make it known that he wanted a bung. I had no choice but to comply and he knew it, not if I want to avoid having my name dragged across all the headlines denouncing me as a paedophile."

Angela didn't say anything, but her mind was full of questions. *What kind of brother sets up his fourteen-year-old sister for sex? Or was she a willing party? Many girls that age would be sexually active. A lot of pop stars' groupies would fall within that age group. But even so, fourteen? At that age, she might find a date with a famous man exciting – but for sex and nothing else? Was she a victim as much as Brendan?* She thought back to the woman they'd met in the house in Peckham. She'd seemed confident and assured, the house and the children has been clean, tidy and well looked-after. But that told her nothing. It would be naive to assume that the lives of all abuse victims fell apart.

There was no point in continuing without a concrete answer to her previous question. "How can you be sure," she asked, "that she was only fourteen?"

A bleak look appeared on Brendan's face. "Totally sure. He had that covered," he said. "He showed me her birth certificate. Gave me a good long time to read it, as well, hold it in my hands, feel it, check its authenticity. And then he left me with a copy." He cocked his head to one side of the room. "It's in a drawer over there. There's no escaping the fact. She was underage."

Angela nodded. Brendan's eyes were fixed on hers, with a kind of desperation in them. He could have been a prisoner in the dock and she the judge about to pronounce a verdict. For the time being, at least, she could put him out of his misery. "I believe you, Brendan," she said.

His shoulders slumped and a look of relief appeared on his face. "Thank you."

"What's this Brother Xavier got to do with it?"

He gave a haunted smile. "Our school was run by the Salesians and he was the physics master. We had one of those days when our regular teacher was off sick and Brother Xavier came in to babysit us. You know what it's like when that happens."

Angela smiled. "Yes, the lessons can turn out to be quite fun and more interesting than usual."

"That's what happened in this case. Terry – you knew I was at school with Terry, right?" Angela nodded. "Terry had a tabloid newspaper and the front page was full of some celebrity who'd been accused of attacking a woman. Actually, I tell a lie, he'd just been acquitted. The case dragged on for months and his name had been smeared all across the headlines. Terry held up this paper and shouted out, 'Hey, Bro Xavvy, what do you think of this, then?' We just wanted to get him talking about anything other than physics, of course. But he was canny, Brother Xavier; he knew what we wanted. He probably didn't want to give a physics lesson either, and we got into this discussion about how the media handled this sort of thing. Looking back, I can see this monk was even more shrewd that I gave him credit for at the time because, really, he turned it into a session on ethics. This celebrity's name had been dragged completely through the mud, people had been talking about it for weeks and in the end he'd been found innocent. And that's the point that's stayed with me. I can still see Brother Xavier holding up this tabloid so that we could all see this poor man's picture. And he tapped it as he spoke. 'This is how it works, boys,' he said. 'Good that he's innocent. But. He. Has. Already. Been. Crucified.'"

Chapter Fourteen

Back at the incident room, the team pooled the results of their morning's labour over a couple of shared pizzas. Rick and Jim took the floor first. They'd finally managed to go and search the victim's property that morning.

"We've come up with two things of interest," began Rick.

"Fire away," said Angela.

"He seems to have had a girlfriend."

"Yes," added Rick. "A neighbour came and knocked on the door while we were there and wanted to know what was going on. He couldn't tell us any more about Oliver Joplin than we've heard from everybody else so far. He said he'd got a grunt once or twice when he passed him on the stairs and said 'Good morning', but that was it. However, the neighbour did say that over the past few weeks he'd been coming back late at night with a woman. He peeped out from his door one time when he heard the footsteps on the stairs, but he only got a sight of someone's back and heard her giggle."

"We've every reason to believe this is Carla, the runner on the crew," said Angela, "It'll all be in our report. What's the other thing?"

"He was either into something dodgy or he just liked holding folding," continued Jim.

Angela and Gary exchanged looks then Angela spoke. "How much?"

Rick look down at the inventory they'd made. "Three and a half thousand pounds," he replied, "in a variety of denominations, used notes. He had wedges stashed in different pockets, a hundred here, couple of hundred there."

"We've heard from some of the backstage crew that he was thought to be into 'something' but they didn't know what," said Angela. "Gary and I have discovered one of Oliver's sidelines. We'll tell you about that in a minute. But he could be more enterprising than we know – he may have had more than one iron in the fire. Amounts of money like this stashed about his person sounds like – what does it sound like, team?"

"Like money you'd have for making a payment that wasn't going to go through anyone's books," obliged Jim.

"Exactly," agreed Angela. "OK, did you find a computer?"

"Yep. We couldn't get into it, he must have a password set up, so we've sent that to the lab."

"Good. What else?"

"His bank statement," replied Rick.

"And?"

"The cash we found in his pockets was only the tip of the iceberg."

"Really?"

"Yep. He's got fifty thousand in a deposit account."

"Wow!" said Gary. "I wonder how much a member of a rock band road crew would normally expect to earn."

"Not that much, I'm sure," said Angela.

"We're also wondering if somebody had been into the flat before us," continued Rick.

"Oh, really? What makes you think that?"

Rick frowned. "That's just it; we've no way of knowing for certain. There was just a feel about the place. It wouldn't have been difficult to get in. If we hadn't had his keys with us there'd have been no trouble forcing the lock, so most other people could have done the same. And then, he didn't seem to be all that tidy. He had clothing, odds and ends and books and what-have-you on every surface and in every drawer, bar one."

"Yeah, that's what made us think someone had been there," added Jim. "It was the top drawer of the desk where the computer sat. There are three drawers to the right and the top one was completely empty." He looked across at his partner. "We thought, since everywhere else was crammed with stuff and such a mess – "

"It could have been cleared out in a hurry," finished Rick. "Some of the mess could have been spread about by an intruder. Hard to say. Anyway – if there has been a break-in, whoever it was took what they wanted but didn't hang around to look for money. There was plenty for the taking."

Angela considered what they'd said. "Hmm, it does sound strange. Perhaps, if you're right, whoever came to the flat was nervous of being caught there."

"If they emptied the drawer out they must have known what they were looking for and gone straight to it," said Jim. "We don't know what was going on, do we? So whoever it was might not have known he was dead, and been keen to get in and get out before Oliver turned up."

"They might have had good reason for haste even if they knew he'd been killed," said Angela. "We now know of at least one very alert neighbour."

Nobody on the team argued with this.

"OK," said Angela. "We'll keep the place sealed for now. If you're right and something was taken away, it could be documents of some sort and the computer might tell us more once the lab has got into it. We might need to pay another visit. Anything else?"

"We took away some photographs with us," said Jim. Some are family snaps – what you'd expect – him with his parents, him with his sister, there are a few of him with some little kids, maybe his niece and nephews."

"We met the sister yesterday. I'm sure we'll recognize

the children if they're the same ones," said Angela. "Any of friends?"

"Just a couple, and he's with the same bloke in both of them. Apart from this man in the photos, he sounds a bit of a Billy no-mates to be honest." Rick passed the photographs around the team, starting with Gary.

"Ah!" said Gary. He passed the photograph to Angela.

"Oh yes," said Angela, looking intently at it. "Are we beginning to join up the dots, do you think?"

"I reckon so," he replied. He looked round at the others. "On the night of the murder I went to a concert at the Apollo."

"Yes, I remember," said Rick. "That's why you were on the scene so quickly."

"Yes, well, before the show I was waiting for Maddie in the foyer and I saw this bloke outside, touting tickets." He passed the photograph round so they could all see it properly. "I got a good look at his face – but these…" He brought his hand over the top of the second picture and pointed to the memorable tattoos.

"Very distinctive," said Rick.

"What are they? Oh, I see," added Leanne, peering closely at the photograph. "They're like elongated hawks swooping down his arms."

"So we know he's a tout and he's a mate of the victim," finished Jim.

"Ah!" exclaimed Gary. They all remained silent as his face showed him going through some thought process. "Ping! Or 'Bingo!' as Angie might say." He grinned across at her.

"What are you thinking?" she asked him.

"I hadn't thought before about the whole context of seeing him at the theatre. I've just remembered something and it might have a bearing on things."

"Go on, fill us in, then," said Angie.

"I was standing in the foyer looking out through the glass doors to the street, watching for Maddie. I heard a bit of a commotion behind me and I looked round. Some man had brought his daughter and a few of her friends for the concert – a birthday treat from what I could gather – but it turned out that his tickets weren't valid."

"Bought them from a dodgy source?" suggested Jim.

"Sounds like it. He argued the toss a bit with the doorman, protested he'd bought them in good faith and paid with his credit card, but his daughter started crying so he ushered them out into the street, very embarrassed. By that time Maddie had joined me and we both watched as this man – " Gary pointed at the photograph again – "approached him in the street and started talking to him. We could tell what was going on, and we reckoned he'd pay up because he wouldn't want to disappoint the girls."

"He'd be paying well over the odds in that case," opined Derek.

"Cor, yeah!" agreed Jim.

"Oh – just a minute," said Angela. "I think I know where you're going with this. Are you assuming a link between this man's phoney tickets and the fact that a tout approaches him the minute he gets outside the theatre?"

"Yes."

"That looks quite juicy," added Jim.

"Doesn't it just," agreed Angela. "A possible ticketing scam, eh? OK, Gary and I found another connection between hawk-arms and the victim," she continued, "through Joplin's sister. She has a picture of him in her kitchen. It shows him at a party with Oliver but Kay claims not to know him and, if my memory serves, said he hadn't been around for a while; which, of course could also be true – from *her* point of view." Angela paused for a moment. She remembered the constantly grounded conversation with Kay Joplin and began to wonder if the woman had deliberately stonewalled them. She took the picture showing the two men together from Leanne. "Stick that up on the board, Jim," she added.

"You look like something's bothering you," said Gary.

"I think there might be, but I can't get what it is," Angela admitted. "There's something about our interview with Oliver's sister. Never mind, it might come back to me when I'm not thinking about it."

"Instead, you can think about how he's got a lot more in the bank than one would suppose for a man in his job," said Rick.

"Plus all the cash about the place," added Derek.

"Indeedy," agreed Angela. "OK, Derek and Leanne."

"Yes, guv," they replied in unison.

"Do a bit of research. Try to find out exactly how much someone in his position can expect to make in the normal course of touring, and stay on top of what the lab find on his computer."

"Will do," replied Leanne.

"And maybe check to make sure an elderly aunt didn't die and leave him fifty thousand quid recently."

"Right," added Derek.

"But that's not all," continued Angela. "Gary and I have discovered another little earner he had on the go."

"Seems like an enterprising chap," remarked Rick.

"Oh yes," agreed Angela. "No flies on Mr Joplin, and not many scruples either, from what I gather." She quickly told them about the blackmail of Brendan Phelan and waited for them to digest what they'd heard.

Rick was the first to speak. "Poor bloke; he was paying top whack for his pleasure, wasn't he?"

"And paying and paying and paying," added Jim.

Angela looked across at Leanne and saw she'd gone very pale except for two bright red spots high on each cheek. "What a bastard!" she exclaimed. "Blackmail. The dirtiest crime in the book! Poor Brendan, my heart goes out to him. You know, some of his songs in the past few years have been really haunting, like they've been born out of real pain and suffering. I bet that's the reason."

"Actually, his girlfriend told us he hasn't written anything new in a long while and she can't figure out why. I think this could be the reason," suggested Angela.

"That makes it all the more poignant," said Leanne.

"It certainly takes the edge off our sympathy for Oliver Joplin as victim," agreed Angela. "But our job is to find his killer, no matter what the man's character may have been like. I didn't ask Brendan for a copy of that birth certificate because he seemed so wretched about the whole business, and I didn't want to alarm him that it might become relevant to the case; but, of course, we'll need to follow through on this."

"Want me to get on to it, guv?" asked Leanne.

"Yes, add it to the jobs you and Derek have got. I don't know if she was registered in the borough where she's now living, but it's a good place to start and she would have been born twenty-two years ago. Do a bit of a trawl round the family. I mean, see if you can find out anything else about them."

"Any previous convictions, for instance?" asked Derek.

"Yeah, that, but..." Angela paused. "Maybe any instances of Social Services' involvement as well – child at risk, that sort of stuff. I don't quite know what I'm looking for, but when we met Kay yesterday – full name, Kayleigh, by the way, Leanne – she seemed like a regular young mum with no problems beyond sorting the kids out and running a home. The thing is, this young woman was used by her brother as bait to entrap Brendan Phelan when she was just *fourteen*."

"It makes you wonder about the quality of the home life, doesn't it?" remarked Rick. "And also – "

"Yes?" asked Angela.

"Well, I'm just thinking back to what my younger sister was like when she was that age. She was a mouthy little so-and-so. She would have soon told me where to go if I'd even suggested such a thing."

"Perhaps this one was under her big brother's influence in a completely unhealthy way," offered Leanne.

"She seemed genuinely fond of him, said what a good brother he was."

"I'm not saying it makes it any better or right, even," said Jim. He looked carefully around at them all before continuing. "But some teenagers are very forward and much more grown-up than, well, others."

"It's a good point," agreed Angela. "Brendan had no doubt whatsoever he went to bed with somebody of age."

"Until she turned up two days' later in her school uniform," added Gary. He grimaced. "And that monk at his school was right," he added. "The press *would* crucify him if it came out."

"Wouldn't they just. They'd be like a pack of baying hounds. We go very carefully with this."

"We'll find out what we can, guv," said Leanne. "Leave it with Derek and me."

"Good, that's sorted," replied Angela. "Now, the other thing was that Brendan thought we might consider him one of the suspects. He was half-joking, mind you."

"How would that work?" asked Jim.

"It's a good question. Gary put forward the suggestion after our first visit to him, but it got buried under everything else. He was very tense and we now know why, but even so, let's think about it. Gaz and Derek, stand in the centre of the room facing each other. One of you be Oliver and the other, Brendan. The one who's Brendan, you've got a gun in your hand, right? You're talking to each other outside the stage door. OK – go!"

Gary picked up a stapler from the nearest desk and pointed it at Derek.

"No," objected Derek. "Surely he'd have it out of sight at this point."

"OK," agreed Gary, and put the stapler into his trouser pocket.

"Give me some more money or I'll tell everyone you slept with my sister when she was just a kid," snarled Derek, causing a few giggles to erupt in the room.

"I'm fed up with this. I don't want to pay any more," replied Gary.

"You've got no choice, punk!"

"Punk? Seriously? Oh, right, then! Yes, I have. This is what I say to you." Gary pulled the stapler out of his pocket and pointed it at Derek. "Bang," he finished. Derek began to feign a slump forward. "Oh, no, that's not right," said Gary. "I've got to shoot you in the back of the head. Go back to where I pull the gun out of my pocket." Derek righted himself. "OK. No, I'm not paying you another penny," snarled Gary. With one hand he pointed the gun and with the other he reached out and quickly spun Derek round so that he was facing the opposite direction. "Bang," he said again.

Derek slumped forward again and this time stretched himself out on the floor in the approximate position in which Oliver's body had been found. Gary went round so that he was standing at his head. A ripple of applause ran round the room followed by a brief silence.

"Hmm," said Angela after a moment. "Not very convincing, is it?"

Derek scrambled to his feet, pretending to be offended. "What do you mean? I'm pretty good at the old amateur dramatics, even if I do say so myself." He brushed his clothes down.

They all laughed. "You were wonderful," soothed Angela. "I wouldn't be surprised if you've missed your calling. But I meant the scenario itself. That's probably about the only way Brendan could have done it, if he's the murderer, and the idea is not very tenuous. Apart from that, remember, no gun was found at the scene."

"He could have put it in his pocket," suggested Rick.

"That's true; but the forensic team would have found it. They tested him for powder residue, remember, and took away the clothes he was wearing," said Angela. "Mind you…"

"Yes, even if he'd hidden the gun the whole idea isn't very tenable," said Gary. "I heard the shot from the street and reached the body within a minute. I really don't think it could have happened that way."

"That's a relief," put in Leanne. "I'd hate to think of Brendan as the murderer."

"Bit of a bummer all the same, though," said Jim.

"Why's that?" asked Angela.

"Well, from what you've now told us, he had a fantastic motive."

Chapter Fifteen

Patrick was just lighting the candles on a dining room table set for two when Angela arrived home that evening. He'd used their best linen and the dinner service they'd received for a wedding present. "Ooh! This looks nice," she said, coming into the room. She noted the two place settings. "Isn't Maddie eating with us tonight?"

"No; she rang me from her office. Gary's taking her out for a meal."

"Oh – he didn't say anything today; but then, why should he?" Angela looked at Patrick and raised her eyebrows. "Are they having a romantic candle-lit supper, do you think?"

"I assumed so, but have you noticed she's not very forthcoming about the situation between them?"

"It might be because Gary and I work together. He doesn't say much, either; but then, he's a man, so I suppose he wouldn't – not to me, anyway."

He grinned. "I did try to push her a little. I said, 'Oh, so this is getting serious, is it?' Then, just as she was thinking up ways to change the subject, it occurred to me that *our* last romantic meal in a restaurant was interrupted by you being called to this murder, which put the kibosh on things a bit. But by then the meat had been out of the freezer a couple of hours so I thought, 'Hey, why don't we eat out – in?'" He leaned back spreading his hands to display the scene.

Angela laughed. She loved Patrick very much, but there were moments when she felt particularly blessed in her husband. "What a superb idea, darling. And what's the name of this exclusive eating-out-in restaurant?"

"It's known as the *Chez Nous*. A limited menu, to be sure, but this establishment offers exclusive postprandial delights; Maître d' Costello, at your service." He opened his arms wide and Angela moved across to be enfolded in his embrace. Their kiss, long and deep, came to an abrupt halt when the front doorbell rang. "That'll be yon swain, no doubt," said Patrick, going to answer it.

"Is the bathroom free?" asked Angela.

"Yes, I heard Maddie come out and head for her bedroom at least half an hour ago," he replied from along the passage. "Evening, Gary," he added, as he opened the door. "Come in. I think Maddie's nearly ready. Go into the dining room, we're just in there."

Gary stopped and looked at the table in admiration when he came through the door. "That looks nice," he said, with a grin. "Do you want me to keep Maddie out really, really, really late?"

"You cheeky detective constable! I'll make sure I give you a horrible job tomorrow for saying that," replied Angela, with a laugh. Just at that moment Madeleine entered. Her subtle make-up hit just the right note, her shining chestnut hair fell in soft waves to her shoulders, and her dress – a shimmery midnight blue, with a pashmina in a lighter shade thrown artlessly around her shoulders – presented an exquisite picture.

"Evening, Angie," she smiled at her stepmother and caught sight of the table. "Hey, nice one, Pops!" She turned to her boyfriend. "Gary, we'd better get going; they don't need us here."

Gary wasn't really listening. "You look stunning," he said, hardly able to take his eyes off Madeleine. "That's much better."

The look of pleased satisfaction that appeared on

Madeleine's face quickly gave way to bewilderment. "Thank you – er – better... than what?"

"If you remember, Maddie," Angela cut in, "the last time he saw you, you were wearing your old school uniform and you had your hair in pigtails." As she spoke she remembered Carla Paterson, affecting the dress and mannerisms of somebody several years younger. *Not quite the same thing*, she thought. Carla's reasons were calculated in a most decidedly adult manner.

Madeleine's brow cleared. "Oh, yes – the reunion the other night! That was a great get-together, Gary; we're thinking of doing an 'and boyfriends' evening."

"No problem," he grinned, "just so long as your stepmother hasn't got me on night duty of some sort."

"I'll get my dad to have a word if so," she said, taking his arm and leading him towards the front door. "Night-night, folks; don't get carried away by the romantic ambience. Oh – on second thoughts – get carried away all you like."

The young man emerged from Ladbroke Grove tube station and made his way along the street. His backpack, slung over one shoulder, banged heavily against him with every step, but he didn't seem to care. He stopped at a pub, but paused before entering to roll down the sleeves of his shirt, covering the distinctive tattoos on his arms. He hated concealing these works of art. They were a source of considerable pride for him and he'd been really surprised when Olly expressed reservations about them because they made him so easy to identify. He'd shrugged off his business partner's misgivings and the matter had never arisen again.

Over the past year or so he'd begun to feel that he'd been relegated to the position of junior partner; he didn't like it. They'd started off on an even footing and he couldn't be sure when or how he'd slipped down the ranking. Doing nothing about these tattoos offered a way of silently asserting his authority, his equality. All the same, he was surprised by how much Olly's death had affected him. He felt cut loose, adrift. For a moment he'd felt complete panic, totally unnerved. What was he supposed to do? How could he carry on? So he'd welcomed the telephone call when it came. The caller seemed to know all about the business. Perhaps this could be a way forward, a fresh opportunity. But he had to play it carefully. The other person had to know he was talking to Olly's business partner – not merely an employee. He went over to the bar, ordered a pint of beer and sat on the seat nearest the door, according to their arrangement.

Fifteen minutes later the man he was due to meet came in. He wore a smart overcoat with an expensive scarf hanging loosely around the neck, and carried himself with an air of assurance. The newcomer cast a quick look round and their eyes locked. He gave a barely perceptible nod before buying himself a half-pint of beer and joining the young man with the hawk tattoos, lowering himself onto a stool the other side of the table.

"You're punctual, anyway; that's a good start."

The young man took a mouthful of beer. He wanted to say: "How would you know I was on time when you're late?" But he was unsure of himself, intimidated by these confident people who moved so easily around the stars of the music business. He would most dearly have loved a niche on the inside of that world.

"OK. So what's your full name?" asked the man, briskly. "I only know you as Alex."

"Alex'll do for now," he replied. He wanted to appear cool, but he felt very nervous about hedging and knew he'd crack if the other man insisted on a surname. The newcomer merely gave a shrug and a half-smile.

Alex took another pull at his beer. "So what do I call you, then?"

"H."

Alex frowned. "What? Just 'H'? Like the letter?"

"That'll do. You're going to need someone new to work with, then."

"Hold on a minute. How about a little sensitivity? Olly's not even cold in his grave. He was a good mate of mine," protested Alex.

"I'm sorry for your loss," came the calm reply; not a flicker of emotion. "The king is dead. Long live the king."

"What?"

"Never mind. Look, Alex, I can't hang about. Do you want to deal or don't you?"

"Not necessarily," answered Alex, his mouth suddenly dry. He'd got the stationery and the disc locked away in his flat. He thought he was in a good position to bargain.

The half-smile appeared again, this time accompanied by a gentle headshake. "I haven't come here to play games, Alex. You need someone on the inside – someone who can walk the walk and talk the talk. You hear what I'm saying?"

The necessity of having someone on the inside had also been Oliver's contention. Alex hadn't understood why, then, and he still didn't. When he'd broached the subject with Oliver, he'd been told there were things about the business only an insider could know. He assumed he'd get the same answer now. He could predict the outcome of this meeting and his heart sank. What ingredient made some people big-time while others could barely get a leg-up?

"So, have you brought the stuff?" asked the man.

Alex made a last-ditch stand. "No. I wanted to meet first –

see what's on the table." He injected a note of bravado into his tone, but that was all it was. His drinking companion didn't bother to hide his contempt.

"Nothing's on the table until I get a look-see at the material. Then we'll talk." The man's dark blue eyes stared directly into Alex's grey ones. "You're not in a position to bargain. I know all about your little scam and I could get you taken off the street sooner than you could say Jack Robinson. I'll give you a few days to think about it and see sense. We'll meet here Friday at the same time. Only then you'll bring me the stuff."

"What makes you think there's nobody else interested?"

The man didn't even seem to consider this a possibility. "You play fair with me and I'll treat you right," he said, as he rose to go.

"What's that supposed to mean?" Alex replied, with a hint of belligerence.

"What I mean is, don't mess me about and you'll keep your job," said the man, with the tone of a headmaster holding out the hope of a grammar school place if only the pupil would knuckle down and work hard.

Alex didn't have a great deal of confidence, or the highest of intellectual capability, but he did know when he was beaten. He watched the other man pick up his drink and finish it in one gulp and realized that it hadn't ever been his intention to stay long; another blow to his self-esteem. All he received by way of parting was a curt nod. He sat and finished his drink in a silence that would have been angry without the other thing he had on his mind tonight. He'd been decisive and in control about that, anyway. A smile played around his mouth. He'd show them all. None of them knew he had another string to his bow.

Once outside the man walked slowly back to his car. He

made a call on the way. "Hi," he said once the phone had been answered at the other end. "Went like a dream... Yes, it was a walkover. Yes – don't worry." He finished the call. Smiling to himself he got into his car and drove away, humming the melody from "Battle For Your Love", his favourite of all Brendan's songs.

Carla pasted the picture onto a fresh page in her scrapbook. She'd set aside this evening for the task of updating her records. Quite a few glossy pictures waited to be dealt with. This one showed Brendan and Terry Dexter in country gentleman mode. They wore Barbour jackets, wellington boots and flat caps; each holding a rifle slung nonchalantly over his arm. She assessed the way they held their weapons with a knowledgeable eye. She could handle a rifle well enough. She had won the junior section in her club two years' running, though it wasn't her favourite firearm.

A gentle knock on the door interrupted her reverie. "Come in!" she called.

One of her flatmates, Paige, entered, carrying a tray with two steaming mugs. "Coffee?" she asked, lifting one of them.

"Ooh! You're a star – thanks!" Carla reached out for the proffered cup.

Paige settled cross-legged onto the floor, leaning her back against Carla's bed. "Ohhh – that's a lovely one," she breathed, gazing at the array of photographs awaiting attention. "That's the spread from last week's *Hello!*, isn't it?"

"Yes. Pictures of Bren with firearms don't really do it for me, but I thought I'd include them in my records." Carla's own familiarity with guns gave her the freedom to make comments like this but, in truth, she wouldn't dream of missing out on any image of Brendan, in no matter what pose. She wouldn't admit this, or that she kept a scrapbook like any other aficionado. Working with Brendan gave her a different status from the rest of his fans. This had to be acknowledged.

"You're very good about updating your archive," remarked Paige. She had been well-trained. She gazed on her friend with earnest eyes. She knew she was lucky to be sharing a flat with her.

"Isn't Shauna going to join us?" asked Carla.

"She's popped out for some milk. I used the last for our coffees." Paige using up the milk in making a coffee for Carla, and Shauna going to the corner shop for more, expressed the pecking order of the three flatmates very clearly. Carla, by reason of her perceived relationship with Brendan, ruled the roost; Paige filled the position of trusted lieutenant. Together they lorded it over a loose-knit collection of devoted Brendan Phelan fans, all of them deeply envious of Carla for being even within touching distance of the man.

Paige leaned forward in a conspiratorial manner. "You've got no further news about – you know?"

Carla shook her head. "The shooting has put all the plans out. Brendan's really shocked."

Somewhere along the line the runner had allowed Paige and Shauna to form the impression that it was only a matter of time before Carla and Brendan announced their engagement. She'd sworn them both to absolute secrecy, and they had eagerly and sincerely entered into the intrigue. Paige could hardly believe her luck in belonging to this exclusive inner circle, barely one remove from the star himself. Of course, she would have preferred to be the one chosen for such an intimate relationship; but she was realistic about the improbability of such a thing. She settled happily for the prospect of basking in her friend's reflected glory, when the happy couple could finally go public.

Carla sat back from her task and took a sip of coffee. She gazed into the middle distance, her expression pensive. "He's, like, gone into himself, you know?"

Paige nodded, her face earnest. "Poor Brendan! It's such a shame you can't be with him, to comfort him."

"It's not wise at the moment. He's not in a good place and he can't deal with 'us'."

Paige nodded her head in understanding. These were such personal confidences; the intimacy thrilled her.

"Was Shauna there today?" Carla asked, in a deliberate change of subject.

"She managed to get this morning off and she was there till about one."

"Did she see anything?"

"Oh yes! At one point when the policeman on duty wasn't looking she managed to get round to the side – you know – where there's a back gate. I told you about it, remember, it was ajar and she managed to look through." Carla nodded, concealing her impatience to hear every detail. "Well, she saw the policeman and woman who came the first time – the one whose picture we saw in the paper – remember?"

"Yeah. D.I. Costello, she's the one who interviewed me."

A shiver of pleasure ran through Paige's whole frame. Carla was right in the thick of things; it was just too exciting. "Well, she didn't see them arrive but she saw them leave, and guess who saw them out?"

Carla took a breath. "Nooooo," she said.

"Yes!" Paige beamed. "It was Brendan himself; in his grey jogging bottoms."

"Oh, he knocks about the house in those," said Carla, with a knowing air.

"It was a bit weird, though," continued Paige.

Carla was instantly alert. "What was?"

"Well, Shauna said that after he'd seen the police out, he just stood there on the step staring into space. It's been so chilly today, and he only had a T-shirt – no jacket or hoodie – but he just stood there. For ages."

"There! I told you he wasn't in a good place, didn't I? My poor love!"

"Perhaps," began Paige, choosing her words with care, "you'll be able to call him and cheer him up later?"

Paige knew she came close to crossing a boundary here. Carla frowned. This is where she found it most difficult to maintain the fiction of her relationship with Brendan. In the beginning she'd overlooked the obvious assumption that even if your love affair must be kept secret, there would still be phone calls, text messages, emails, facetime. She'd devised the strategy of disappearing now and again into her bedroom, emerging after half an hour or so with an update: "He's dead beat; he's about to go to bed, bless him" or "The flight was delayed but he's checked in to the hotel at last." That Brendan had not even once called Carla had never been raised between the three housemates. Paige and Shauna wanted to believe the romance she had spun. They needed it as much as she did.

"He needs space to get his head round everything at the moment," Carla explained. "We've decided to give it a complete break while all this is going on."

Paige nodded her understanding, never probing the illogicality of this situation existing between two people who were supposed to be in love. "Anyway, Shauna was really excited at seeing him so close up," was all she said.

Carla smiled and relaxed. They could move on to safer ground. "The jogging bottoms are a good sign. He only wears those when he's truly relaxed."

Paige laughed. "Well, he must have been wearing them

when the police were there, so obviously wasn't too bothered about their visit."

It was time for Carla to reassert her superiority. She nodded her head in the manner of one who knows. "I'm a bit worried about the way the police are going about things," she said, in confiding tones.

Given her place in the hierarchy of Brendan Phelan fans, it seemed only natural to Paige that Carla should have words of wisdom to impart on the progress of the investigation. "Why? What have they said?" she asked.

Carla opened her mouth to reply but shut it again quickly. Voicing her view that the bullet could have been meant for Brendan might not be wise. Casting a fleeting glance into her friend's gullible face, she knew she was right. Any such speculation coming from her would acquire an air of authority among their network and could cause genuine distress. Instead of brushing the matter aside, though, she recognized an opportunity to build her stock a little higher. "Oh, sorry," she grimaced in apology. "I was talking out of turn. Something was said when the police were questioning me, but I shouldn't really repeat it."

"Ooh." Paige's eyes twinkled in the excitement of it all. "Maybe you'll mention it in court, though."

Carla studied her fingernails. "Oh, I expect so," she replied. The idea of appearing in court excited her. She would be in the papers – the front pages, most likely. The scene played out in her mind: Carla walking along the street near the Old Bailey, Brendan on one side of her and one of those legal people with a wig and gown on the other. A journalistically concise headline: *Brendan Fiancée Gives Evidence in Roadie Murder Trial*. She didn't give a moment's consideration to who might be the defendant. The whole of her imagination was taken up with the prospect of herself on the front page with Brendan.

Then Shauna returned with the milk and the conversation passed to other topics.

Brendan Phelan gazed out into the night sky above Hampstead Heath. He smiled up at the stars. He felt good. His tormentor was dead and Tilly was coming over. They were going to have a long, leisurely meal. Brendan realized she had probably never seen him completely relaxed. None of his last few girlfriends had. He wondered if she would remark on it.

The door behind him opened and Desmond came in with a telephone in his hand. "Call for you, Bren."

"Thanks," he replied, taking the instrument. "Hello?" he said into the receiver as he walked back across the room to the sofa.

Silence.

"Hello?" repeated Brendan.

"Brendan Phelan?"

"Yes. Who is this?"

"I'm a business associate of Oliver Joplin."

Brendan stopped dead. An icy sliver of fear grasped at his entrails. "What do you want?"

"I just want you to know that nothing has changed. You'll be hearing from me."

The line cut off. Brendan stood with the phone pressed to his ear. Several minutes passed before he could put one foot in front of the other and move out onto the landing.

Chapter Sixteen

"You know what I think I'd find helpful?" Angela asked of her team the following morning. She gazed up at the whiteboard with a frown on her face.

"No, what?" asked Rick, on behalf of them all.

"I'd like a visual reminder of the scene of the crime. I can close my eyes and picture it, but each time I do that I also remember how late it was and how tired I felt and the image fades."

"We can set the scene and take some photos," he suggested.

"I'm very keen on photography. I can do that for you," volunteered Derek.

"I don't think you need to be David Bailey, Derek. Some snaps taken on a mobile will do, as long as they give the exact layout of the crime scene."

"I'd be glad to help, though," replied Derek.

"Thanks. Well, I'll take you up on that." She looked around. "Gary, we'll need you to be involved. You were first on the scene."

"Yes. There was a bit of coming and going. A packed crate – sorry, flight case – already standing by the van. So we'll need a picture of that. Then loads of people – at least, it seemed like a lot at the time – came charging through the door, wondering what was going on. I was trying to talk to you on my mobile and keep an eye on them all at the same time. On top of all that, the production manager, Jack Waring, started pushing another flight case out to park by the first one. I told him to take it away again. I could hardly hear you on the phone with those castors clattering and rumbling across the concrete."

"Yes, I remember that," said Angela. "OK. Can I leave you two to set that up?"

"On it, guv," replied Derek, a satisfied smile on his face as he picked up the nearest phone.

Angela gazed at him, arrested by the pleasure she sensed he was feeling. "Why are you looking like the cat that got the cream, Derek?"

Derek blushed as Leanne laughed at him. "You've just given him his dream job, guv," she said. "He'll be able to go backstage at the Apollo while Georgia Pensay is rehearsing."

Derek smiled sheepishly, his blush deepening as the rest of the team joined in with the merriment, and good-natured comments of "Sneaky!" and "Nice one, Del-boy!" echoed around the room.

Angela laughed. "Quite a result for you in that case, Derek. But," she added, "don't be surprised if Gary starts talking about magicians sawing ladies in half while you're doing all this."

"You what?" asked Jim, looking up from his console.

Gary laughed. "It's those cases. They call to mind a magic show I remember watching when I was a kid and it's the first thing I thought of on that night."

"I used to like those shows. I remember having a fantasy about my form mistress being cut in half," said Rick.

"Goodness! I presume you weren't the teacher's pet, then," remarked Angela. "Mind you, talking of magic, are we looking for some legerdemain in this murder?"

"Ledger-what?" asked Jim.

"It means 'sleight of hand'," explained Angela. "It's the magician's real art. Apart from Gary's childhood reminiscence, it turns out the production manager started out as a magician's lad."

"Oh, that explains something at least," said Rick.

"What?" asked Angela.

"When we did the preliminary interviews, a bunch of blokes was sitting around in the crew room doing card tricks on each other."

Angela remembered the people she'd seen in the auditorium with packs of cards on the night of the murder. "He probably started the trend," she agreed. "OK, everybody, let's get going. Gary, I've been thinking about that interview we did with Kay Joplin."

Gary made a face. "It was like getting blood from a stone, wasn't it?"

"It was indeed. I'm wondering now whether that wasn't deliberate on her part. I think I've realized what struck me at the time. A couple of times during that interview I sensed her becoming suddenly alert, though – from our point of view – we made no headway at all."

"Ah yes, I remember her getting annoyed when I pointed out the photograph of Oliver and that man at a party."

"Hmm, yes – there were a couple of moments like that. The thing is, her brother's been killed and she appears grief-stricken. You'd expect that in normal circumstances. Given what we know about them, I don't think this brother/sister relationship *was* entirely normal, but let's accept it at face value: she's in mourning."

"For all we know, Angie, little sis begged and pleaded for a chance to go with Brendan. Some fourteen-year-olds can be very precocious."

"This is true. The more I think about it, the more I'm asking myself if I'm bypassing the obvious here. What are we investigating?"

Gary's face took on a puzzled expression. "A murder."

"Yes. Who's been murdered?"

"Oliver Joplin, one of the roadies for Brendan Phelan –

though there's the suggestion of Brendan being the intended target."

"What's wrong with that theory?"

"Barring some personal vendetta that we know nothing about yet, it looks like an insider must have done it. And if anything happens to Brendan they all lose their jobs, so why kill him? Plus, nobody liked Olly but they all like Brendan."

"Quite."

Gary thought for a moment. "From my view of the scene, and what I understand to have happened just before I got there, I would say it would be very difficult for someone to have shot Brendan right then. OK, there are some very sharpshooters on that crew by all accounts, but even so I wouldn't choose such a moment to kill Brendan, if I wanted him dead."

"And why is that?"

"Because there would be too much risk of hitting Oliver instead."

"Exactly! So what conclusion do we draw?"

"Oliver Joplin *was* the intended target all along."

"This is exactly what Tilly Townsend said when she came to see me. I have to say, I think she's right. And given that premise, what do we know about Olly?"

"He was a highly dubious character."

"And what does someone like that often keep?"

"Highly dubious company?"

"Bingo! We need to delve a bit more into Mr Joplin's life. And we do have to put Brendan in the frame."

"Brendan? But how could he have done it? We went through that yesterday."

"Yes, but as Jim pointed out at the time, Brendan has a fantastic motive. He could have hired a hitman."

"Surely that would mean a stranger wandering around backstage? Somebody would have noticed."

"Not if he was a member of the crew."

Gary thought for a moment. "You mean, like, someone undercover, posing as one of the crew?"

"He could have been employed as a regular member, but had a special arrangement with Brendan. Being a crack shot would raise no eyebrows on that particular crew. So long as he could hump scenery and lights around, or whatever, all he had to do was get behind Oliver when he had his final 'conversation' with Brendan."

Gary nodded. "That's doable, but wouldn't Brendan then have had to be involved in his recruitment?"

"Yes, and I know what you're thinking. Jack Waring does the hiring and firing – *normally*." Angela raised a finger to emphasize her point.

Gary got her drift. "Yes. Even *he* couldn't do anything about Oliver's name recurring on the crew list."

"Exactly. We have some more questions to be answered there, I think."

"Yes. I do hope Brendan's not involved, though."

"Madeleine will forgive you," smiled Angela.

Gary laughed. "It's not that. I've quite taken to the bloke myself. I wouldn't like him to be guilty."

"Well, perhaps he's not. Let's hope so. Now, we also need to trace this man with the tattoos on his arms. Have you and Madeleine got any more concert visits planned?"

"No, but I can trawl the gig venues before the shows. I think there's a big one in Brixton tonight."

"Wembley's got something on tomorrow," said Jim. "My brother's going."

"Fancy giving him a lift there and mingling among the crowds beforehand?" asked Angela. "You'd recognize him from the picture, wouldn't you?"

"I'm sure I would. But if I wasn't certain, I could shoot off a couple of stills for you to look at."

"Good idea," agreed Angela. "It can't be that difficult for us to catch up with him."

"Do you want us to bring him in, Angie, if we get hold of him?" asked Jim.

"You may ask him to accompany you to the station," cautioned Angela. "But go gently. Remember, it's not illegal to sell tickets."

"It is if he hasn't got a street traders' licence," put in Derek.

"Which is more than likely the case, but there's no need to push that angle. Either get him in or get his contact details. We just want a word. Don't anyone mention anything about ticketing scams. We've got no evidence; what Gary saw before Brendan Phelan's concert could just have been coincidence. In any case, those scams can be very sophisticated enterprises. This man is probably just a lowly foot soldier way down the pecking order."

A deafening silence filled the room.

Angela became aware that her entire team had stopped working and were looking in her direction. "I just said something noteworthy, didn't I?"

"I think you may have done, Angie," said Rick.

"'Very sophisticated enterprises', I said."

"We could be talking *very* big business," added Gary.

"I went out on a raid during my first year in the force," Jim put in. "*That* was a ticketing fraud case, sporting events. There was even a shoot-out, nearly scared the you-know-what out of me. I started wondering about doing something else for a living."

"OK," said Angela. "It's an interesting thought and we need to look at it properly; but let's consider, first, what we've already got."

"We know Oliver Joplin was a blackmailer," said Leanne.

"But that puts Brendan right in the frame and I can't believe – "

"We've got to be dispassionate, Leanne. If blackmail is the motive, then we have to put Brendan in the frame."

Leanne nodded her head with obvious reluctance.

"Brendan might not have been his only victim," suggested Rick.

"Yes – good point. You don't need to be rich and famous to have something you don't want everyone to know about. Right; moving on to the other aspect?"

"The only person who looks anything like a friend of Oliver Joplin is thought to be a tout," said Derek.

"So is he a lone operator or part of a much larger organization?"

"He looked a bit seedy to me," said Gary. "I wouldn't be at all surprised to find he's just one man on his own."

"But we can't assume that. We need to find out for sure."

"Yes, of course."

"OK, Gary, you go and play 'I Spy' at Brixton tonight; and Jim, you're doing the same tomorrow at Wembley. I'm sure we'll run into this man before too long. I want to go through what we've got so far; make sure I'm up to speed." Humming to herself, she went over and sat at the console she habitually used when in the incident room.

"Have you remembered what that tune is yet?" asked Gary.

"What tune?"

"The one you were just humming. The manager, Jack Waring, was whistling it when we went to see him at that warehouse the other day."

Angela looked at Gary and smiled. "I had no idea I was humming," she said, "but to answer your question; no, I haven't remembered. Have you?"

"No, 'fraid not."

"Have we seen the report on the gun, yet?"

"No; at least, I haven't. Do you want me to chase it up?"

"Yes, please, Gary. Oh – might you be passing by the coffee machine on your way back?"

Gary grinned. "Yep, no probs."

Angela got stuck into the case file. When Gary put a cup of coffee on the desk beside her some moments later, she looked up at him with a quizzical expression.

"What?" he asked.

"I've just thought of something we haven't given enough attention to."

"Yes?"

"A member of the crew who might have been better acquainted with Oliver than the rest."

"Oh, really, who's that?"

"Carla."

"Of course, we're assuming she's the woman Oliver's neighbour heard coming back to the flat with him, aren't we?"

"Yes – and she did openly admit to cutting a deal with him that was supposed to get her a chance with Brendan. However, perhaps it's a woman thing, but there was something in her expression when we first spoke to her that I didn't take much notice of at the time. Some sort of – er – dislike."

"All too understandable if, having 'obliged' him, he then didn't fulfil his side of the bargain."

"She wasn't around the stage door at the relevant time, though, was she? You need more than dislike to kill someone, anyway."

"No, I'm not saying she did it, but we're trying to get an angle on Oliver and I think we haven't asked her the right questions."

Gary thought for a minute. "Well, she's the one that told us Oliver supplied Brendan with his women, and now that I'm thinking about it, she's the only one who seems to believe this."

"Exactly; he spun her this line in order to play his own little power game with her."

"That makes sense. OK, shall we pay her another visit?"

"Yes, let's pop out there now. We've got a bit of time in hand."

Chapter Seventeen

The front door of the house where Carla lived opened on
the second ring of the bell and the two police officers found
themselves face-to-face with a young woman. Earnest, large blue
eyes peered at them from behind spectacles which she pushed
further up her nose before speaking. "May I help you?" she
asked. Angela performed the usual introduction and displayed
her police identity badge. The woman's eyebrows lifted above
the level of her thick lens and she gave a little gasp. "Oh! I – er
– I haven't done anything. I didn't go through the gate."

Angela checked an immediate inclination to pursue an
enquiry about the gate. "May we come in?" she asked.

"Well, yes," said the woman, standing back. "As you're the
police, I suppose it's all right."

Angela had received many less welcoming invitations
in her career. She stepped across the threshold, followed by
Gary, and they were led through into same room where they'd
last spoken to Carla.

"My name's Shauna," she said, going ahead of them. "I live
here with Carla and Paige."

"Nice to meet you, Shauna. What was that about a gate?"
she asked, as Carla's flatmate indicated seats for them.

The woman blushed. Angela noticed that she was rather
spotty and her hair somewhat greasy. She wondered if bad
grooming or unfortunate hormones could be the cause. "Oh,
that," Shauna said, sitting down after the two officers had
done so. "I was up at Brendan's house the other day, keeping
a kind of vigil, you know. We're all very concerned about how
he's faring with all this shooting business."

"I saw quite a crowd there when I went up to interview him," recalled Angela.

"Yes; well, there aren't so many now. That makes it better in many ways. It's nice to meet up with other fans and chat, but when there are just a few of us, we feel like… like there might be more chance of seeing him."

The logic of this was lost on Angela. "*Did* you get through his gate, though?"

"Oh, no!" Shauna gave a giggle. "When I was up there, one of the others noticed that it was ajar. One of them went right up to it and peered inside. I was really scared. I couldn't do anything like that. Anyway, his brother came and locked it very soon after that. But I did wonder; he might have made a complaint."

"Oh, I see," replied Angela. "The thing is, we were hoping to have a word with Carla."

"I'm afraid she's not here at the moment."

"Ah. Do you know when she'll be back?"

Shauna shook her head. The way she did this, raising her eyebrows upwards and assuming a somewhat disparaging expression, gave Angela pause. She changed her mind about ending the conversation there and then, leaving a message for Carla to get in touch. "She didn't tell you where she was going?" queried Angela, injecting a sense of conspiracy into her voice, wondering if Shauna would take the bait. She did.

"I don't get told anything," she said. "I just get to run errands. Paige gets all the inside info. I get the crumbs that drop from the table." The resentful note was unmistakable. Angela settled herself in her seat and Gary took out his notebook.

"I presume you mean information to do with Brendan Phelan?" she said in her most inviting tone.

"Yes. I wouldn't mind, but I was a fan before any of them.

END OF THE ROADIE

I've liked him since he started. And this flat is in *my* name. *They* actually live here with *me*."

But you'll put up with it to maintain this very tenuous contact with Brendan, won't you? speculated Angela, silently. "We're trying to get as complete a picture we can of how they all interacted with each other – you know – the backstage crew, the band, Brendan Phelan and his management team."

"Doug Travers is his manager and Jack Waring works for him and takes care of the stage production," said Shauna. "Do you want the names of the band and the crew?"

I wouldn't be surprised if you could furnish me with all their collar sizes, thought Angela, smiling at the young woman. "No, that's all right, thank you, we've got all that kind of information. We're really trying to get an angle on the relationships. Did Carla ever talk about the atmosphere backstage, for example?"

"She'd say things now and again, but I don't think she picked up much gossip or anything like that."

"I find that hard to believe; it's quite an enclosed world, isn't it?"

"Yes, but they minded their p's and q's in front of her because of the situation with Brendan."

Beside her, Angela sensed Gary raise his head from his notebook, but she kept her eyes fixed on Shauna and allowed no surprise to appear on her face. "Ah yes! Can you fill me in about that?"

Shauna shifted to make herself a little more comfortable. "I'm sure it's all right telling you – you're the police, after all. It's a *mega* secret, of course, because if the papers got hold of it, well – phew! You can imagine."

"I can," agreed Angela, playing the sense of conspiracy for all she was worth.

"I mean, she's been discreet, but we could tell she was seeing someone; only she wouldn't say who, at first. Paige and I really had to prise it out of her. We thought maybe a band member or one of the crew. She was really secretive but we kept on and on at her. You could have knocked me down with a feather when she finally came out and told us who it was. Paige and I were absolutely beside ourselves. Never in a million years would we have guessed it would be… him." She paused and gazed at the police officers, gauging the effect of her words.

"Brendan Phelan." Angela very deliberately made it a statement.

"Yes! They're secretly engaged. They're waiting for the right moment to go public with the news."

Angela paused. She'd come across some bizarre things in the course of her career up to that point, and this notion wasn't the craziest. "What about Tilly Townsend?" she asked.

"Well, that shows what a super person Brendan is," replied Shauna. "I mean, he couldn't help falling for Carla, and obviously, he wants to follow his heart; but he recognizes that he owes it to her – to Tilly, that is – not to just dump her unceremoniously. That's partly why they're keeping it a secret for the moment."

"I see," nodded Angela, thinking she very probably did. "And when do Carla and Brendan actually get to – er – go out?"

Shauna gave a smirk. "Stay in, more like, if you see what I mean. She'd text Paige that she wasn't coming straight home from the show, and we'd look at each other and we'd know what that meant."

"So when did this romance begin?" asked Angela.

"It all kicked off towards the end of the tour, so it's still a new situation. She told us, though, of course. Obviously I wish I was in her shoes but, well, it's still very exciting to be in the know."

Angela nodded absently as she and Gary looked at each other. She could tell they were thinking the same thought. If they substituted Oliver for Brendan, this story confirmed they were right in assuming Carla to be the woman Oliver's neighbour heard him taking up the stairs.

Angela rose to go. "You've been very helpful, Shauna," she said. "We won't wait for Carla right now. Depending on how we get on, if we need to speak to her again we'll phone beforehand next time." She smiled. "We'll see ourselves out."

Alex stepped off the bus, made his way along the street and after about two minutes' walk, turned in at a front gate. His ring at the bell brought a child's feet running along the passage inside, and a familiar voice called out, "Hang on, Tyrone, I'm coming." The door opened and he found himself looking at Kay, one child by the hand and a younger one perched on the other hip. "Hi, Alex," she said and turned, leaving him to follow her into the house and shut the front door behind him. She was sitting at the kitchen table when he joined her. The eldest child went back to playing with a small, cheap Transformer toy, while the younger child busied herself with a tiny tricycle.

"How are you doing?" he asked, as he sat down opposite her.

She shrugged. "How do you think?"

"Are you all right for money?"

Fury flared behind her eyes and he winced. The anger died as quickly as it had arisen. "Sorry, Alex, it's just that Olly always said that."

"I know. I was trying to – well, we were partners... I was trying to..."

She nodded. "I know." A brief silence ensued, broken when the eldest child asked for his favourite DVD. Kay took him into the front room, followed quickly by his little sister, and was back within a few minutes. "That'll keep them amused for all of ten minutes, if we're lucky. The kettle's just boiled; want a cup of tea?"

Alex nodded and she went over to the kettle. "I'm trying to see you right," he said. Kay turned away from what she was doing, looking questioningly at him. "You know," he continued, "I'm not your brother, but we were partners, him and me. I know how he supported you." Kay raised an eyebrow and turned back to her task. "I mean, I know *how* he supported you," he repeated. A cautious note had appeared in his voice and his eyes followed her every move.

"Oh yeah?" she queried.

Alex took a deep breath. He was no longer in the pub with that man in the smart clothes and superior attitude. He could assert himself here. "You could get him for it, you know; child abuse."

Alarm flared in her eyes as she put a steaming cup down in front of him. "Through the proper channels, you mean?"

"Yeah, why not? It happened, after all. And there's a lot of it going on now – being sorted, I mean. Ever since all that stuff came out about Jimmy Savile and the way he carried on. All sorts of things are coming out, people being accused, and that; some of them are going to court. You must have seen it on the news."

"Yes, but a court case? All those questions? I don't like the thought of that. And they're not all found guilty, are they?"

"No, well, they haven't all done anything, have they? Some people are ready to make all sorts of accusations against a celebrity if they think there's money in it for them. That's bound to happen. But it's different with you. You know you'd be taken seriously. You'd have a good case, I reckon."

"I… I don't think I'd be able to cope with the ordeal of it," she replied in the manner of one repeating a well-worn line she'd learned. "I just used to let Olly handle it." She paused and looked at him. "He wanted to spare me any further hurt. He said it would be too humiliating."

Again, it sounded like a quotation. Looking at her, Alex wondered about her relationship with Olly. When the dead man had told him Kay would do anything he told her to, he didn't really believe him. But now he began to wonder. Olly had told him she'd been a bit fearful at first, had a couple of scruples, even, but Olly had brushed them aside. "It's no skin off Brendan's nose," he'd said to her. "He's loaded. He can easily afford to stump up. It won't make any difference to him." After that, she'd made no further protest and just got on with following her brother's lead. Alex saw her expression soften as she looked at him. "I was only a kid, remember," she said. "If you're his business partner…?" She let the implication hang in the air.

He smiled and picked up the thread. "I thought you'd say that. I'm OK with it. It makes sense doing it this way. I mentioned to Olly once or twice about going through the proper channels, but he insisted all the court could give you would be compensation. They can't heal the trauma, that's what he said. It's not like they can make the thing un-happen. And *his* way of getting compensation was more efficient." He nodded to emphasize his point. "Yeah. I know Olly looked after you."

"That's right," she said. "He looked after me." She smiled and relaxed, apparently pleased he'd arrived at the place where Oliver had left off. "So…?"

"Already made a phone call, didn't I?"

"Yeah? How did it go? What did he say?"

"What could he say? He didn't argue, that's for sure."

A shrewd look appeared in Kay's eyes. "How are you going to get the money? It's not like you're on his crew."

Alex made a business of blowing steam away from his cup before answering. That thought had occurred to him, but he hadn't yet come up with an answer. "Just you leave that to me," he replied, wallowing in the approval and trust he felt emanating from her. It was a nice feeling after his encounter in the pub.

"How much are you going to ask for?"

Alex was emboldened now. "I won't be asking, Kay. I'll be telling, remember."

"Yeah, 'course. So…?"

Alex took a slurp of his tea. This was a thin-ice moment. "The same," he said eventually.

"Right," said Kay, nodding in a knowing manner and trying to hide any hint of a further question in her voice.

A brief, awkward silence ensued in which it occurred to Alex, for the first time, that Oliver had most likely not passed all his ill-gotten gains on to his sister, in spite of his avowal that he was doing it for her.

"Oh," Kay said. "Where are my manners? I didn't even offer you a biscuit."

Alex beamed. The moment had passed. "That'd be great, ta," he answered. He leaned back, satisfied with himself. He'd make sure Kay got a fair whack, but this could turn out to be a nice little earner for him.

Chapter Eighteen

The management at the Apollo agreed for two officers to come and take the required photographs. An assurance of minimum disruption to the work of the theatre was given, and Derek had just enough time to dash out, buy a disposable razor and shaving gel, and spruce himself up before Gary called out it was time to go. He was still trying to slick his hair down while popping mints into his mouth as he passed through the incident room.

Angela and Leanne watched him disappear before turning to each other and exchanging smiles.

"Mints?" queried Angela. "How close does he think he's going to get?"

Leanne gave a good-natured shrug. "He'll be lucky if he even sees her. They're only going to take pictures outside the stage door, after all. But if he gets even a scintilla of a chance to meet her, he wants to be prepared."

Angela laughed. "A scintilla is all you need sometimes."

The report on the murder weapon appeared in the incident room just after lunch, but did nothing to further the investigation. Every gun owner connected to the case handed their firearms in to the ballistics department. All had been checked. The gun that killed Oliver Joplin wasn't among them. Angela placed the report in the case file, glad to tick *firearms* off her list. A nasty experience with a gun on a recent case had moved her from mere disinterest in them to decided antipathy. She looked up to see Rick coming towards her with some papers in his hand.

"It looks like your theory's holding up," he said.

"Pull up a chair. What theory's that?"

Rick dragged a nearby chair across and sat down next to her, putting the pages on the desk in front of her. "The ticketing scam one. The lab people got into Oliver Joplin's computer and they've printed up what they found."

"Oh, good, let's have a look." Angela's eyes followed the direction of his pointing finger. "Yikes! It's a ticket for one of Brendan's shows at the Apollo." She bent closer. "I must say it looks the business."

"Yes, it seems completely authentic." Rick turned the page over to reveal a similar one.

"The O2 Centre?" queried Angela. "Oh look, that's for the concert Brendan cancelled because of the shooting."

"Yes, and there are others," replied Rick, rifling through the top pages and setting them to one side. "They cover all the gigs from the entire tour."

"Are there any for other artists or shows?"

"No, he seems to have kept things close to home." Angela looked quizzically at him. He smiled. "Seems a bit like fouling your own doorstep, is that what you're thinking?" he asked.

"It did cross my mind. It's either that or a case of sticking with what you know," she replied.

"I wonder how they worked it?" he mused.

"What do you mean?"

"Well, did the person buying a ticket from them download it, or was it sent to them?"

"It would be sent to them, wouldn't it? When Patrick and I have ordered tickets for things, we set it all up online and then received the tickets through the post."

"Yes, but it doesn't have to be like that, does it?" Rick smiled at her. "When was the last time you went abroad on holiday, or took a train anywhere?"

Angela thought for a moment. "Last year we – oh, I see

what you're saying. You're right. With the last few trips Patrick and I took, we printed up our own tickets and presented them at the check-in desk."

"I wouldn't be surprised if Oliver had things set up in the same way."

"It'd save on printing costs and on postage, wouldn't it?"

"Yes, seemingly; and the bogus ticket agency wouldn't need to have any stationery, either."

"And if he thought he was being rumbled, it would be very easy to close the site down. Have we found the site he used?"

"Yes. It looks like he set up this website here, look," said Rick, picking up another one of the pages.

"'Concert Sales'," read Angela. "He didn't knock himself out trying to think up a catchy name for the business, then. So I suppose the punter accessed the site and went through an ordering process." She looked at the remaining pages.

"There's nothing there," said Rick, interpreting her look. "But there must have been some sort of program. You know what it's like. The customer has to put in the date, the venue, the price range, seat preference, stalls or circle, all that stuff. The lab people couldn't find anything like that in the computer."

Angela rubbed her chin with her forefinger. "Silly question, but I'll ask anyway; I don't suppose anybody's overlooked the presence of a disc in the computer, or a memory stick?"

Rick gave a small laugh. "No such luck. And we didn't find either anywhere in the flat."

"Just that suspiciously empty drawer you told us about."

"I reckon it must have been cleared of something."

"Hmm. I wouldn't be surprised if you're right. So what have we got here? Oliver Joplin doesn't seem to have been the gregarious centre of a large and lively social circle. If the indications are anything to go by, it's just him and this chap with the hawk tattoos, whose mugshot was stuck to Kay's fridge. I think I'll be paying her another visit before too long."

"If he only scammed the Brendan Phelan concerts, is it worth Gary trawling the crowds at Brixton tonight, or Jim doing Wembley?"

Angela nodded. "They still ought to go. You're quite right, from this it looks unlikely we'll see this man. But Stanway's bound to ask if we checked, and I'd rather be ready with an affirmative answer."

"Fair enough; that makes sense. Besides, when you work a particular circuit you get to know the others doing the same thing. Who knows? This bloke might have friends or contacts among the other touts. He might turn up to see them anyway."

"Good point," agreed Angela.

"The rest of these pages are emails," said Rick. "They might tell us something."

"OK, let's have a look."

"A lot of them are to do with buying tickets. Some of them are irate."

"Angry customers, no doubt," said Angela. "OK, leave these with me, please, Rick. I'll go through them and see if they can tell me anything."

Much to Derek's disappointment, Barry Grieves met him and Gary when they arrived at the Apollo, and led them straight round to the stage door. They never even had the chance to pass through the auditorium and see whoever might be on stage rehearsing. They could hear, though. As they followed the front-of-house manager along the corridor, they couldn't mistake the identity of the strong-voiced alto rejoicing to be with her "may-yan". Derek inclined his head towards the sound as they progressed, a dreamy expression on his face.

"Ah, this is one of my favourites," he said, half-turning to

Gary as they walked. "She sang this at the Grand Ole Opry last year."

Gary, about to remark on the number of diphthongs he could hear, looked at his colleague's face and bit back the comment. He was sure it would come across as sarcastic and he didn't want to mar a good working relationship.

"Has your van arrived yet, do you know?" asked Barry, as he led them through a door leading to a dim passage. Georgia Pensay's voice faded as the door swung shut behind them.

"I've arranged for it to be here by now," replied Gary, looking at his watch. "I'll need to supervise the parking so it's in exactly the same place as the one on the night in question."

"Just through here," said Barry, opening yet another door into what Gary recognized as the passage leading out to the stage door.

"Oh, I nearly forgot," said Gary. "We'll need to borrow a couple of those crates – er – flight cases. Would that be possible?"

"We don't keep any here," said Barry.

Gary stopped, looking very puzzled. "But – aren't the flight cases where all the equipment for the show is stowed? There were a couple outside the stage door on the night of the shooting. We'll need them for the reconstruction."

"Oh yes, that's what they use for transporting the equipment," confirmed the manager. "Virtually every artist who performs here brings their equipment packed into flight cases. So once they've finished it all gets packed up and taken on to the next venue." He left a brief pause. "That's the point."

"Ah, I see," said Gary. "I should have thought of that. All your equipment belongs to the theatre. It's at home, so to speak."

"Quite."

"Er…" began Derek. Both men turned to him. Gary

noticed the delicate flush that had worked its way up from his neck. "Perhaps – er…" he coughed. "Perhaps Miss Pensay… er, her concerts here are part of a national tour, aren't they?" Gary hid a smile at Derek's diffidence. He knew without a doubt the singer was in the middle of a tour of the British Isles. He could probably have reeled off the complete itinerary, if pressed to do so.

"It's worth asking, I suppose," answered Barry. "I'll take you round to where you can get into the auditorium. You'll find a cowboy sitting a few rows back from the stalls. You can't miss him, he's in full regalia, buckskin jacket, rhinestones. He might even be wearing his Stetson. He's the tour manager. He's the one to ask. But I do stress the importance of being very quiet."

"I quite understand," said Derek. His flush had deepened to crimson. Barry nodded Gary towards the stage door and left him to go and check on the van. Looking as though he was about to receive first prize in a competition, and surreptitiously slipping another mint into his mouth, Derek followed the theatre manager back the way they had come.

After a little manoeuvring, with the help of the uniformed driver, the van stood in the correct position as far as Gary could remember it. He'd just begun to wonder how Derek had fared when the stage door opened and the "cowboy in full regalia" stepped through into the alley. Barry Grieves had only referred to the man's mode of dress. He hadn't mentioned the pleasant smile and the affable manner.

The cowboy smiled. "Mornin'. I'm told y'all want to do some ree-construction here."

"Yes, sir," answered Gary. "I'm sure you heard about that dreadful event."

"Sho' did," affirmed the man, with a slow nod. "Awful business. So y'all want a flight case, right?"

"If you wouldn't mind."

"OK, let's get that dang thang out here."

Gary blinked. Dang thing… thang – it actually rhymed. "Er…" he said, "There were two around at the time. Both about the same size. This big." He sketched out the size and shape with his hands.

Another slow nod. "OK. Well, I left your man at the side of the stage. I'll have him and Chuckie bring them through. Georgia's about to take a little break, so it won't disturb her none."

Gary thanked him. He smiled at a mental picture of Derek, glued to the side of the stage, hardly able to believe his luck in being so close to his heroine.

Chuckie, when he arrived, was every bit as pleasant and obliging as his employer. The flight case he wheeled out was more or less identical to the one in the alley at the end of Brendan's concert. After a few moments Derek followed with another, very similar. His colour had returned to normal but there was a very faraway look in his eyes.

Now he was here, the events of that night came back vividly to Gary. He remembered his nervousness at coming upon a serious crime, and the relief he'd felt once he'd made contact with Angela, and once another officer had appeared on the scene. He even recalled, with a smile, the magic show of which the whole tableau had reminded him. Whistling a cheery melody, he took on the role of Jack Waring. He wheeled the case through the stage door, positioning it next to the one already there. Under his direction, Derek took photographs throughout, except when Gary made them swap places so that he could see he'd set the scene properly. Gary was completely unaware he was whistling until Derek pointed it out to him, asking about the tune.

Gary stopped and thought for a moment. "What tune?" he asked.

"The one you've been whistling."

Gary shook his head. "I don't know. I didn't even realize I was doing it. I bet it's the one Jack Waring was whistling the day we went to see him at the warehouse. Angela's been humming it as well."

"I'm not surprised," said Derek. "It's very catchy. Have we finished here, then?"

Gary looked at Derek with a quizzical expression. "Why? Are you in a hurry?"

Derek blushed. "It's just that these cases are stored in a particular place at the back of the stage, and Georgia Pensay will be back from her break soon. So it's probably a good idea to get them stowed away before then, so we won't disturb the rehearsal." In spite of the blush, Derek made a very creditable attempt at sounding matter-of-fact. Gary hid a smile. He had no doubt Derek's main motive was to be on stage when the chanteuse arrived, just so he could drink in the sight of her; but he didn't begrudge him the opportunity.

"Yes, I reckon we've got enough here," he replied. "You might as well put the cases back now."

"OK," said Derek, suppressing his pleasure at the prospect. He pushed at the case and it slewed round on its castors and moved off in the wrong direction. "Oops," he said, righting it.

"Yessir," remarked Chuckie, who'd been watching the action. "They can run away from you when they're empty." He went over and pushed the other case in through the door after Derek. Gary thanked the uniformed driver of the van for his assistance and watched as the vehicle backed carefully through the gates out onto the street.

Their conversation in the car all the way back to the incident room was completely one-sided and contained only a single topic. Derek waxed at length and lyrically about the voice, the looks, the style, the everything of Georgia Pensay. Gary listened politely as he concentrated on driving, grateful that all he had to do was to nod here and there, saying "Really?" and "Wow!" on occasion. Country music was not his first choice in entertainment but he liked quite a few of its offerings. They were halfway there before he realized that something was nagging at the back of his mind. Something having a bearing on the investigation had occurred to him during the reconstruction, of that he was certain. He went through every detail of it in his mind. He thought back carefully over the events of the actual murder scene again. But try as he might, the significance of what he'd seen eluded him.

Chapter Nineteen

Angela was still poring over emails from Oliver's computer when Gary appeared by her side after his expedition to the Apollo. "Oh – hi, Gary," she said, looking up. "Mission accomplished?"

"Yes, I took quite a few photos. Do you want me to upload them here?"

"Yes, please." Angela moved away from the console on the desk. "Look – I've been puzzling over these emails."

"I've got a puzzle too," he replied, plugging his camera into the computer.

"Really? Tell me."

"I wish I could. Hang on, let me just get these sorted. The reconstruction went very smoothly except I hadn't realized the theatre wouldn't have its own flight cases. Still, it was all right because Georgia Pensay's people were very helpful. They let us use two of theirs."

"Oh, that's good. Did Derek get to meet the lady?"

Gary smiled. "I don't think so, not really, but he managed to be on stage – in the wings – when she was rehearsing. He was full of it in the car on the way back. You should have heard him."

"I can imagine."

Gary clicked on the mouse a few times and after some moments the pictures he'd taken at the theatre appeared on the screen.

"It looks very different in daylight, doesn't it?" remarked Angela. They went methodically and silently through the entire collection that had now been loaded onto the computer.

"It is helpful," she said, finally. "We'll need some printed out and put on the board." She clicked on three. "Those, I think."

"OK, I'll get them done," replied Gary.

"Great. So, what was your puzzle, then?"

Gary blew out his cheeks. "I wish I knew. It didn't strike me immediately, just later, when we were driving back. I suddenly realized I'd missed something."

"Go carefully over the sequence of events and what you saw."

"I've been trying to do that. It wasn't easy with Derek going on, but even so, I don't know that it would have come to me."

"No clue at all?"

Gary creased his brow. "I think it's something I've seen that isn't quite right. Now, whether it's not quite right from today's reconstruction or whether it wasn't quite right on the night of the murder I couldn't say, and it's driving me crazy."

"Never mind; it happens," sympathized Angela. "You know how to deal with it, don't you?"

He grinned. "Yes, put it right out of my mind and it will pop back when I'm least expecting it."

"Exactly," beamed Angela. "Now, you sort out those photographs. When you've done that, you can go over these emails from the victim's computer."

Half an hour later, Gary laid the pages down in two piles and looked up at Angela, standing by the desk. "Anything strike you?" she asked.

"I've only managed a brief look but..."

Angela smiled and nodded. "Go on."

"In the first place," Gary tapped the pile. "The ones I've seen so far are all emails sent to a bogus booking agency. I wonder why he saved them to his computer. He must have copied and pasted them into documents. OK. The most recent name is 'Concert Sales' but he's also used the name 'Hot-Hot Tickets' and 'TicketsGalore'."

"Yes, I expect he had to change them on a fairly regular basis to avoid being caught. Some of those customers are furious, aren't they?"

"You can't blame them. It's very distressing. I felt really sorry for that man I saw on the night I went with Maddie. It was a birthday treat for his daughter and her friends. They must have been looking forward to it for ages."

"How long beforehand did you and Maddie book?"

"About three months." He gave a small smile. "It was a tad embarrassing, actually. We'd only had about two dates when the subject came up and it was, like – er – we're making this arrangement but we don't know if we'll still be together by then."

Angela laughed. "Patrick and I had a similar experience when we first met. Sometimes you just have to take the risk."

"Absolutely; by the time the concert day came round we decided to turn it into our three-month anniversary."

"Oh, that's nice! So – what have we got? He's changed the name a few times, which must be par for the course when you're running a scam. And we don't know how big the operation is, but we're pretty certain his tattooed friend was working with him."

"I reckon it was fairly small-time," suggested Gary. "It looks like they were just working the Brendan Phelan concerts."

"I think you're right. And having done the sale online, Oliver would have to be backstage working on the show."

"Which just leaves his friend trawling the crowds in front, knowing – "

"Yes, indeed. Knowing exactly how many punters would turn up with dodgy tickets."

"A nice little earner, really," agreed Gary. "They seem to

have kept it simple. I suppose they sold the authentic tickets at double their face value – "

"Only double? I'm sure that's a modest estimate. I bet they charged whatever they thought they could get away with. Yes. Right, let's see what we've got. Brendan's on our radar because of the blackmail. That's one motive, right? What are you thinking now?" she asked, as she saw Gary frowning again.

"Hmm… it's just – well, given that Brendan's been quietly paying the blackmail for all these years, my question is; why wouldn't he go on paying it? I don't suppose he was happy about it, but it wasn't breaking him. He must have learned to live with it. Why kill Oliver now?"

"From what his girlfriend says, it was affecting his whole life – remember? He was stuck in respect of his relationship with her, stuck in his musical output – this was ruining everything."

"Good point. But now we know Oliver was running a ticket scam as well as the blackmail."

"What an enterprising bloke."

"He was. Might that not provide an equally likely motive?"

Angela grimaced. "Hmm. Except this little ticket business seems to have been very contained. Who would want to kill a small-time ticket scammer?"

Gary laughed. "Nobody, I would have thought, except maybe a big-time ticket scammer?"

Angela waited until he'd finished laughing and then waited some more. Gary straightened his face, considered the matter and frowned as the thought took hold. "That's quite an idea," he said, eventually.

Angela nodded. "As we've already discussed, some ticket scams are very big business."

"And ruthless."

"Oh yes. And what makes big-time criminals unhappy?"

"Small fry muscling in on their territory."

"Bingo, Gary. It's a nuisance to which they don't take very kindly at all. And they usually do one of two things, don't they?"

"Yep."

"Which two things are they?"

"They either take over the small-time businessman or they eliminate him."

"Exactly! Now let me show you something." Angela selected some of the pages and spread them out on the desk.

Gary leaned over and looked at them in turn. "'*You bastard!*'" he quoted. "'*I'm going to find out who you are and sue the backside off you!*'" Gary glanced at Angela. "I wonder how much that person got ripped off?"

"Look at this one: '*You completely ruined my wedding anniversary and quite possibly my marriage*'," read Angela. "'*I'm going to make it my business to see you shut down.*'"

"Empty words," said Gary. "Oliver had probably shut himself down by that point, and moved on to another address."

"Quite; there are a couple more measured ones which claim to have reported the site to the police."

A pause ensued.

"Er…" mumbled Gary, "they're not all dissatisfied customers, I see."

"You're right. These ones," she said, tapping the relevant pages, "come from people claiming to be pleased with the service they received. Have you noticed something else?"

Gary scrutinized the pages again but shook his head, bewildered, after a few moments. "I'm still not sure what I'm looking for, specifically."

Angela smiled. "Stop looking at the content of the emails and concentrate on the provenance."

Gary gazed again at the pages. "Well, I don't know." He put his finger on one. "This one's from somebody called d.buckley@buzzmail.com. That rings a bit of a bell for some reason, but I don't know… Oh!" Gary opened his eyes wide. "Hang on, the manager of the support act – Don – his name's Buckley. He seemed like a straight, honest bloke to me. He was very helpful, I remember."

Angela merely smiled and tapped the pages. "If you look, you'll find a few more familiar names."

Gary looked back at the desk. "D. Travers? Ah, Brendan's manager… J. Waring – well, we know him all right; the production manager. Here's C. Paterson – that would be Carla – and T. Dexter… and – look! That one's a bit odd, if you ask me," he finished, pointing to yet another familiar name.

"Which one have you got there?"

"B. Grieves. That must be Barry Grieves, the theatre manager. But he works at the theatre. He helped Derek and me this morning. All the rest of the names would have been involved in the tour."

"Good point; what else do you notice?"

Gary glanced rapidly through all the emails. "These names are all so satisfied with the service they received they've taken the trouble to write and say so." He checked the dates. "The most recent ones even say they'll be booking with this company again." Gary paused and looked at Angela.

"What does that suggest to you?" she asked.

"Given what we know, most of Oliver's correspondents would have been ripped off like everybody else."

"So why write and praise the ticket agency?"

"It's sarcasm. Somebody's on to him and they're letting him know it."

"That's exactly the conclusion I reached," agreed Angela.

"Look at that one," she said, pointing.

Gary leaned over and read it out. "'*I really loved the concert. It's been a pleasure doing business with you and I'll be dealing with you in the future.*'" He looked up at her. "That could be taken as a threat, when you think about it."

"Oh yes." She stood up. "Distribute these among the team. I want a powwow about it. But right now I'm going to get myself a coffee. Want one?"

"No, I'm fine, thanks," said Gary, gathering up the sheets of paper.

While she was in the kitchen pouring hot water onto a generous heap of coffee granules, Angela's mobile rang. "D.I. Costello," she answered, manoeuvring the milk out of the fridge with her free hand.

"Inspector? I – er – I…" The voice broke. It sounded familiar, but Angela didn't immediately recognize it. She had no doubt about the sense of strain, though.

"Hello caller," she replied, making sure no sign of impatience appeared in her voice. "Take your time. I'm listening."

The voice began again. "Sorry… I – it's Brendan Phelan."

Angela stopped what she was doing. If an intelligent, articulate and talented man couldn't string a sentence together, something calamitous must have taken place. "What's happened, Brendan?"

She heard him take a deep breath. "My nightmare goes on."

"Are you talking about the blackmail?"

"Yes." His voice caught on a sob.

She made an instant decision. "Look, Brendan, I've just got a meeting with my team and then I'm going to wrap things up for the day. My D.C. and I can come up to see you."

She heard the relief in his voice. "I'd be grateful if you would."

"God and the London traffic allowing, we'll be with you by about six-thirty," she said. She finished the call, hurriedly slopped some milk into her coffee, kicked the fridge door shut and dashed back into the incident room. "Gary," she said as she took her place in front of her assembled team. "I hope you haven't got any firm plans for the early part of this evening."

"I was going to trawl the crowds going to a gig at the Brixton Academy, if you remember."

"Oh, yes. I think you'll still have time to do that. But we've got a date in Hampstead."

"Aw, guv," wailed Leanne. "If Gary's busy..." She looked across at him. "Or if he breaks both his legs in the next ten minutes, which can be arranged..."

"Sorry, Leanne, I know you'd love to come with me, but it sounds as though something's happened to upset Brendan and it's best to keep continuity in terms of the persons dealing with it. OK, everybody. You've all had a chance to see what the lab found on Oliver's computer. I'm sure you'll agree he was an enterprising chap."

"Yes," said Rick. "A ticket scam as well as blackmail."

"And he didn't give up the day job, did he?" remarked Jim.

"Indeed. Hence all that lolly in his bank account. Did you find out about the provenance of that, by the way, Jim?"

"Yes, he hadn't been left any money or given any gifts. Apart from what he banked of his wages, it looks like ill-gotten gains from his sidelines."

"Right. Even so, it's a lot to believe *all* the people supposedly sending him emails were actually involved in some kind of plot to shoot Oliver Joplin."

"And setting up a buzzmail account is just about the easiest thing to do on the Internet," said Derek.

"Absolutely, so let's proceed on the basis that there's one person behind all these names and see where that takes us."

"We're still going to have to talk to each of these so-called satisfied customers, aren't we?"

"Yes, but that's for tomorrow. Jim, you and Rick take Don Buckley and Carla Paterson. Leanne and Derek, talk to Barry Grieves and Doug Travers. Gary and I will speak to Terry Dexter and Jack Waring. As well as the usual questions, sound them out about each other. Somebody might not be on their guard and you could get something. OK, team. We'll all meet up first thing tomorrow — by which time Gary and I will be able to fill you in on our meeting with Brendan Phelan."

Chapter Twenty

END OF THE ROADIE

We're still waiting to hear about these so-called satisfied customers, aren't we?

Yes, but that's for tomorrow. Jim, you and Rick take Don Buckley and Carla Paterson, Leanne and Derek, talk to Barry Cheves and Doug Travers. Gary and I will speak to Terry

Somebody must have been watching for them; as the Homicide Assessment Team car arrived at the Hampstead house, its gates slid smoothly open and they drove through into the now-familiar curving drive. When they drew up at the house, Brendan was standing in the open doorway, silhouetted by the hall lights behind him. He led them through to the kitchen, where a pot of coffee, one of tea and a plate of biscuits had been set out at one end of the central island.

"No Desmond tonight?" asked Angela.

"He's meeting up with some friends," confirmed Brendan. "I'm sorry you've had to come back here, but I'm a bit hesitant to go out at the moment." He indicated the pots and the biscuits.

The price of fame, thought Angela. "Thanks, I'll have a coffee," she replied, helping herself to a biscuit. She noticed the strain around his eyes and sensed the fragility of his smile. She decided to launch straight into the reason he had called her. "You said your nightmare goes on."

Brendan set down the pot because his hand was shaking. He took a deep breath. "Yes. It's worse than ever."

"Worse? Is the blackmailer asking for a lot more money?"

Another deep breath. "No. He hasn't asked for anything yet. He just said he was Oliver's business associate, that things haven't changed and he would be in touch. It seems worse than ever because I thought I was free of it."

Angela nodded. She could understand that. She felt for him in his evident torment. "It's not as bad as it sounds,

Brendan," she replied. "This could be easier to deal with than it was before. Did you recognize the voice?"

He looked puzzled by the question. "No. Should I?"

"It's just that Oliver was a member of your road crew; would this caller be another member, do you think?"

His brow cleared. "Oh, I see what you mean. I didn't recognize the voice, and I think I would if it had been one of the crew. The current lot have all done at least two tours with me."

"The thing is," Gary put in, "Oliver was able to come up to you backstage and ask for money; but if this new bloke isn't on the crew that's the first thing that'll be different."

"Yes," added Angela. "Getting the money from you just won't have the convenience of the previous arrangement."

Brendan's expression lightened. "I hadn't thought of that."

"He's going to call you again," said Gary. "We can put a trace on the phone for a start."

"Yes, and we can work with you on the money angle so we can arrest him when he comes to collect."

Brendan's face, which had begun to express the start of a beatific smile, suddenly fell. "No!" he almost shouted.

Angela and Gary exchanged perplexed glances. "But," said Angela, "we can put a stop to this thing."

Brendan dropped his head into his hands and a low moan escaped him. "Oh, no – no!" He looked at them, his face a picture of misery. "It can't be done. I can't press charges."

"But – I don't understand," said Angela.

Brendan took a deep, shuddering breath. "I know what you're saying, and believe me I'm grateful, really I am. I think I might have got you here on false pretences."

"Then why – ?" Gary was perplexed.

"You can tap my phone and stake-out the handover. You can even arrest him and charge him, but you won't be able to stop him leaking what he's got on me – and I can't face that. I just can't!"

Silence reigned in the shining kitchen.

"Public crucifixion," said Angela, after a few moments.

Brendan nodded. "No nails, no cross; but it would be just like that – you *know* it would." Angela and Gary could only agree. "I'm in a good place now. I'm established. My fans are growing with me. Sure, I'm rock 'n' roll and that's where my roots are, but my audiences are expanding. I get families coming to my shows. Some of the appearances I'm being asked to make – well, I just wouldn't have got those invitations a few years ago. My career is on the up. I just can't risk it."

Gary nodded in sympathy, his expression glum. "Yes, the media doesn't hold back. We've seen quite a bit of it in recent years, haven't we?" He didn't say any more but he didn't need to. They were all familiar with the headlines he was referring to; celebrities pilloried, their privacy invaded and their lives made miserable, regardless of whether they were guilty or innocent.

A bleak silence followed these words. Angela didn't see how they could persuade Brendan to move from his position, and couldn't really see a way forward; but she didn't want to leave the matter there. She wanted to hold out some hope to this man. "Look, let me think about it," she said. "There might be another way to manage things without any risk to your reputation." *To be honest*, she thought, *I don't see how it can be avoided and my advice is to call your blackmailer's bluff. But that's easy for me to say. I don't have a glittering show business career to defend.*

Brendan, his tread heavy, his shoulders slumped, led them back to the front door. "I'm sorry to have wasted your time," he said, as he opened the door.

"You haven't," Angela assured him. "We need to know there's a blackmailer out there. If we come up with anything, we'll be in touch."

He gave a grim smile. Angela didn't need to be told he had no hope of that happening.

A short while later the HAT car was heading south through Swiss Cottage. "You know, every time I hear that tune in future, I'm going to think of this case," said Angela.

"Was I humming it?" asked Gary.

"Yes," smiled Angela.

Silence reigned in the car until she spoke again after a few moments. "You've got to feel really sorry for Brendan, haven't you?"

"I should say. I noticed you didn't tell him his precious secret might all come out anyway."

"Yes, well – I didn't want to alarm him."

"But if this blackmail has any bearing on the murder, we'll need to take a very close look, won't we?"

"Absolutely. We'll have a lot better idea once we've caught up with this bloke with those tattoos. We can get something in place, though. I haven't pushed this, and we've all had plenty to do, but first thing in the morning, I'm going to ask Leanne to get a copy of that birth certificate."

Heavy traffic slowed them down. It took an hour to reach Angela's home. "Are you seeing Maddie tonight?" she asked, as the car pulled up in front of the house.

"We left it open once I knew we'd be going to Brendan's. I said I'd call her just as soon as I'd got home and showered."

"You might as well come in and sort out your arrangements with her now," said Angela. She got out of the car and led the way, calling, "Hi, darling, I'm home," as she pushed her way through the front door.

"In the living room, Angie," came Patrick's voice.

"I've brought Gary in with me," she said, going over and planting a kiss on his mouth.

Patrick smiled. "Evening, Gary, take a seat. Her ladyship's upstairs."

"Want a drink, Gary?" asked Angela.

"I wouldn't say no to a coffee," he beamed. As Angela went to make it, she could hear Gary once again humming the elusive melody as she walked along to the kitchen. He was still at it when, coffee in hand, she arrived at the living room door just as Madeleine came down the stairs. Gary looked up at their entrance and fell silent.

"Don't stop, that brings back happy memories," said Madeleine, going over to greet him with a kiss.

"You know, I was just thinking something similar but couldn't remember why," added Patrick.

"Don't stop what?" asked Gary, taking a steaming mug from Angela.

"You were humming again," said Angela.

"He was," agreed Patrick. "If you hang on, I'll tell you what it was." He screwed up his face in the effort to remember.

"Mum," said Madeleine. "It reminded me of Mum."

"Ah yes!" exclaimed Patrick. "Hang on, hang on, it's coming."

"*Fantasia!*" they both said at once.

"Oh, that's right!" Angela chimed in. "Walt Disney! I remember seeing Mickey Mouse getting in trouble to this piece of music."

"My goodness, you've got a good memory, Maddie," remarked Patrick. "Louise and I got this and a few other films to take on our holiday one year to keep you entertained in case of bad weather. I don't remember any rain or such, as it happens, but we all watched it together one afternoon. You could only have been about seven."

"Yes. I was. It was the last holiday we had before Mum got ill," replied Madeleine.

"So it's fixed in your memory," said Angela. "My situation was also related to kids; well, it would be with a Walt Disney film, wouldn't it? I had to babysit my niece and nephew on the day their next sibling was expected. I don't know who enjoyed it more, them or me."

"I haven't seen the film at all," smiled Gary. "I just heard Jack Waring whistling it. Anyway, I'm glad the mystery's solved."

"Talking of music, Gary," said Madeleine. "Did you say something about going to Brixton Academy tonight?"

"Ah, yes – but it's work-related. I wanted to trawl the crowds before the concert. We're trying to catch up with someone who might be able to help us." He looked across at Angela. "To be honest, though, we're not very hopeful."

"Why don't we do it anyway? We can get a takeaway and go on to your place afterwards."

"OK," he said, standing up and gulping down some coffee. "It's not too late. Let's go for it." He headed into the hall followed by Madeleine, blowing kisses as she went.

"Send me a text if you strike lucky," Angela called after them.

Later, no text having arrived, Patrick and Angela spent a quiet evening. At about nine-thirty Patrick wrote in the final answer to the newspaper's daily crossword and leaned back in his armchair. Angela sat curled up in the other one, hemming a blouse she'd made. "What on earth must that poor bloke be going through?" he said.

"Yes, Pads; he was set up then hung out to dry. He's in a wretched state, only just holding it together."

"Do you suppose it's this bloke with the tattoos who's now trying to collect?"

"We can't be certain, of course, but we haven't come across any other associates of Oliver Joplin; so it's the natural conclusion to jump to."

"Yes, I see that. But I'm surprised about the young girl in all this. Well, I say young girl; she'd be about twenty-two now, wouldn't she?"

"If she was fourteen eight years ago, yes; why do you mention her?"

"Well, it's just that since this happened there's been all that brouhaha over Jimmy Savile and a whole variety of other people hauled up before the courts."

"And a good many of those on completely trumped-up charges," replied Angela.

"Yes, indeed. But this wouldn't be a false accusation. Brendan admits to having sex with the girl. His defence is that he thought she was of age."

Angela threw him a puzzled look. "Where are you going with this, Paddy?"

"Well, obviously the brother and the sister were in it together. Given that she was so young, we can assume she was acting under his influence. The thing is, now he's dead and she's twenty-two, the situation can't be the same. Whoever made that call to Brendan can't have the same influence over her, surely?"

"Something along those lines had occurred to me," she answered. "It's not going to be so easy to collect the money, but she can still go to the police and make a formal complaint about historic sexual abuse." She gave a bleak smile. "I didn't say any of this to Brendan, but he's a bright chap. He'll think that one through himself soon enough, if he hasn't already done so."

"This birth certificate – I don't suppose there's any chance it could have been doctored?"

"That's what I'm hoping to find out. I'm going to get Leanne chasing that one up tomorrow."

Chapter Twenty-one

At the morning briefing, Jim and Gary reported no success among the concert-goers at Brixton or Wembley. "Saw a few touts," remarked Rick, "but none matching the description of the bloke we're looking for."

"Ah well," said Angela, "we've tried, at least."

"There'll be other gigs," said Jim.

Angela looked at him and nodded. "Yes, all the time. I bet you anything you like, if we went to them all we'd find touts among the audience doing good business. I'm not sure we should spend too many hours on this just now, though." She turned to the back of the room where D.C.I. Stanway sat, leafing through the pile of emails. "What do you say, sir?" she asked.

Stanway looked up from his perusal. "I'm glad you've given it a go, of course, but I'm inclined to agree with you, Angie," he replied. "It's not as if we don't have other avenues to explore." He waved the sheaf of papers at no one in particular. "This is definitely promising. I presume you're all of the opinion there's only one person behind this collection of names and buzzmail addresses."

"That's the premise we're working on, sir."

"And what bearing, if any, does the blackmail of Brendan Phelan have on things?"

"Ah, sir, there's been a development in regard to that. Gary and I chased it up last night after everybody had been dismissed for the day."

"Yes?"

"We can't say for sure there's any tangible link to the

murder, or to the ticketing scam, but Gary and I went to see him yesterday. He'd had a call from someone claiming to be an associate of Oliver Joplin, who told him to expect the demand for payments to continue."

"And?"

"Well, the fact is that friends and associates of Oliver Joplin seem to be rather thin on the ground."

"What about the rest of the crew or the band?"

"That's just it; he didn't really mix with them."

"Ah, a bit of a loner, was he?"

"Seems like it, sir. We think he worked the ticket scam with this other man, the one we're trying to trace. And I'm assuming, until I learn otherwise, that it's this same man who's now continuing the blackmail."

"You've got a kind of two-pronged attack, haven't you? Following up these emails and trying to find this man."

"That's about it, sir."

"All right, I'll leave you to it," said Stanway, rising to go. You've got quite a bit of trawling around to do between you."

As the door closed behind him, Angela turned back to her team. "OK, everybody, see you all back here later today."

The mobile phone lying on her bed hummed into life. A familiar face appeared on the screen. Her pulse raced as she picked it up and pressed "answer". "Jack?" Her voice was nervous. Jack was her only connection to the crew that worked with Brendan.

The tone of his voice reassured her immediately. "Hi, Shortcake, told you I'd keep you in the loop, didn't I?" he began, by way of a greeting.

Carla let out a sigh of relief. "Is it more concerts?" she asked, not bothering to hide her eagerness. "How many?"

"Whoa," he laughed. "Steady on; it's a bit too soon to be

planning another tour. The poor bloke's got to have some rest. It's just a one-off. You know Brendan had to pull out of that charity gig because of the shooting?"

"Yeah, loads of his fans were upset about that."

"Yes, I'm sure. Anyway, the same charity has managed to set up another evening. A couple of other acts couldn't do the last evening because of prior engagements. They're available now, so it's all going ahead for next weekend, the Saturday night."

"Brendan's headlining, I presume."

"Yes, of course."

"Have you put me down for runner?"

"Who else, babes?"

Carla smiled. "Thanks, Jack. Where is it?"

"We're at the Apollo again. It's come free unexpectedly. Some American band got sent back at immigration." Carla remained silent for a moment. A shiver went through her. "You OK with that?" asked Jack.

"Yeah… yes, of course I am. Just for a moment, going back there was a scary thought, but I'm all right now."

"That's it. Stuff happens. You have to deal with it."

"I know," Carla gave herself a mental shake. "I'll be fine," she replied.

"That's the spirit," said Jack. "Doug and I are still fine-tuning the details. I'll let you know when it's sorted and what your call time is, OK?"

"OK. Thanks, Jack."

Carla threw the phone on the bed, stood up and took a deep breath. This was going to be good. Only yesterday Shauna had asked if she'd been in touch with Brendan. Carla had allowed a little impatience to creep into her voice, to indicate the question shouldn't have been asked. She had explained, again, how he needed space to assimilate what had happened. Usually that would be the end of it, but almost immediately she'd intercepted a raising of eyebrows between Shauna and Paige. For the first time she wondered if they totally believed in her relationship with the star. To be exposed would ruin everything, and the humiliation would be unbearable. This gave her what she needed to reinforce her credibility. She pushed through into the living room where her two flatmates were listening to Brendan's latest CD. They looked up expectantly.

"I've just had a call," she announced. "Hot off the press. Brendan's doing a charity gig to make up for the one he had to pull out of."

"Oh, wow!" Two excited faces beamed at her, the doubts she had accurately sensed forgotten for the moment. "Ooh, tell us!" they pleaded.

"He's just called me," she said, flopping down onto the sofa and drawing one leg up underneath her with a nonchalant air.

"So he's coming out of his – you know – shock?" asked Shauna.

"Oh yes; I knew he'd bounce back," said Carla.

"When are you going to see him again?" queried Paige.

Carla studied her nails wondering if a one-off gig would do the job she needed it to do. Still, it was all she had to work with. "He reckons the press are still hovering about watching his every move, so we're going to wait until he goes into rehearsal. He thinks he'll be back to his old self by then, bless him."

Chapter Twenty-two

Angela gazed out at an idyllic view across Buckinghamshire fields. She and Gary had been waiting fifteen minutes for Terry Dexter to finish a telephone call and join them. She thought back to her two previous meetings with him – the 'Mr Angry' of the first occasion and the much more pleasant individual of the second. "I wonder," she mused aloud.

"You wonder what?" asked Gary.

"If I had that sort of relationship with a celebrity, same as he does… I wonder if I'd feel more like second fiddle or first minister."

Gary laughed. He left his perusal of the bookshelves on the far side of the room and joined her in contemplating the landscape. "Neither, I would think. Like the manager; he's got a good gig and I expect he knows it."

"You think?"

"Yes. They were best mates at school, remember. And performing together ever since. It must mean he has a firm friendship with Brendan." Gary looked across to where several pictures adorned one wall. They could see the two men smiling out at them in a variety of poses; with arms about each other's shoulders, standing four-square facing the camera, with and without rifles, with and without braces of pheasants.

"It looks as though Brendan comes out here to shoot." Angela turned back to the room and followed the direction of Gary's gaze. "I wonder if the friendship is really mutual."

Gary gave her a puzzled look. "You mean, he thinks more of Brendan than Brendan does of him?"

"Well, Brendan's got to be the goose that lays the golden eggs, don't you think?"

"I didn't think you were a cynic when we first met." Angela and Gary jumped at the sound of the voice. They turned to find Terry Dexter had entered the room by a door they hadn't seen before. He came towards them, smiling, a phone in his hand.

"I'm not, normally," replied Angela, returning his smile which, she could tell, wasn't in the least offended. "But, I'm afraid, in my job I have to consider every option."

"Quite right; I expect nothing less from the police," he agreed, reaching them. "Can I get you something to drink?" Angela and Gary refused politely, and Terry led them to where some comfortable chairs were grouped in front of an imposing Yorkstone hearth.

"It's genuine," he said, sitting down and indicating they should too. He glanced around the well-appointed room. "Our friendship, I mean. Eleven, we were; our first day at senior school. That's when we met. We got stuck side by side in class. The master, Brother Xavier, spent the first part of the morning introducing himself and trying to get an angle on us all. You know the sort of thing. 'Who likes football, boys?' And he put his fingers into his ears to make like he was blocking out the loud cheer that went up: 'YAY!' 'Who wants to try out for the school team?' More noise. 'Me, sir – me, sir – me sir!' 'That's good. Did you know we play a lot of rugger here too?' And back went the fingers in the ears. It was all good fun, but I couldn't help noticing Brendan's responses were the same as mine; merely polite, just enthusiastic enough not to appear uncool on our first day. But when Bro Xavvy mentioned the school orchestra, we couldn't keep our hands down. That made us laugh – to realize we had something in common, and there we were sitting side by side among all these footballers and aspiring scrum halves. We became friends from that moment. And no, I'm not."

"Not what?" asked Angela.

"Jealous of him. I'm a very competent musician, Inspector; a worthy member of the band. I don't have Brendan's voice. Neither do I have his charm. I'm not without talent, but I'm fully aware thousands of people wouldn't pay vast sums of money to come and see me in concert. It's something I accepted a long time ago." He flashed a sudden smile. "It no doubt helps me to maintain what little humility I have."

"Do I hear Bro Xavvy speaking there?"

Terry smiled. "You do. Now, there *was* a humble man; humble and holy, and there aren't too many of those about. You wouldn't think those qualities would make him popular, would you, but I can't think of anybody who didn't like Bro Xavvy."

"I think Brendan remembers him fondly as well," said Angela, carefully.

Terry threw her a shrewd glance. "Yes, he's had cause to remember some things he said with particular clarity over the past eight years."

"Ah."

Terry nodded. "Yes, Inspector, I do know about the blackmail."

"How many other people know?"

"Not many. Des, Brendan's mum and me."

"Not even Tilly? As few as that?"

Terry nodded. "It's a very closely guarded secret. To be honest *I* wouldn't even be in the know but for the fact that I once overheard Oliver making his demand, and I asked Brendan what was going on. He didn't want to tell me but I pressed him. Oliver was clever enough not to get too greedy.

Brendan said he could cope. He said as long as the status quo remained he could put up with it, and maybe he was right, but it took its toll on him all the same."

"Really?"

"Inspector, you can't go on like that year after year. It wore him down slowly." He paused. "He... he hasn't written anything new in several years, and for Brendan that says it all. He was even beginning to have difficulty tweaking the old stuff. He'd reached the end of his tether." A look a raw anger flashed across his face. "The bastard!"

Angela thought for a moment, aware of being on delicate ground. She only had Terry's word for how he came to know of the blackmail, and no way at all of knowing if he was aware it looked set to continue. *In any case*, she reminded herself, *I didn't come here to talk about that*. "Unless he's prepared to make an official complaint, I can't do anything to help."

"He won't do that. He's terrified of what the media would do to him. Especially the way things have been in the last few years. The situation has become quite ridiculous in some cases, but Brendan did at least sleep with the girl. His defence would have a hard time."

"Yes, unfortunately," agreed Angela. "I actually wanted to talk about something else."

"Oh, really?"

"Yes. This might sound a daft question, but would you mind giving me your email address?" Terry raised his eyebrows but made no comment as he reeled off an address that sounded nothing like any of those received by Oliver. Gary wrote it down slowly, making sure he had it correct. "That's your only one, is it?" asked Angela, when he had finished.

"Yes."

"Have you ever heard anything about a possible ticketing scam related to Brendan's concerts?"

He opened his eyes wide at this. "Never. I mean, I've seen touts out in front of the theatre, of course, but – no."

"What I'm thinking of is deliberate fraud."

"Wow! It's the first I've heard of it. Was Olly involved? I can just imagine that; bleeding Brendan backstage and ripping off his audience out front."

Angela gave him an enigmatic smile. "We're not sure of anything yet, Mr Dexter; the investigation is still in its early stage. I think that'll be all for the moment." She rose and Gary did likewise. "Thank you for your cooperation."

"Oh, yes – yes, of course." Terry got up and led them through to the front door.

"What do you reckon?" asked Gary, as he belted himself in behind the steering wheel.

"Oh, he's got a motive, all right," replied Angela. "He's spent the last eight years watching his best friend being slowly destroyed. And as well as making a good living from him, I should think Terry Dexter is very loyal to his friends."

As Angela and Gary were leaving Terry Dexter's estate, Rick and Jim were being shown into the neat, cosy living room of Don Buckley's house.

"A buzzmail address? No, I haven't got one," he said, in response to their query. He brought up his personal details on his mobile phone and handed it to Rick. "That's my email," he said.

"Thank you." Rick wrote it down. "Have you ever received an email from this address – or any like it?"

Don looked blank and shook his head. "Sorry, it means nothing to me. It must be another D. Buckley. It's not like Smith, but even so there are loads of Buckleys about."

Rick and Jim exchanged looks, wondering where they could take this conversation. Jim had suggested as much on the way. "I mean," he'd said, "I know this email address business is important and we have to check it out, but it's a long way to go for just one question. And whoever was trying to get in on Oliver's scheme is going to deny having one of those addresses anyway, aren't they?"

Rick could only agree; then it suddenly occurred to him, though they'd noted everyone's movements on the night, nobody had been asked about their perception of where other people had been. He decided it could be an interesting path to pursue. "Do you remember the scene outside the stage door at the time of the shooting?" he asked.

Don narrowed his eyes as he thought. "Your colleague was already there when I came out to see what was going on. Apart from Brendan, of course. To be honest, my attention was mostly taken up with Brendan. D.C. Houseman asked me to get him a chair and something to keep him warm – for the shock. I know loads of people came out of the stage door just about then. Your bloke told them to go inside. Poor old Jack had to tug a flight case back through the door after struggling to get it outside."

"When you went back inside for the coat, did you pass anyone?"

Don thought for a moment. "No. I'd decided the best idea would be to fetch my own coat for Brendan, otherwise I'd have to chase up someone with the key to Brendan's room and that could all take time, so I went straight to our room. I was aware of other people going past me in the direction of the stage door – word got out very quickly. By the time I came back it seemed everybody was there and it all became extremely confusing."

Rick and Jim thanked him for his time, and drove across London to Carla's address. They found her sending emails, and she handed her phone over so they could check for themselves. As they expected, she had no buzzmail address. She didn't even look up as they left.

In his office at the Apollo theatre, Leanne and Derek were observing the same blank-faced bewilderment on Barry Grieves's face as he answered the same question about his email address. "Sorry, I can't help you," he said, raising his shoulders and letting them fall again. "I can only assure you this is not mine."

Like Rick and Jim, Leanne and Derek felt the need to prolong the interview beyond one simple question. Taking into account the most recent development, they took a slightly different route from their senior colleagues.

"Do you get many touts here?" asked Derek, as they were escorted back through the foyer. Before them, through the glass front door, they could see the concrete pillars of the Hammersmith flyover.

Barry Grieves grinned. "I've never bothered to count them, but I should think there are plenty. I don't usually spot someone's a tout unless I see them actually trying to sell tickets."

"Have you ever been approached?"

"Oh, goodness, yes; I think we all have – every member of the staff here, I mean. It's just a question of hurrying past and saying, 'No, thank you.' In the early days I used to stop and tell them I worked here and could see every show for free. But I don't bother any more."

"They earn enough from it to keep coming back," mused Leanne.

"It seems so," agreed Barry. "Of course, I've got to know one or two of the faces, but I'm sure what I see is only the tip of the iceberg."

"Would you have ever noticed a young man with distinctive tattoos down his arm?" asked Leanne.

Barry rubbed a hand across his chin. "Distinctive tattoos? Nothing springs to mind; distinctive in what way?"

"They're an unusual design," replied Leanne. "A hawk swooping down each arm."

"Oh, that would be distinctive, wouldn't it? But I'm sorry, I can't help you there. Is he a tout?"

"We think he might be," answered Leanne, with care. "We just want to ask him some questions."

"Oh, I see. Well – " Barry pushed the door to let them go through – "a hawk swooping down each arm would certainly be noticeable. If I come across him, I'll be in touch."

Leanne and Derek thanked the theatre manager and found themselves standing in the street. "Good thinking with that last question, Leanne," said Derek. Just at that moment, his mobile beeped. "Oh," he said, looking at the screen. "It's a text from Angela. Don't bother to go and see Doug Travers. She and Gary have caught up with Jack Waring and the two men are together."

"Oh, good. Let's get back to the incident room, then," said Leanne. "I sent for a copy of Kay Joplin's birth certificate and it might have arrived by now."

When Jack Waring answered Angela's call and explained that he was already with Doug Travers, she was glad of the convenience. Two birds with one stone. They found the production manager sitting in the outer office playing with a pack of cards. He looked up and smiled in greeting as they came through the door. "Doug won't be long. He's just tying up some details for a gig for Brendan."

"A one-off?" asked Gary.

"Yes – it's related to the charity show he couldn't do because of the murder. Lots of fans bought tickets just because he was in it, and it's a shame for them to miss out."

"Better than having to give all the money back," said Angela. She watched, fascinated, as the cards moved in Jack's hands.

"Something like that," he agreed. "The charity has approached us, so we're setting it up."

"Either that's a really obscure game of patience, or you're practising card tricks," she said.

He grinned. "Card tricks. What else? You've got to keep your hand in."

"Do you produce coins from behind ears and rabbits from hats as well?" asked Gary.

"I've never bothered with the rabbits," replied Jack. "But producing coins and other objects is bread-and-butter stuff. I've done a bit of children's entertaining here and there – birthday parties and the like, you know. You need to have it in the repertoire. I wouldn't be without the card tricks; but it's the big illusions that really fascinate me."

"Like sawing the lady in half," said Gary.

"Yes, though of course, it's one of the better-known ones. I'd really like to pull off something unusual. That's always been my dream. Bit late now. I should have stuck to magic if I'd wanted to do that." He smiled wryly, and with an astonishingly deft movement brought the cards together into one single stack.

"Don't ever invite me to play poker with you," said Gary.

Jack laughed. At that moment the door to the inner office opened and Doug Travers emerged. "We're good to go, Jack," he said. "I'll get the publicity rolling. The band are all on board; you set up the crew. We'll need the equipment you were going to take to the O2."

"No problem," said Jack.

Doug turned towards Angela and Gary. "Sorry, Inspector, how may I help you?"

"Not at all, Mr Travers. We're sorry to disturb you again, but we've come across something in Oliver Joplin's inbox that surprised us." She explained about the email addresses but received, as she now expected, a puzzled expression and no answers. Five minutes later, she and Gary were on their way back to the office.

Chapter Twenty-three

"OK, everybody, your attention please." Angela stood ready by the whiteboard displaying all the case details. Her team turned away from their various occupations to face in her direction. "I know it's late. We've probably all got arrangements for this evening. But my feeling is we have only a few loose threads left to tidy up on this case. Before we knock off for the day, I thought we'd go through what we've got so we're all singing from the same hymn sheet." The opening of the door distracted her and she looked across to see D.C.I. Stanway enter the room. "Sir?" Angela made as if to move away from her position, but Stanway waved her back to it and took a seat at the side of the room.

"I've just come in to touch base with you all and see where you've got to."

"We're about to have a brainstorming session, sir."

"Excellent! Excellent! Don't mind me, just carry on."

Angela turned back to her team. "Right, so what have we got?"

"One dead roadie," obliged Jim.

"The indisputable fact," agreed Angela. "Just to put Carla Paterson's theory to bed; do we think he was the intended target?"

"It's more likely than the alternative," said Rick.

"Yes," added Gary.

"That's true," put in Stanway. "And from what I gather, there are some crack shots among these people. Whoever did the deed would make sure the correct target got hit."

"OK; agreed," said Angela. "So where does this take us?"

"How did anybody know they were outside having one of their famous 'chats'?" said Gary.

"Interesting point, Gaz. I mean, we know these little meetings went on between Oliver and Brendan, and we now know why. Given the reason for them, I don't suppose they were advertised among the other people on the tour, were they?"

"That's right," said Jim. "Most of them said they'd seen the two of them have a quiet word now and again, but that would have been in passing. I don't suppose they knew when a confab was planned."

"Somebody could have overheard them making the arrangement to meet later," suggested Gary.

"Yes – possible," agreed Angela. "But that makes it sound a bit random and I think this murder was planned."

"The perp could have planned the murder but not the timing, Angie," said Rick. "He or she must have stuck close to either Brendan or Oliver to find out when they were going to be alone and then swung into action."

"Yes, waiting for an opportunity," suggested Derek.

"That makes sense," agreed Angela. "So we've got the premeditated murder of Oliver Joplin."

"Why?" asked Stanway.

"Yes, that's the next question, isn't it; what's the motive?"

"We know he was blackmailing poor Brendan," said Leanne immediately, her mouth set in a tight line.

"This is a very good motive, but we've already established that Brendan probably couldn't have done it."

"He could have paid for someone else to do it," suggested Jim, with a nervous glance across at Leanne. She glared at him but said nothing.

"We have to consider that possibility," said Angela, gently. "But we'll only know about that once we've caught the killer, so let's put that on the back burner for the moment. Do we have any other motives?"

"The ticketing scam looks likely," ventured Gary.

"Yes, I'm inclined to agree. All those emails with the familiar names indicate that someone was on to his little game – that's all I think it was, by the way; a small-time operation. And it's reasonable to assume, from their content, the sender was signalling his intent to muscle in with a view to taking over."

"All those emails create a real smokescreen," put in Stanway.

"Definitely, sir," agreed Angela.

"So who have we got in the frame?"

Angela ticked off the names on her fingers as she reeled them off. "Don Buckley, Doug Travers, Jack Waring and Terry Dexter are the front runners, sir. We can place them all in the vicinity before, during and after the shooting. A few other faces came piling out of the stage door, but from what we can tell, they'd come up from either the crew room, the band room or the dressing room area, once they'd either heard the shot or got wind of something going on."

"Hmm," muttered Stanway. His team waited as he ruminated on what he'd heard. "It seems to me you have two options and you've got to follow them both. If Brendan Phelan took out a contract on Oliver Joplin because of the blackmail, then we've got to lean on him and hope he cracks. However, if the motive is this ticket scam, we've got a bit of a conundrum because matey is hiding behind several aliases and we've no easy way of finding out which one."

"That's about it, sir."

"And the only lead seems to be this elusive young man with the hawk tattoos. Am I right?" Several heads nodded. "And it's possible he's the same person who's now planning to carry on blackmailing Brendan," continued the D.C.I., demonstrating, should any of the team have doubted it, that he kept his finger on the pulse of the investigation.

"We think so, sir."

"Have you asked for Mr Phelan's cooperation?"

"We did, sir. He's determined not to press charges, should we catch up with the blackmailer, because he's terrified of the repercussions in terms of publicity. I can't say I blame him, to be honest. We've been very gentle with him so far."

"But…" cautioned Stanway.

"Yes, I know, sir. This is a murder enquiry."

Stanway nodded. "Yes," he said. "I think you're going to have to be a little firmer with him, Angie."

"Yes, sir," replied Angela. She suddenly felt quite depressed. "We will, sir. He was very distressed last night so I didn't push it, but I've put Leanne onto getting a copy of Kay Joplin's birth certificate." She looked across to where Leanne was sitting, and received a confirmatory nod.

"Thinking Joplin might have doctored the one he gave to Brendan, eh?"

"Yes. It would make life simpler for us if we could find something like that – and for him."

"Indeed." Stanway got up and moved towards the door. "Well, it's all coming along, Angie. Keep me up to speed." He moved out into the corridor.

"OK, everyone," Angela said to the room in general. "You all know what you're doing, so get on with it." She looked at Gary. "I'll be right with you, Gary. I just need to see how Leanne's got on." She nodded at Leanne and beckoned her over to a secluded desk in the corner of the room.

"OK, Leanne," she began, sitting down. "What have you got? You're looking rather flushed, by the way. Are you all right?"

"Yes, guv, I just keep thinking about poor Brendan and

what he must be going through."

"I agree; the poor bloke's been well and truly set up. Anyway, let's look at this birth certificate. It might tell us something we don't already know."

But it didn't. The document bore out in every detail the information Brendan had been given about Kay, née Joplin. It confirmed her birth had been registered in the borough of Southwark twenty-two years previously. The only addition to what they already knew was her full name. She had been registered as Kayleigh Emma.

Angela sat back in her seat, "That's it then, Leanne. I don't know what I was hoping to find, but it's all in order, isn't it?" Leanne nodded. Her flush had deepened and Angela suddenly became aware of a sense of quiet excitement emanating from her. She raised her eyebrows in a questioning manner. "Have you got something up your sleeve, Leanne?"

Leanne nodded and fidgeted in her seat. The words burst from her. "Yes, guv! I don't know how I've managed to contain myself since I found out, but I wanted to wait until I had your undivided attention." A broad smile spread itself across her face. In the manner of a magician producing a rabbit from a top hat, she laid another piece of paper on the desk.

Angela bent over to read it, puzzled. "What's this?" She frowned. "Hang on – I don't understand." She began at the top again and read the page carefully. When she'd finished she looked back at Leanne, who nodded triumphantly and shifted on her seat as if she couldn't help herself.

"I'm right, aren't I, guv?"

"You are indeed, Leanne. Good work!" She looked back down at the page.

"I couldn't believe it at first, guv. I made the woman on the phone read it out to me about three times."

Angela smiled. "Did you follow this through?"

"Ahead of you, guv." Leanne laid yet another sheet of paper on the desk.

Angela read it through carefully and exhaled slowly as she took in the implications. She stood up. "Can you let everyone know about this, Leanne? Another trip to Hampstead is on the cards before Gary and I knock off. We shouldn't delay on this."

Desmond, back from his day off, opened the door to the star's home an hour later. "I'm sorry," he began. "Brendan didn't mention any appointments today. He's busy in his studio and normally doesn't like to be disturb – "

"He'll see us, I'm sure," said Angela. "If you'd just let him know we're here." She had made a point of not ringing ahead to announce their visit. She wanted to spring a surprise.

The unscheduled appearance must have intrigued him, because ten minutes later Desmond was showing them upstairs and ushering them, once again, into the living room-cum-studio.

Brendan moved away from his piano towards the sofa as they entered. "I thought I might as well try to exercise the muse," he said. He attempted a smile of greeting but gave up after a second.

"How have you been?"

"Not good, I'm afraid," replied Brendan, throwing himself down onto the sofa. "I thought I could live with it, but I now realize it's been slowly wearing me down for several years. At least Oliver had the good sense not to get too greedy. To find I'm not free, as I thought, has brought the horror back ten times worse than it ever was." It seemed to Angela that he blinked back some tears.

"We've been digging into this matter," she said, coming over and standing in front of him.

"Oh, really? And what have you dug up?"

Angela took the birth certificate out of her bag and handed it to him. "Is that the same as the certificate Oliver Joplin gave you when he first started blackmailing you, eight years ago?"

Brendan took the document and looked it over carefully. "Yes," he said eventually, looking up at her. "Of course, mine's a photocopy but, as I told you, he showed me the original in the first place. I can't tell you how many times I've gone over it, looking for some evidence of forgery."

"There isn't any," replied Angela. "It's a genuine document."

Brendan gave a mirthless laugh that sounded more like a sob. "Then I don't see – "

Angela took the other piece of paper out of her bag. "We've got a very thorough researcher on our team," she told him. "Her name's Leanne Dabrowska and she's like a ferret when she gets going. She presented me with this today," she said, handing it to him.

Brendan took it, a puzzled look on his face. He read it through quickly, looked up at Angela, frowning, and looked back again at the document. Angela watched as enlightenment slowly dawned, saw hope flicker into life and then die because he didn't dare to believe. Finally, with shaking hands, he held the documents side by side, looking from one to the other.

"OK," he said, his voice a croak. "Am I seeing what I think I'm seeing?"

Angela smiled. "You are."

He gave a sudden choke. "Dare I say it?"

"Go on," Angela encouraged him.

"I have here in my right hand, Kayleigh Joplin's birth certificate." His last words were almost hidden in the strangled sob that escaped him. "And in my left I have her death certificate."

"That's it," said Gary. "She died at the age of three months."

Brendan nodded. Angela and Gary waited. Brendan leaned back, tears gathered in the corners of his eyes. The only sound in the room was the deep shuddering breaths that seemed to rise from the depths of his entire being. "So I didn't sleep with a fourteen-year-old girl."

"No; we think you slept with her big sister. We took the precaution of getting a copy of her birth certificate as well. She would have been twenty at the time."

Brendan rose up and moved towards Angela. He put his arms round her and lifted her off the ground. "Thank you, thank you, thank you, thank you," he breathed. "You have no idea what this means."

"I think I've got an inkling," smiled Angela as her feet touched the ground again. *Carla Paterson, eat your heart out*, she thought. She cast a quick glance at Gary, who smiled and raised his eyebrows.

At that moment, Desmond came in bearing a tray of coffees. As he put it down, he cast a concerned glance towards his brother. Angela didn't think Brendan had registered his presence, but she was wrong. "The day we wondered would ever come has arrived, Desi! The monkey's finally off my back! I'm home free!"

Desmond straightened up; he looked a little puzzled but quickly picked up the jubilation in Brendan's voice. "What? You don't mean...?"

"Yes! I do!" Brendan could hardly keep his feet on the floor. "The blackmail – it was all a scam. Olly had a little sister who died as a baby and he'd used *her* birth certificate." He held out the document Angela had shown him.

Desmond took it and read it through quickly. "Yay!" He shouted. "It's over!" he beamed. The brothers caught each other up in a bear hug and swayed together.

"We'll crack open a bottle of fizz tonight," said Brendan, when they separated.

"Indeed, indeed. I'll put one in the fridge, and if I might suggest, I've got a couple of very nice fillet steaks – "

"Perfect," nodded Brendan, his voice gaining its normal register. He glanced again at the death certificate. "What's this – Edwards' syndrome?"

"It's very rare, I gather," answered Angela. "Children who are born with it very often don't make it to their first birthday."

"As this poor child didn't," he muttered, going over the document again. He looked up at Angela. "Honestly, the day Olly came here with his sister, she had her school uniform on – her hair was in plaits and she made her eyes look so big and innocent. I mean…"

"A woman can drop a lot of years quite easily," said Angela. Her face was still pleasantly flushed from her surprise hug. "It's no wonder you were taken in. Why shouldn't you have been?"

"So who is this grown-up sister who allowed me the pleasure of her body?"

"Her name's Katie-Jane. We went to see her a few days ago. She answered to 'Kay' when we were there. She did admit she's sometimes affectionately known as Kadey or Kadey-Wadey." Angela remembered the woman taking a call in her kitchen, when they were there, and passing it off as a pet name. "We'll need to see her again."

"I don't know what to say. I can't thank you enough."

"Well, there is something you can do."

Brendan's eyes crinkled into a smile. Angela's heart lurched as she was reminded of Patrick. It gave her an insight into the fascination Leanne and Madeleine felt. "Ah yes," he said. "This blackmailer still wants to collect, doesn't he?"

"Yes. It would help us enormously if you could play along with us there."

Brendan leaned back into the sofa and extended his arms. She realized he looked truly happy for the first time since she'd met him. "Oh, Inspector," he said, a broad smile splitting his face in two. "It would be my pleasure."

Chapter Twenty-four

"What a result!" exclaimed Gary, once they were back in the car and heading south.

"Yes, indeedy," agreed Angela. "We might manage to close up the gaping hole in the middle of our investigation if this blackmailer is who we think it is."

"He's probably not the murderer, though," added Gary.

"It doesn't seem likely. Mind you, Oliver could have sneaked him in backstage for reasons best known to himself – but I'm sure somebody would have noticed and mentioned seeing him."

"If I was the actual murderer and I saw him hanging around backstage, I would definitely mention it in my statement. I'd want to cast suspicion on him, for a start."

"Exactly!"

They continued in silence for some minutes. "I just wish I could remember what I saw that was important," remarked Gary, eventually.

"What, the thing you picked up on when you did the reconstruction?"

"Yes. I'm sure it's nearly flashed into my head a couple of times, but when I tried to grasp the memory, it disappeared."

"It's very irritating when that happens. All you can do is relax and not think about it. You never know," she added, "it might turn out not to be important at all."

"That's true," mused Gary.

"Let's go back to this list of names that sent Oliver emails," said Angela. "The presence of one of them puzzles me. Can you guess which one?"

"Er…" Gary thought for a moment. "Barry Grieves?"

"Yes. He's not a member of Brendan's management team, nor one of the regular crew."

"Neither is Don Buckley."

"That's true, but he and Foursquare were on the tour with Brendan."

"Oh yes, of course. OK, so why do you think the inclusion of Barry Grieves is odd?"

"It might not be, but I'm curious. I'm sure show business is like any other industry; some people you get to know better than others. If, as we think, a bigger ticketing fraud gang was muscling in on Oliver's little operation, it might just be that whoever's running it knows Barry Grieves, and decided to use his name as well. The fact that it was the last gig of the tour and he runs the Apollo might be significant."

"Possibly," replied Angela. She remained in thought for a few moments. "Actually…"

"What?"

"I know you saw this incident of the man and his daughter and her friends who had the duff tickets, but I don't think you've ever described the scene to me."

"Haven't I? There's not much to describe. I became aware of this man talking with one of the front-of-house staff and I could hear from the tone of his voice that he was half-embarrassed, half-angry. The man checking the tickets was blushing like you wouldn't believe. He looked young and I got the impression he couldn't handle it very well, but Barry Grieves came over and obviously he's got a lot more experience and clout. He dealt with the man; very regretful and polite, but firm. The poor bloke still wasn't going to get in to the concert, not on those tickets, anyway."

"Well, he's got to be like that, of course, hasn't he? He can't let people in on fraudulent tickets."

"Yes. He did it very smoothly, I must say."

"Probably gets a fair bit of practice. So then what happened?"

"The party went out, the birthday girl was crying, I think, and probably wishing the ground would open up and swallow her. They'd just got to the edge of the pavement when I noticed the man with the hawk tattoos. Maddie had joined me by then and we both watched him approach the girl's dad and they started talking. We didn't watch any more. We went in to find our seats at that point."

"Oh, right. Thanks, Gary. That's all a bit clearer for me now."

In the exclusive area of Mayfair, two men sat nursing drinks in the dimly lit corner of a hotel bar.

"Do you think we can relax yet?" asked one, the larger of them. He had slicked-back blond hair and a smooth complexion.

His companion, slighter of build, crinkled his eyes with amusement. "I wouldn't like to call it, but it seems to me the police are going in a straight line looking for the murderer."

"That's what you'd expect, of course, but I'm still concerned –"

"I know what you're concerned about," cut in the smaller man. "But you don't need to worry. You're prone to panic, that's your trouble."

"The police found those email addresses on Olly's computer –"

"So what?" He picked up his drink and took a sip. "They can't trace them to us."

"Are you sure? I got such a fright when they asked me about my email address. It gave me a real turn."

The smaller man quelled a momentary impatience. "They

asked me, too. No sweat. It's a dead end, I keep telling you."
He studied his companion for a moment, noticing the beads
of sweat on his upper lip. "Are you getting rattled?"

The larger man took out a handkerchief and wiped his
face. "No, no, of course not; it's just that when I signed up for
this, I didn't sign up for – " He cast a glance round the bar,
nearly empty at this time of the day, and lowered his voice.
"Murder!"

The melodramatic way in which he uttered the word
brought forth a smile from the other man. "Keep calm. You
signed up for a nice little earner and it's worked well so far,
hasn't it?"

"Yes, but – "

"But what?"

"Well, I'd have thought it obvious; Olly's dead."

"He was muscling in on our territory and it had to be dealt
with."

"Yes, you said that, but I thought you were only going to
frighten him off."

"Somebody offed him altogether, didn't they?" The smaller
man paused, a smile playing round his mouth. "Did you
think it was me?"

A horrified look appeared on the smooth, well-fed face.
"Oh no! Of course not! I mean… It wasn't you, was it?"

The other man laughed outright at this. A couple of heads
on the other side of the bar looked briefly in their direction
and turned immediately away again.

"Of course it wasn't me. Do you think I'm stupid?"

The large man wiped his forehead with his handkerchief.
His fellow drinker was completely cool and unruffled. He
even seemed amused by the turn of events. He had to admit,
this sangfroid was one of the reasons he'd thrown in his lot
with him. The man exuded confidence. He didn't expect to

ever find him wiping sweat from his face. He took a deep breath and told himself he was imagining problems where there weren't any.

The smaller man nodded, the smile very visible in his eyes as well as his mouth. "That's better; you just calm down and rely on me. I've seen you all right so far, haven't I?"

"You have. I have to admit it. I'm puzzled about one thing, though."

"What's that?"

"Why do you want this disc and that stationery from Olly's friend?"

"The stationery's not so important. Olly was probably only using it when he started, to print his own tickets and send them out. He must have stopped doing that a while ago. It's the disc I want. It's got the program on it that he'd got together, you know, for setting up the duff tickets."

"Yes, I realize that; but we've got our own system."

"Yes, but we need to make sure his is out of circulation."

"Of course."

"In any case, I always like to know how my business rivals operate. I don't think Olly was too bad at the old IT stuff. Might have had some good ideas; could even be a better program than ours."

"That makes sense."

"He was a silly boy, though, doing Brendan's concerts."

"That surprised me, I must admit. Bit close to home, wasn't it?"

The other man nodded. "Rule number one: protect your own patch. And there's another reason I want that disc." He tapped the side of his nose. "We've got to let his 'business associate' know who runs the territory."

The big man smiled, completely relaxed now. "Shall we use him, do you think?"

A shrug. "We'll see. Depends how amenable he is to doing what he's told, doesn't it?"

"I've got to hand it to you; you know what you're doing. And you know how to keep your cool doing it."

The man smiled slowly, self-satisfied. "That's what it's all about, isn't it?" He held up his glass. "Chin, chin."

They clinked their glasses.

The journey from Mayfair to Ladbroke Grove didn't take very long, but a huge social divide separated the two places. Alex sat in the same dingy corner of the pub he'd been in three days earlier. He wore the same grubby anorak, and his hair, pulled back into its customary ponytail, looked greasy. He wondered why he was doing this. The person he'd met on the previous occasion had made it clear he wanted Oliver's disc. And here he sat, waiting to hand it over, and he didn't quite understand why. He had an uncomfortable sense in the back of his mind that Olly wouldn't be doing this. Olly would ask a few questions, make his own demands, talk money. It always came down to money with him. Alex remembered the time he'd asked for a bigger cut. He'd been told in no uncertain terms that if he didn't like the arrangement, he knew what he could do. The trouble was, he *didn't* know what he could do; he had no other experience than a life of petty crime. Meeting up with Oliver and becoming part of the ticket scam had been a career step up for him – the closest thing he'd ever done to steady work.

Thinking about Olly cheered him. He could just imagine Olly in this situation. He might very well see the value of handing the business over to a bigger firm, but he'd be no pushover. He'd play hard to get; then he'd hedge. Hedging would become haggling, then bargaining, and finally negotiation, leading to a reasonable deal. That's what happened in industry all the time. Yeah, he shouldn't wonder that a takeover bid had been made. It was only natural. Olly had a product worth selling.

The door opened and he saw the other man enter. He wore an expensive-looking raincoat with a pure wool scarf slung round his neck. Alex sat up a little straighter, smoothed his hair back and ran a hand over his ponytail.

He swallowed. No longer Olly; *he* held the marketable commodity. He'd offer him a drink and start with some small talk. That was the way to do business.

The man didn't approach Alex's table immediately. He got himself a drink, a tonic water, and sat down opposite him. "Well?" he began.

Alex raised his own glass in a toast. "Evening, Mr H; cheers," he said, with a small smile.

The other man barely moved a muscle in his face. He raised his glass and took a sip. "Have you brought it?"

"I've got it nearby," replied Alex. He patted his pocket and cursed inwardly when the other man's eyes flew straight to that pocket.

"Let's have a look, then."

"We need to talk a bit first."

"What about?"

Alex swallowed. "This program didn't come cheap."

"Yeah, right," came the reply. The man didn't even bother to hide his disdain at this.

"I've got a couple of other people interested," continued Alex, but even he could hear the nervousness in his voice, and he knew it would be obvious to the other man.

"Of course you have." Disdain had been matched with unbelief. "Look, I haven't got time to play games. Hand it over."

"It's got a price tag," said Alex in a near-squeak.

This brought forth a weary smile. "Listen. You either hand it over here and now or you find the police on your doorstep tonight. The choice is yours."

Alex gulped, took the disc out of his pocket and laid it on the table between them. The man flicked his eyes down at it but didn't pick it up. In spite of himself, Alex was impressed. Cool. The man took a long swallow of his drink and put the glass down on the table. "OK, now you're acting sensibly. I like that. Do you want to work for me or don't you?"

"I might; if I'm free." The man laughed outright at this. A surge of resentment reared up in Alex. "This isn't my only business."

The man cast an appraising glance over him. "What else are you into, then?"

Alex shrugged in a hollow show of nonchalance. "That's for me to know."

"You'd better not be peddling drugs. My operation steers clear of that."

"I'm not peddling drugs."

"Doing 'em yourself?"

"No."

The man nodded. His hand came out and the disc disappeared into his raincoat pocket. "Make sure you don't," he said. "I don't tolerate that among my operatives. We'll have a cooling off period. I'll give you a call in a couple of weeks." He downed the rest of his drink, stood up and was gone.

Alex was left staring as the door swung shut behind him. A familiar sensation crept over him as he saw his erstwhile drinking companion move unhurriedly past the window near where he sat. He'd been shafted. He never knew how it had happened until the process was almost complete, by which stage any protest would be completely useless. He took his mobile phone out of his pocket. He had one small crumb of comfort to bolster his crushed ego. As he'd said to the man, he had an alternative business on the go. He scrolled through his contacts until he came to the number he had for Brendan Phelan.

Chapter Twenty-five

Brendan Phelan pushed his empty plate away from him, downing the final mouthful from a bottle of vintage champagne. He set his glass down on the table and beamed at his brother. He'd done a great deal of beaming throughout the meal. Every so often the memory would come to him afresh, and an involuntary smile would light up his face. "That was magnificent, Des; who'd have thought my brickie bro would have turned into such a good cook."

Des smiled and took a sip from his own glass. "I think I could have done beans on toast with mouldy cheese tonight and it would still have tasted good to you."

"You've got *that* right. It still hasn't sunk in." Brendan closed his eyes for a moment and let out a long, slow breath. "I'm free! I'm actually free!"

"We must phone Mum later. She's been praying for this day."

"Yeah, I'd given up hope, I really had; but she never did." Brendan remained in silence for a moment. "I know it's small-minded of me, but would you believe I have one slight regret in all this?"

"What's that?"

"That I didn't know the truth when Olly was alive so I could deal with him directly. I'd have loved to see his expression when I threw it all in his face. Then I'd have got him sorted once and for all and booted him off the crew."

"I can understand that temptation," said Desmond. "It's a shame you're going to be denied that pleasure but it's a small price to pay for being free at last."

239

"I wonder what he's going to think up for collection? With Olly it was like a drugs deal, a slapping of palm on palm and over in a minute before anybody could be sure they'd seen a thing. But, of course, that won't work now, will it?"

"It wasn't always that arrangement, though, was it? What about those times when you weren't touring?"

"Yes, you're right. I had to put him on the guest list for a TV show once, didn't I? Remember how I had to hand the money over in the dressing room and you were in the en suite?"

"Yes, and he narrowly missed having Doug walk in on him as well, if I remember rightly."

"Yes, but he was always going to find a way. As a crew member it didn't attract anyone's attention, but now…" Brendan shrugged.

"Well, I hope he thinks up something dramatic; in the middle of the Heath at midnight or some such scenario."

"So you're still OK with that?"

"Oh, absolutely! The more cloak-and-dagger it is, the better I shall enjoy it. The very idea reminds me of all those adventure stories we read when we were kids. I hope the police will let me lurk in the bushes and watch what goes on after I've done the drop."

Brendan smiled. "I love that – the idea of you lurking in the bushes."

Des smiled back and pursued the image. "I thought, a false moustache and glasses; what do you reckon?"

"Go for it! And a red wig."

"Oh – a bit over the top, don't you think, bro?"

Brendan laughed outright at this. "You might be right."

"I hope he doesn't take too long getting back to you with his demands."

"So do I; I wonder what the police will do when they catch him."

"At the least, they'll have to arrest him for attempted blackmail," surmised Des.

Just at that moment, Brendan's mobile, on the table near his plate, sprang into life. "Ah! It's Tilly," he said, looking at the screen.

"I'll just start clearing, then." Des stood up and began collecting the empty plates.

"Hi, Tills," said Brendan, into the phone. "Hold on a minute." He pressed "mute" and turned to his brother, a look of wonder on his face. "I've just realized, Des."

Des paused. "What?"

Brendan waved the phone in the air. "It's *all* going to be different now. I'm not… I can move forward."

"You're free."

"Yes!"

Des gave a small smile. "Move forward with caution, little brother. New-found freedom is heady stuff."

"I hear you, Des," grinned Brendan, pressing the button and bringing the phone up to his ear.

"I bet he's enjoying his evening meal tonight," said Patrick, picking up a spare rib and gnawing at it.

"Paddy, you could almost see the weight falling off his shoulders," answered Angela.

"I'm not surprised. What a parasite, though; blackmailing somebody for something they actually did is a bad enough crime, but to set up an innocent man, make him think he's guilty and *then* blackmail him; it doesn't bear thinking about!"

"I'm trying to put that in a separate box in my head," replied Angela.

Patrick looked across at her. "Yes, I know that feeling. I had the same thing once or twice back in the day. You're investigating a murder, and the more you get to know about the victim the more you find yourself thinking, my goodness, if I'd met him or her in life I'd have been tempted to murder them myself."

"I'm trying to stay focused. My job is to do my very best to find his killer, no matter what type of man he was. I'm trying not to judge him."

"I always found that bit easy, after all…"

Angela smiled at Patrick. "Oh yes, he's come before the ultimate judge now, hasn't he?"

"You took the words out of my mouth."

"I must keep reminding myself of that," replied Angela.

For a few moments they ate in what would have been complete silence if Angela hadn't been humming to herself. "He turned out some amazing work over the years, didn't he?" remarked Patrick, eventually.

"What? Sorry. Who?"

Patrick grinned. "Walt Disney."

Angela gave a small laugh. "Oh – was I humming from *Fantasia* again?"

"You were. You seem to have picked up the habit from Gary."

"Actually, he stopped once we realized where the music came from; but now that you mention it, it's been on my mind for most of today. I've got this sense of a loose thread relating to it, somehow."

"We can watch it later, if you like. I've still got the disc and it's a film I enjoy."

"Oh, what a good idea! That'll be fun, and maybe I'll be able to tie up the loose thread."

"You might, indeed. Any breaks on the rest of the investigation?"

"Not so far, but I hope that will change just as soon as this would-be blackmailer has contacted Brendan again."

"What if it turns out to have no bearing on the murder?"

Angela grimaced. "That's the trouble, Pads. Oliver is the only connection between these two sidelines. I'm disinclined to believe blackmail was the motive, so it looks like the ticket fraud."

Patrick grinned. "He didn't have a third iron in the fire, then?"

Angela made a face. "Oh, please! Spare me!"

"So, finding the blackmailer won't necessarily lead you to whoever was trying to cut themselves in on his ticketing scam."

"That's about the size of it; but we've got to chase it up."

"Absolutely, it's the only lead you've got."

"And we haven't got very far with trying to find out who set up the email addresses."

"Have you spoken to all the people named now?"

Angela sighed and looked at him. "Oh, yes. Wide-eyed surprise all round. Every one of them assured me about their addresses, none of which was a buzzmail one."

"Somebody among them, or someone very close to one of them, is a cool customer."

"You're not kidding!"

"Any chance of tracing an originating address or computer?"

Angela raised her shoulders and let them fall again. "We've given that task to the lab, but I'm not holding my breath. I wouldn't be surprised if they can all be traced to a computer in an Internet café somewhere."

As they sat mulling over these thoughts, the front door opened and they could hear Madeleine and Gary coming in.

"In the dining room!" called Patrick, and the young couple appeared in the doorway. "There aren't any more spare ribs," he said.

"Not a problem," replied Madeleine. "We had a pizza out. You know what, Ange," she continued, cocking her thumb at Gary without turning round to him, "this 'ere bloke's going to make one very discreet detective."

Behind Madeleine, Gary smiled and shrugged at Angela. Angela looked puzzled. "Really, why do you say that?"

"Because he doesn't tell me a *thing* about this case and it's very frustrating."

Patrick and Angela cast surreptitious glances at each other, each thinking of the conversation their entrance had interrupted. "He's just doing his job," Patrick said.

"I know," replied Madeleine. "I wouldn't care if it was Joe Bloggs the burglar, I wouldn't even *want* to know, but he accidentally let slip that you've been up to Brendan Phelan again today, Angela, and then went all *shtum* on me – and he knows how I feel about Brendan. How do you like that?"

"Sorry, Angie," said Gary. "I didn't mean to blab."

Angela laughed. "Don't worry, Gary. Mads, our enquiries are proceeding and at some point, all will be revealed. But I can tell you we have no reason to believe Brendan guilty of any crime."

"Of course he's not guilty of anything! He's the sweetest man ever," said Madeleine. "Oh, I say, is that lemon meringue pie?" The small trolley at the side of the room had riveted her attention. "We didn't have dessert at the restaurant."

"Yes, there's plenty of that if you want some," answered Patrick, standing up and going over to it. "We're about ready for it now." He manoeuvred the trolley away from the wall and pushed it towards the table.

"*Ah!*" Every face turned towards Gary, arrested by the unexpected shout. Angela dropped her fork onto her plate with a clatter as concern filled their eyes – had he hurt himself?

"No need to get excited, Gary; it's just a regular lemon meringue pie!" Patrick said.

Gary blinked. "No. Sorry to make you jump!" He looked at Angela. "I've just remembered what it was that struck me when Derek and I went to do that reconstruction at the Apollo."

"Ah!"

"Look, Detective Constable Gazza," said Madeleine, assuming the manner of a superior officer. "This pie is cold anyway, so it won't spoil. You go and get your notebook and write it all down, every aspect of it while it's fresh in your memory – including why you think it's significant; everything you can think of. What?" she asked as three pairs of eyes swung towards her. "Do you all think I learned nothing, growing up as the daughter of a policeman?"

They all laughed simultaneously. "Yes, ma'am," said Gary, as he went out to where his raincoat hung in the hall.

"You can save it for the briefing meeting in the morning," Madeleine called over her shoulder. "And whatever you do, don't share it with your girlfriend, or you'll end up directing traffic." She turned back to Patrick and Angela and grinned. "It's all right, I know you two discuss Angie's cases all the time, but you're an ex D.I., Dad, working for the coroner, so that's different."

Angela was saved from the necessity of making any comment by the ringing of her mobile phone. "Oh!" she said, excited. "I wonder if we have lift off?"

Patrick, close enough to see Brendan Phelan's name appear on the screen, poked his head into the passage where Gary stood, still extricating his notebook from his raincoat. "Scramble, Gary!" he called. "It looks like you might be back on duty."

Gary hurried back into the dining room. "Is it?" he asked Angela.

She nodded and looked at Patrick.

"Deal with it in the living room," he advised. "Best do the thing properly."

Gary turned and went ahead of Angela. Once inside, she shut the door and mimed the need for a pen and some paper. Gary opened his notebook at a blank page and presented her with a pen. Angela pressed the speaker button. "OK, Brendan; tell me what was said."

"The call came through just now," he said, gabbling in a high-pitched voice. They heard him pause and take a deep breath. "I didn't realize I'd be so nervous," he said. "Des and I were talking about it over dinner and joking, would you believe? We were, like, this is a regular boys' adventure, great fun. And then when I picked up the call and recognized the voice from before, just for a second all the horror came back to me." He paused. They could hear him taking another deep breath. When he spoke again, his voice had attained its usual timbre. "So, I've been told to have the money ready for tonight."

"How much?"

"Eight hundred."

Angela and Gary looked at each other. "That's less than Oliver asked for," she said.

"I think our friend is new to this and was busking it," replied Brendan. "I asked him in what denominations he wanted the notes, and I don't think he quite realized what I meant at first. There was this long pause and I'd just begun to say, you know, fives, tens, twenties, when he said, 'Oh, yeah, yeah, yeah, just mix it up. It doesn't matter.'"

"He didn't ask for used notes?"

"No."

"How is the handover meant to take place?"

"I've got the name and address of a supermarket in west

London, out near the A40, I think." They could hear the rustling of paper as Brendan consulted his written instructions. "I've to drop it into a trolley on the outer perimeter of the car park, would you believe."

"Good grief!"

"Quite. I don't predict a glittering criminal career for this man. If you catch him and lock him up, you'll probably be saving him from himself."

Angela laughed. "And what time is this supposed to take place?"

"What he said was, 'on the stroke of midnight'. I wouldn't be surprised if he's got a bit of poetry in his soul."

Angela and Gary could tell Brendan had fully recovered from his initial apprehension and was beginning to enjoy himself. She agreed with him about the likely poetic streak, and told him they would pick him up at eleven. She finished the call and looked across at Gary with raised eyebrows.

"Sounds like a rank amateur, doesn't he?" said Gary.

"He certainly does," she agreed. "So, Gary, it could turn out to be a long night. Before we get started, since we're alone in here and you didn't get the chance to write it down, you might as well tell me what sparked your memory about the reconstruction."

"It wasn't just the reconstruction," he said. "I've realized that's only the catalyst for showing me something I saw at the time of the murder without really *knowing* that I'd seen it, if you get what I mean."

"I do," she reassured him. "So tell me about it."

Gary cleared his throat, marshalled his thoughts and began to speak. Angela wrote it down in his notebook as she listened.

What he said threw a whole new light on the case.

Chapter Twenty-six

Ten minutes to midnight.

Angela and Gary, with Brendan crouched low behind them in the back seat, watched Brendan's silver BMW with the tinted windows nose its way past the brightly lit front of the all-night supermarket, cruising gently among the few stationary cars. It moved as if the driver couldn't decide where to park the vehicle, heading away from the well-lit central area to the shadowed edges of the car park, and eventually gliding to a halt in a gloomy corner made even darker by the branches of an overhanging tree.

After a few moments Des emerged, gazing all around. If he recognized the Homicide Assessment Team car parked alongside a warehouse on a side street opposite, he gave no sign of it. His eyes swept across them and continued to search. They sat low in their seats, the car concealed in the deep shadow thrown by a lorry parked on their other side. Des ambled casually towards a supermarket trolley standing abandoned, half-in and half-out of the car park. The neighbourhood, heavily industrialized and no doubt a hive of activity during the day, still showed signs of life at this time of the night. Darkness hid the grime and the dust but couldn't disguise the litter, the unkempt feel to the place, the potholes in the roads.

Moving cautiously behind them, Brendan leaned carefully forward, keeping his head ducked low.

"I don't know why, but I'm feeling nervous," he murmured.

"I can understand that," replied Angela. "I think it's only natural." They watched in silence as Des reached the trolley and glanced about. Apart from the BMW, no other car stood within a fifty-yard radius. The only signs of human life were those of the late-night customers at the supermarket across the vast expanse of empty parking spaces. Des took a bulky A4 manila envelope from inside his coat, placing it very clearly and deliberately in the trolley. He took another sweeping glance around, then started slowly back towards the BMW. He got in, started up the engine and drove back the way he had come. He kept his cool throughout; completely unhurried, just as he'd been instructed.

Angela pressed a button on the radio device. "Rick?" she asked in a very soft voice, once her signal had been answered.

"We're in position, Angie," came Rick's answer, equally low. He and Jim had stationed themselves behind a bus shelter, on the other side of the main road in front of the supermarket. "From where we're standing we can see Leanne and Derek sitting on the bench in front of the supermarket, looking like a couple in love."

"I don't think that's going to tax their acting skills to any great degree," smiled Angela.

"I heard that," said Derek.

Angela gave a gentle laugh. "I should hope so. OK, we play a waiting game now, team."

The radios fell silent. Brendan stretched himself out along the back seat and Angela and Gary made themselves as comfortable as they could in front.

Ten minutes past midnight.

"What's that?" asked Gary. He'd yawned and pushed out his arms in front of him to stretch, but arrested his movement in the middle of the action.

Angela had heard the same noise, but Brendan was the first to answer. "It sounded like a tin scraping along the ground," he said, very low, resuming his crouching position, head close to the front seat.

"I think you're right," agreed Angela. "It seemed to come from round the front of this warehouse." Automatically they looked to their right but could only see the brick wall of the building. A few moments later a figure passed in front of the car, staggering and lurching, a beer can clutched precariously in his hand. "Ah," said Angela. "Must have been sitting on the ground or on the wall round the front."

"Yes, he probably scraped the can when he got up," added Gary.

"Do you think he's our bloke pretending to be a drunk?" ventured Brendan.

"It's a possibility," answered Gary. "But if the blackmailer is the man I saw touting in front of the theatre on the night of the murder, then no. This one's a bit shorter and stockier, for a start."

They all watched as the drunk lurched forward towards the car park entrance where the trolley was positioned, his erratic progress punctuated by frequent stops to take sips of his beer. His back was towards them. As he reached the pavement he blocked the trolley from their view.

Angela opened up her radio. "Everybody there?" she asked, and received a soft chorus from Jim and Derek in the affirmative. "Can you all see what we're looking at?" she asked, to another gentle chorus assuring her they could. "Nobody do anything rash," she whispered. "He could be a genuine drunk. Keep your eyes peeled because at the moment, from where we're sitting, he's blocking our view of the trolley." The man reached the trolley and swayed over it. "What's he doing, Rick?" asked Angela.

"He must have come to the end of the can because he's squashing it now," replied Rick.

"Ah, yes," said Angela. "We can hear the crunch, and he's swearing."

The can clattered into the trolley, and Gary and Angela immediately opened the doors of the car. The drunk continued to sway over the trolley.

"What's happening?" asked Angela, frustrated at only having a back view of the man. She and Gary moved a leg carefully out of each side of the car. "Is he picking up the money?" she asked. She could see he was doing something with his hands but couldn't tell what.

"It's OK," came Rick's voice. "He's just getting another can out of his jacket."

As he spoke, Angela saw the drunk turn slightly. He got to work on the ring pull and brought the new can up to his mouth. She and Gary drew their legs back into the car and closed the doors silently. "All right, everybody, false alarm," she said, as they all watched the man move away from the trolley towards the supermarket, leaving the empty can in it with the manila envelope.

A different voice came on the radio: Jim. "I don't think that's a completely false alarm," he said.

"You're going to have to explain that," said Angela.

"I was keeping my eyes peeled," he replied. "When that drunk turned up and started swaying about, I think I saw something. It wouldn't have been in your and Gary's eyeline, Angie, because there are all those recycling bins between you and that part, but it looked to me like someone moved from behind the trees where the car park goes up the side of the shop. I couldn't make it out properly, but just as we realized that the man was a genuine drunk and he started moving on, the shadows went back to normal. I could be wrong, of course."

"I bet you're not," replied Angela. "He's got to be watching the trolley. He's got eight hundred reasons to see that nothing happens to it. OK, everybody. Let's settle down."

They didn't have long to wait. Fifteen minutes later, a man came walking across the car park, dressed in a fleece with the logo of the supermarket on the breast. He moved at a steady pace, giving the impression of a worker sent out to round up all the stray trolleys in the area. As he reached the trolley, he turned slightly to take hold of the handle, and they could see the ponytail hanging down his back. "Oh, yes. I think so," whispered Gary.

He and Angela opened their doors again and began to slide out of the car. "OK, everybody," she said into the radio, "Gary's given me the nod. Can you all see what's happening?" She received another chorus of answers and this time Jim and Rick appeared from behind the bus shelter. Derek and Leanne stood up and began to move in the same direction as the newcomer. "Gently does it," cautioned Angela. "We mustn't let that trolley out of our sight."

The "worker" glanced all around. He began pushing. But instead of heading for the trolley park by the main doors, he kept going towards the side of the building where the recycling bins stood – exactly where Jim had already thought he'd caught sight of him.

They followed him round the back. Several overflowing waste bins lined the service road behind the shop. He pushed the trolley away from him, moving into the pool of light shining down from the bulkhead lamp over one of the back doors. Rick, Jim, Leanne and Derek had all managed to hide behind the bins. Angela and Gary moved to stand behind one of several delivery vans parked along the road. Angela looked about, making a speedy reconnoitre. One end of the service road was covered by the team, but if the quarry turned out to be quick on his feet, the minute they approached he could sprint to the other end and disappear. She tapped Gary on the shoulder and, using hand signals, indicated the problem. He nodded to show he understood and she set off, moving stealthily behind the line of vans. Gary followed. Once in place, they poked their heads gingerly out from behind the last vehicle.

The would-be blackmailer was still absorbed in his task. Apparently savouring the moment, he slowly undid the flap of the envelope, the smile of anticipation on his face revealed in the lamplight. He peered into the envelope and punched the air in triumph. They all heard him say, "Yes!" and watched as he began to extract the notes. The money was in eight bundles of £100 each, in mixed denominations. Angela waited until he'd put two of them into his jeans' pocket before speaking into her radio.

"Gary and I are covering the far end of the road. Move in!"

Rick and Jim stepped out from behind their bin. "Police! We'll take that, thank you," said Rick.

The man's head jerked up, a horrified look on his face. He recovered from the shock and reacted very quickly. "No way, you filth!" he yelled, and tore off at a very impressive speed, straight towards Angela and Gary. Rick, Jim, Derek and Leanne chased after him, and he made the big mistake of concentrating more on his pursuers than who might be blocking his way ahead. Angela and Gary stepped out in front and straddled the narrow space. The man turned to face forward just at the same moment he banged into Angela. "Out of my way!" he shouted, as the collision checked his flight.

"I don't think so," said Angela. Whatever else she had been about to say died on her lips as she saw the man's hand dive into his pocket; a familiarly shaped object inside it suddenly pointed straight at her.

A pit opened at the bottom of her stomach but in the split second before she spoke, her only thought was a very pragmatic, *Oh no, not again.*

"OK, everybody, freeze!"

Instant stillness settled over the service road.

The man straightened up slowly. He waved the gun in his pocket to indicate she and Gary should move to one side. "Out of my way," he ordered.

Angela mingled silent prayers with a firm reassurance to herself: *This is not the same as last time; this is not the same as last time*. She looked at Gary and they cautiously began to move.

Angela remembered this feeling, this dryness of the mouth, the pit opening up in the stomach.

A fear like no other she'd ever experienced.

Nobody moved.

Time stood still.

Then Leanne suddenly came forward. Quickly she came right up to the man. "Don't worry, guv," she said, in an astonishingly normal tone. "He's not going to shoot you."

"Leanne! What are you doing? Don't try any heroics!" cried Angela, in a horrified voice. But as she spoke she immediately saw the shoulders of their quarry slump; a look of chagrin crossed his face. Leanne put her hand into his jacket. And pulled out a banana.

"You couldn't see it from your angle, guv," she said, with a grin. "But his pocket flops open a bit and I caught a glimpse from behind."

"We were held up by a man with a banana!" exclaimed Angela, in amazement. She burst into laughter, as much a reaction to the sudden horrific fear that had gripped her as to the humour of the moment. "Are we ever going to live this down?"

Jim, sarcastic smile on his face, stepped forward and grabbed the man's arm. "Very funny, sonny," he said. "Now it's our turn to take you for a ride."

"Oi! Get your hands off me! I ain't done nothing! This is police brutality, this is."

Jim brought him to a halt in front of Angela.

"We need to ask you a few questions," she said. "Do you have any ID on you?"

"I'm saying nothing."

"No matter," said Angela. "We'll sort everything out at the station." She looked across at the rest of her team.

"Do you want me to go and bring the car round, guv?" asked Derek.

Angela nodded at Leanne. *Derek got the opportunity to breathe the same air as his idol. Why shouldn't you get your chance to meet Brendan Phelan?* she thought. "You go, Leanne," she said. "Tell Brendan that he can now call Des to come back and get him. He's only parked round the nearest corner. Tell him we'll call on him tomorrow."

A broad smile stretched itself across Leanne's face. She even gave a small hop of excitement. "Righto, guv," she squeaked.

"Make sure you introduce yourself, or he might think you're a fan who's happened to recognize him in passing."

Beaming, Leanne set off. Even before she got to the corner of the road, they could see she'd pulled a comb out of her bag and was running it through her hair.

Angela turned back to the man they'd caught. The way Jim was holding him had pulled up the sleeves of his fleece and the hawk tattoos could clearly be seen. *Hey! Look at that ink*, she thought, experiencing a burst of excitement. She had to stop herself punching the air in a display of triumphalism as she met his resentful gaze. "Right, Mr Hawk-arms, would you like to explain about this £800 you're carrying?" she asked.

"How do you know it's – " He realized his mistake a split second too late. "I didn't know what was in the envelope. I just opened it out of curiosity. You're trying to trap me, that's what you're doing."

Why would we waste our time when you're already doing such an efficient job of it yourself? thought Angela. "It's a lot of money," she added. "You wouldn't earn that much, stacking shelves in there." She nodded towards the supermarket. "Shall we go in and have a word with the manager?"

"I don't work there," he said, and saw Angela's eyes move to the logo on his fleece. "I just borrowed this from a mate who does."

"So you borrowed the jacket so that you'd look like an employee here in order to pick up £800 in blackmail money."

"Who told you it's – ?" He stopped, a horrified look stealing over his face as he realized he'd trapped himself again.

So, thought Angela, *not the sharpest knife in the drawer. I expect you'll be the despair of the duty solicitor before we're all very much older, but that's not my problem.*

"What's your name?"

"Alex Lindsey."

Angela suddenly felt very sleepy. She nodded across at Rick. "Arrest him, Rick. We'll talk to him tomorrow at the station."

"Oi! What am I under arrest for?" he shouted. "Since when has it been a crime to find money in an envelope?"

"I'd do you for impersonating a shelf-stacker, but unfortunately it's not a crime," replied Angela. "Go on, Rick," she said. "Attempted blackmail; it's past my bedtime." Followed by Gary she walked along to the end of the building and reached the road. After a few moments' wait, Leanne rounded the corner in the HAT car and pulled up in front of them.

"Guv! Oh, guv," she breathed, as she got out and stood on the pavement.

"So you got to meet Brendan at last," smiled Angela.

"Oh, guv, yes! It was fantastic… magic. I don't know what to say. Thanks for sending me there."

A thought occurred to Angela. "I hope you didn't try to take a photograph of him or ask for his autograph."

Leanne giggled. "Give me some credit, guv. I'm a professional woman on duty."

"That's all right, then. He's a nice bloke, isn't he?"

"The tops; I can still hardly believe it. You'd never guess what he's done, guv."

Angela thought she probably could, but decided to let Leanne enjoy the telling of it anyway. "What's that, then?" she asked.

"Well, I knocked on the window and he opened the door and just for a second I thought I was going to wet myself. '*Get a grip, Leanne*,' I thought. So I said, 'Excuse me, Mr Phelan, I'm D.C. Leanne Dabrowska. I work with D.I. Costello. We've apprehended the man who came for the money and Inspector Costello says it's now OK for you to call your brother to come back with the car. You can go home and she'll be in touch tomorrow.'"

"Yes?"

"So he got out of the car and he said, 'Did you say, Leanne Dabrowska?' so I said, 'Yes' and, guv, he reached out and took my hand, like, in both of his. I thought, '*Now I really will wet myself*.' I could hardly believe it. *But then!* He put both his arms round me and hugged me. Me! Brendan Phelan had his arms round me!"

Angela smiled. "He knows it's you who found out about Kayleigh Joplin's death certificate, and broke the threat hanging over him."

"I was just doing my job, guv, but I'm really glad it was me doing that bit of it. He told me he's got another charity gig coming up soon." Leanne grinned. "To be honest, I already knew from his website. It's being set up because he had to pull out of the O2 one last week. He asked me to call his manager and get my name added to the list of his special guests. I can take a friend and we're going to have really good seats, *and* we're invited to the reception afterwards."

"That's wonderful. He's very grateful."

"*He's* grateful? Guv, I think I've died and gone to heaven."

Chapter Twenty-seven

When Angela, followed by Gary, walked into the interview room the next morning, she could see Alex had maintained his ill-humour overnight. A morose expression on his face, he slouched on his chair beside the pleasant fresh-faced duty solicitor assigned to him.

Angela introduced herself and Gary to the solicitor, and turned her attention to the accused. "Good morning, Mr Lindsey. I trust you slept well?"

"How could I, when I've been banged up all night? Wrongful arrest, that's what this is, and it's causing me stress. Stress can cause a lot of health problems – I hope you know that, because I'll be suing. You'll be hearing from my – " He glanced quickly at the young woman by his side. "From her," he said.

Angela's eyes briefly met the suggestion of a smile in the otherwise impassive gaze of the young solicitor, but remained silent. It wasn't her job to point out where the bailiwick of the duty solicitor began and ended. "OK, let's get on, shall we?" she said. She switched on the tape and spoke the necessary introduction. "Tell me how well you knew Oliver Joplin."

"What?" The question clearly surprised Alex. "Why do you want to know about him?"

"Arresting you last night for attempted blackmail is just part of a bigger picture."

"I don't know what you're talking about. And I wasn't trying to blackmail no one," he grunted.

"Mr Lindsey, you must surely be – " She stopped. "You might not be aware of this, but what happened last night arose directly as a result of our investigation into Oliver's death."

Alex sat up suddenly, a look of alarm on his face. "Oi! You ain't pinning that on me – no way! I've got nothing to do with Olly's death. We was mates."

In spite of having had a very refreshing night's sleep, Angela suddenly felt her energy drain a little. "Nobody's accusing you of killing him." She fixed his eyes with her own. "We're trying to find his killer. Have you got any idea how serious a matter it is to obstruct our investigation?"

Alex leaned back in his seat. "We've been mates since school."

Angela made a note. *Some people make deep and lasting friendships at school and even go on to build musical careers. Others do… other things*, she thought.

"Mr Lindsey, you were apprehended in possession of £800 which had, earlier in the day, been demanded as a blackmail payment."

"Was it?" he asked. "I just found it in the envelope."

"I believe you know it was. I believe you made the call for the money."

"I didn't make no call. And you had no right to take my phone from me last night. I'd better get it back in perfect working order, or else."

"Very well; would you like to explain what you were doing in that supermarket car park at midnight, wearing the uniform of one of the shop's employees?"

"I already told you. I borrowed the jacket from a mate. I was cold. Anyway, it's a free country. I can go where I like, day or night."

"You are aware that blackmail is a very serious crime?"

Alex shrugged, an insolent smile on his face. "Yeah, and you ain't pinning it on me; no way."

"What makes you so sure?"

His smile became smug. "Look, you can't pin it on me, all right? Can I go now? You've got nothing."

A wave of anger shot through Angela. *OK, Angie baby, go for it,* she thought. *See if you can smoke him out.* "You think you're going to get away with it because Olly could, is that it?"

"Of course." He stopped and blinked. "No! I don't know nothing about no blackmail. You're trying to trap me. Entrapment, that's what this is."

"I'd advise you to say nothing more, Mr Lindsey," said the solicitor. Angela sensed within her a slight distaste for her client.

Just at that moment, the door opened and Jim entered. Gary leaned over and advised the tape of this fact. "What is it, Jim?" asked Angela. For an answer, Jim leaned between her and Gary and put a sheet of paper on the table. She glanced down to where his finger was pointing, then looked back up at him, nodded, and explained what was happening for the benefit of the tape, finishing with, "Well done; thanks, Jim." Jim nodded and left the room. Angela turned back to Alex again.

"You might just as well tell us all about it," she continued, "because we know anyway."

"You know nothing and I'm saying nothing," insisted Alex.

"Yesterday evening at approximately nine-thirty you made a call to Brendan Phelan's mobile. I believe that you demanded he leave the money in the supermarket trolley, where you picked it up later."

"No, I never, and you can't prove it."

"We can prove you made the call," replied Angela, tapping the page on the desk. "What do you think this is?"

He shrugged again. "Dunno, some police harassment

document, I suppose; something to try and scare me into making a false confession."

I'm beginning to wonder if you should be allowed out on your own, thought Angela. Glancing quickly at the solicitor, she felt pretty sure the same thought was passing through the other woman's mind. "It's a printout of all the calls made from your mobile last night. It's very clear. You made the call to Brendan. It lasted three minutes."

"Oi! I never! That's a lie. You've planted that evidence." He leaned over the table. "There's no way you could have got that, 'cause I deleted everything!"

Silence.

Too late he realized, once again, that he'd trapped himself out of his own mouth. He looked aghast at Angela and didn't notice the solicitor turning her face to the wall, raising her eyebrows and blowing out her cheeks in disbelief.

"We didn't need to check your phone, Alex," said Angela. "We got in touch with your network provider this morning."

The sulky look returned. Alex threw himself back into his seat. "You can't do me for it, anyway," he mumbled.

"Oh, really, and why is that?" asked Angela, even though she was fairly sure she already knew the answer.

"He ain't going to press charges, is he? He can't afford to let this get out. Look how it's been for all those famous people getting done for sexual stuff – goes back years ago, some of it does. He won't say anything. He doesn't want his career ruined, does he?"

What a nasty parasite you are, thought Angela. "On the contrary," she said. "Brendan Phelan hasn't the slightest problem with the whole world knowing he had sex with Oliver's sister."

A flicker of uncertainty crossed Alex's features but he quashed it. "You're bluffing. You can't pull one over on me.

He'll soon change his tune."

"However," continued Angela, as if he hadn't spoken, "Oliver's sister might end up not only very embarrassed but facing serious charges as an accessory to blackmail if the story gets out."

The uncertain expression remained this time. Alex looked into Angela's face as if trying to gain some direction. "You're bluffing," he said again, but his voice lacked conviction.

"You know her as Kay, do you?" asked Angela.

Alex's puzzlement deepened. "Yeah, what of it?"

Angela leaned across the table. "Oliver didn't keep you fully in the loop, did he, Alex?"

"'Course he did. We was mates – partners."

Angela looked at him without speaking for a moment, to let the doubt settle in and take root. "Right, let's leave that for a minute. After all, if anybody's going to be prosecuted now, it'll be Katie, aka Kay. You trying to make the pick-up last night is just a footnote for a very nasty, sordid story."

Puzzlement creased Alex's forehead afresh. "Kay, prosecuted? She ain't done nothing. She's the one that had the trauma." He gained fresh energy. "He's been paying for causing her trauma all these years, that's all; only right, too, if you ask me."

"Look, I'm a busy woman, Alex. I'll just spell it out for you. I can assure you there'll be no prosecution for underage sex, but there may very well be one for blackmail, and it will be Oliver's sister, Katie stroke Kay, facing a serious charge." Angela let a moment pass. "Let me say again: blackmail is a very serious crime, Alex. And it carries serious consequences."

Alex licked his lips and studied Angela as he considered this. She could see his mind working, going over everything she'd said. He eventually arrived at her final comment. "Oi! No way! You're not bringing me into this. I was just helping out, just the once. I've had nothing to do with it all these years. I'm not going down for this!"

"I thought that's how it might be," replied Angela, with care. "We might be able to help you. But we can only do that if you cooperate with us."

"What d'you mean?"

"This partnership with Oliver; it involved the selling of tickets, didn't it?"

Alex started on his seat as if he would escape. He cast a frightened glance at the solicitor. "There's no law against touting," he said.

Angela paused to gather her thoughts. Alex Lindsey had no towering intellect and she wanted to be sure he grasped what she meant. Somebody had been trying to worm their way into Oliver Joplin's ticketing scam, and she hoped finding out the name of that person could crack open the murder case. "You're right, Alex," she replied, as if he'd made a very astute point. "It's not against the law. But selling fraudulent tickets is."

"I never sold duff tickets!"

"No." Angela kept her voice low and steady. "I wasn't accusing you of that."

"Everything I sold was kosher."

"Yes, I understand that, Alex. You're not in trouble for touting, but I need you to tell me how it worked."

"Olly gave me the tickets, didn't he? He's in the business, he's got contacts. He never had no trouble getting tickets."

Angela cast a glance at Gary, which he correctly interpreted. "I saw you selling tickets," he said, "at Hammersmith, before the show."

Alex gave forth a sound which could only be described as a chortle. "Ain't no point in selling them afterwards, is there?"

Angela and Gary laughed with him. "No, you've got me

there," acknowledged Gary. "So did you just stand out the front and wave your tickets around?" he asked, knowing this wasn't the case.

Alex sat up a little straighter in his chair and assumed the closest he'd come so far to looking businesslike. "It can't hurt Olly now," he said, "and it was a brilliant scheme. See, he'd know exactly how many tickets he'd sold through his program." Both police officers pricked their ears up at the mention of a "program", but didn't want to interrupt the flow. Angela quickly made a note and resumed her attentive expression. "So, like, he'd say to me, 'There are at least eight people coming tonight with duff tickets.'"

"At least?" queried Gary.

"Yeah, well. He would only know about the ones he sold through his program, but of course there could be others."

"Oh, of course."

"So, I watched," said Alex. "I'd see them try to get in and get turned away. They either looked really upset or angry, or both. I'd let them get out onto the pavement again, and they'd stand there wondering what they were going to do; then I'd go up to them."

Gary nodded. "A very simple operation."

"Where did he get the authentic tickets?" asked Angela.

Alex shrugged. "He had an allocation, being on the crew, like. Sometimes he could get them from other crew members who weren't going to be using theirs. He even bought them, proper-like, now and again."

"Did Brendan have any knowledge of this scam?"

"No way!" Alex seemed horrified at the thought.

"A nice little earner," said Angela. "Did he set up ticket selling websites?"

Alex nodded. "Yeah; he had to keep closing them down and starting again, mind, but that wasn't a problem 'cause he was really good at computer stuff. He developed a program. It was tops; reckoned he had a really good bargaining counter."

"Was he planning to sell it?"

A frown crossed Alex's features. "I don't know nothing about the business side of things. I just sold the tickets for him."

"But as his partner he must have discussed it with you," said Angela, hoping he'd fall for the blatant flattery.

Alex's glance, from under half-closed lids, suggested that he recognized the tactic. "Somebody was trying to buy him out. He told me he was getting emails that showed someone was on to him but he didn't know who they were. Whoever was behind the emails was close, though – he guessed that. He was ready for them because he'd hacked into other programs, and he said his was better. He wanted to do a deal. He'd only worked the scam on Brendan's concerts to see how it went, but he wanted to be part of a bigger outfit and he knew he had something to offer."

"Did he have this program on a disc?" asked Gary. This question was met with a sudden silence. A shadow passed across Alex's face, and he found something to absorb him in his fingernails. Angela and Gary looked briefly at each other. A memory rose up in Angela's mind and she wrote rapidly on her pad. Gary glanced at the words "flat-search, empty drawer" and nodded. "Alex?" asked Gary, after a few moments.

"Yeah, 'course he did, didn't he? Stands to reason don't it? If he was opening up and closing down websites, he had to be able to work the same program."

"Where is this disc now?" asked Angela.

Alex remained silent for several moments. "I don't know," he said, eventually.

"Did you ever have it?"

Another long pause followed. Angela recognized that

Alex's chief emotion at this point was embarrassment. "Yes," he said, finally.

Angela began to feel tired. "Where did you last have it?"

Alex studied his fingers again as he spoke. "In a pub near Ladbroke Grove."

"So what happened to it in this pub?" asked Angela, but she already had a suspicion she knew the answer.

Alex slapped the table in his frustration. "Look, I was trying to do the deal, wasn't I? Same with the blackmail," he added, forgetting his previous assertion that he knew nothing about it. "I was carrying on where Olly left off. He had it all sorted, Olly. He was *ace*, I'm telling you. He wanted to buy into a bigger outfit and I was trying to... I was doing it for Kay."

Angela and Gary looked at him in silence. They didn't need any explanation. Alex's complete inability to negotiate his way forward, to make any inroads into the world of organized crime, was plain to see. They ignored the final comment as a pathetic attempt to ascribe noble intentions to his underhand activities. "How did you set up this meeting in the pub?" asked Gary.

"I was rung up, wasn't I?"

I might have guessed, thought Angela. "Who did you meet?" she asked.

Alex looked at her and shrugged. "I don't know his name, but I saw him once on the tour. I was having a drink with Olly, and a load of people he knew came into the pub. He said they were part of the team. We didn't join them, though."

"So," said Angela. "Just to be clear; this man is connected with Brendan Phelan's tour team in some way, and he came to meet you in a pub?"

"Near Ladbroke Grove, yeah."

"And he now has the disc with Oliver's ticketing program on?"

"Yeah." Alex looked almost grateful that Angela didn't ask for details of how that had happened, but she didn't need to. *It must have been like taking candy from a baby,* she thought.

"And you don't know his name?"

"No, well, 'H' was all he said."

"The initial 'H'?"

"Yeah."

Angela sighed. *If I was a criminal mastermind and you wanted to be a part of my organization, I would recommend you go and find some gainful employment,* she thought.

"Right," she said. "We're going to show you some photographs. We want to know if you recognize this 'H'."

Chapter Twenty-eight

Stanway leaned his elbows on his desk and steepled his fingers as he listened to Angela. She'd recounted the outcome of the stake-out at the supermarket, brought him up to speed on what Gary had finally remembered, and put before him a scenario of how she thought the murder had been committed.

"Hmm… What you've said makes a great deal of sense, and I'll certainly get a search warrant organized for you. We'll need forensics on that, because it's going to be pretty specialized. Of course, if we find anything, we'll need DNA samples to compare."

"Yes, sir, I'm aware of that."

"OK, then." He beamed at her. "Good work, Angie."

Angela smiled back at him. "Do I sense a following 'but', sir?"

"You do. The scenario you've presented me with is ingenious and it works. It could even be the solution. *But.* If you're correct, we might be looking at a different motive from somebody merely trying to muscle in on the ticketing scam."

"Yes, I had thought of that."

Stanway looked down at Angela's open notepad on his desk. "As motives go, though, it's still the front runner and you've got to chase it up. And there's no question Joplin had come to the attention of some rival scammer."

"Or scammers, sir."

"Yes, indeed. Well, this Alex chap has definitely fingered one of the suspects, so we've got to follow it through. How much store do you set by this initial 'H'?"

"I think it's a bit like the flourish someone might add to a signature, sir, but it does tie up with my theory."

"Yes, I can see that it would, but we have to move with caution, Angie. Theories are wonderful things, but they aren't necessarily facts. You'll need to keep a very open mind on this."

"Don't worry, sir, I will."

"We don't know that 'H' is the perp."

"I'm aware of that, sir. We can only be sure of his involvement in the ticketing scam. We've still got most of the main players knocking about in the vicinity of the stage door at the time of the murder."

"Motives?"

"Hmm, that's a tricky one. Don Buckley has a bit of history from way back when his band was struggling to get established. Oliver latched himself on to them but used their gigs to peddle dope. It nearly ruined their fledgling career."

"So, an old score to settle there, maybe?"

"It's possible. The band seemed to have recovered from the scandal, and Don doesn't strike me as the vengeful type, but you can never tell. For all I know, Attila the Hun was kind to his granny."

"What about these two on the management team, Doug Travers and Jack Waring?"

"Protecting their star would be my first guess. Brendan was under the impression nobody knew about the blackmail, but Terry Dexter had found out about it – so why couldn't they, as well?"

"Yes, indeed; everybody not telling everybody else what they know, yet making plans to remove the threat. Are you assuming the same motive for Dexter?"

"Yes. He and Brendan go back a long way and their friendship is very deep-rooted. I should think he was the most aware of all of them about the strain this was having on Brendan. He probably felt very angry about it. I mean, it had affected Brendan's ability to write songs."

"It sounds as though things might have been coming to a head when the murder occurred."

"I think it's possible, sir. I reckon Brendan thought he'd spend the rest of his life paying for Oliver's silence. A status quo had been established he'd learned to live with. But if his music was suffering, then things couldn't go on as they had, could they?"

"And yet he would have seen no way out – the situation was hopeless. He couldn't possibly have foreseen Leanne finding out the truth behind that birth certificate."

Angela remained silent for a moment as she thought about this last point. "Are you saying I should keep Brendan on the suspect list, sir?"

Stanway rested his chin on his steepled fingers. "I think we've established he couldn't have actually pulled the trigger, but that doesn't mean he wasn't involved in a conspiracy to get rid of this particular thorn in his flesh." Angela's shoulders sagged and she let out a sigh. Stanway cast a quizzical expression at her. "Become smitten with the man, have we, Angie? I gather he can do no wrong in Leanne's eyes."

Angela grinned. "It's not that, sir, although I have to admit, I've warmed to him more each time we've had to go and see him. It's just – if you're right – who was in on it? One of them? All of them? What a nightmare to try to untangle."

Stanway laughed and tapped Angela's notebook. "Well, it looks to me like you've got your work cut out with these latest developments. You and Gary can chase them up while the rest of the team tries to unearth a plot with Brendan Phelan at the centre of it." He closed the book and handed it to her.

"I'll let you know when the warrant is in place, and I'll set up the search team."

Thank you, sir," replied Angela, taking her notebook and heading towards the door.

"By the way, Angie…"

Angela stopped and turned back. "Sir?"

"Another thing we mustn't forget; this murder was a shooting and we've got a recent unfortunate history with guns, haven't we?"

After the clutch of fear she'd felt when she thought Alex Lindsey had a gun, Angela hardly needed reminding of that previous investigation when an unstable and desperate suspect had taken a shot at her.

"Yes, sir."

"This isn't just one poor, deluded man pointing a pistol. Most of our suspects in this case are very familiar with the use of firearms. Some of them even have prizes to prove it."

"You're right, sir, but the real guns are all locked away somewhere."

"I know I'm right and I don't care how secure they are. Once we're satisfied about the evidence we will move with extreme caution and we *will* have an armed response unit standing by."

"Sir."

Stanway gave a small grin and nodded. "That last 'do' could have gone so wrong for us. I'm not taking any chances."

"Understood, sir."

"What are the team doing this morning?"

"They're all going out on a DNA hunt."

"Yes, of course; you'll need matches, won't you? OK, then, Angie. Keep me in touch," he finished by way of dismissal.

Back in the incident room she took the team through the morning briefing, gave them their instructions and passed on

Stanway's cautionary advice. "Any questions?" she asked, after she'd finished.

Leanne frowned. "Suppose someone doesn't want to give us a swab, guv?" she asked.

"They have the right to refuse, of course," replied Angela. "But given that they're all in the frame, the person refusing would only be directing a spotlight onto themselves. I think they'll all cooperate."

"No problem, guv," said Leanne, rising from her chair. "I think Brendan and his team will be rehearsing this charity gig."

"The one you've got special guest tickets for?" said Jim, with a grudging smile. Leanne blushed and couldn't help giving a self-satisfied smirk. "How're you going to get his sample, then?"

"OK, everybody," Angela cut in; she could see the conversation deteriorating. "You all know what you're supposed to do. Rick and Jim, you chase up Don Buckley and his band. Derek and Leanne, get over to wherever the rehearsals are going on and ask Brendan and his lot. If anybody refuses to cooperate, don't insist, just tell me about it."

They all got up and went to get their coats. Within five minutes, Angela and Gary were the only two people in the room.

He looked at her. "So what do you want me to do, Angie?"

"We're going to go over everything we've got so far, Gaz. I think this is as watertight as it can be without the forensic findings, but I need to be sure."

"So we've got a brainstorming session, then?"

"Not immediately."

"Oh, really?"

"Yes," she smiled at him. "I've got a loose thread hanging on this case and it's annoying me. Before we do anything else," she drew a small plastic wallet out of her bag, "we're going to watch a DVD of *Fantasia*."

Jack Waring stood just behind the glass-panelled front doors of the Apollo theatre in Hammersmith, gazing out at the street, so lost in his own thoughts he didn't hear the approach of Barry Grieves. He jumped slightly at the sound of Barry's cough, looking round and nodding in acknowledgment of the other man before turning back to his contemplation of the scene before him.

"How are the rehearsals going?" asked Barry.

"OK." Jack shrugged, then thought about what he'd said. "Actually, more than OK."

"Oh, really?"

"Yes, Brendan's in really good form and that's making for a good atmosphere."

"Is he not normally in good form, then? He's never struck me as one of these prima donna types."

"No, he's not. He's pretty stable, is Bren, but he's firing on all cylinders today. I can't remember the last time I saw him so buoyant."

"That's good." Barry stood facing the same direction as Jack. "Not a view with which you're familiar, I should think," he said, after a moment.

"True," replied Jack, turning his attention upwards towards the flyover passing above them a short distance away. "I don't often come front of house; too busy backstage, usually, especially at show time. How did Georgia Pensay do?"

"Very well. We had full houses every night."

"Lot of cowboys turning up?"

Barry laughed. "Not exactly, but I did see quite a few obvious country and western types. Watching the audience arrive never ceases to fascinate me," said Barry. "I watch them meet and greet and queue and wait. You really do see some strange sights."

"You get some pretty weird happenings at the stage door as well." Jack checked himself. "I don't mean like the recent event."

"I know what you mean," said Barry. "And I suppose you must, fans trying all sorts of tricks to get in and things like that." Just at that moment he became aware that one of his staff had approached with two other people. He turned. "Are you looking for me? Oh, hello," he added, as he recognized Leanne and Derek. "You have some more questions?"

"Yes, sir," replied Derek. He looked at Jack. "We need to have a word with you, Mr Waring," he said.

Jack raised his eyebrows and moved away from the front doors. "Let's go backstage," he answered. "I think better there, where I belong. See you, Barry," he said, as he led the way through the auditorium in the direction of the pass door. The noise from Brendan, the musicians and the backing singers working on one of the songs made conversation impossible, but Jack led them to the empty green room behind the stage and they were able to put their request.

"DNA?" he queried, once he'd heard them out. "May I ask why? Olly was shot, by all accounts, from a bit of a distance. I don't see how DNA samples are going to help you."

Leanne took refuge behind her junior rank. "I'm sorry, sir, it must be something to do with the way the investigation has progressed, but you'll need to ask D.I. Costello if you want any further information."

Jack shrugged and smiled. "It's no problem," he replied. "It just seems a bit bizarre, that's all. Do you want to do everybody?"

"Yes, we're afraid so," said Derek.

"OK, start with me and I'll go and round up the others," said Jack.

Leanne thanked him and Derek started to unpack the kit they'd brought with them.

Don Buckley blinked as he looked at Rick and Jim. It seemed he didn't know whether to be amused or annoyed by their request. "You mean, like a lock of my hair, something like that?"

"It's more usual to take a swab from the inside of the cheek," said Rick.

"Yes, but I was there, wasn't I?" said Don. "I came out of the stage door first and went over to Brendan. Then I got a chair, a coat and a drink for him. I passed Olly lying on the ground a few times. I mean, my DNA's bound to be somewhere around at the scene."

"Yes, sir," said Rick. "We know that, and obviously it will be taken into consideration."

"This is for elimination purposes," added Jim.

"Well, I suppose if you must," answered Don, finally. "I think I'm damned if I do and damned if I don't."

"You do have the right to refuse," said Jim.

"I know that and I refer you back to what I just said."

"Thank you for your cooperation, sir," replied Rick. "It really is a very simple procedure."

Chapter Twenty-nine

Stanway addressed the entire team the following morning. He faced them all with a grave expression and made it very clear they should all listen closely. "You've all done a thorough job," he said. "And we've got a case that hangs together very well. I fully expect we'll be winding it up today at this place." He looked across at Angela. "Where is it, Angela?"

"The Apollo theatre, sir, in Hammersmith."

"But I understood Brendan Phelan and this other band are rehearsing. Don't show business people usually rehearse in some obscure, out-of-the-way place?"

"That's often the case, but Georgia Pensay has just finished there and it's dark again until next week. That's why it's available for this charity gig."

"Dark. I see. Yes." Stanway didn't ask for an explanation of what "dark" meant. Angela hid a smile as she caught a look at Jim and realized he had been hoping for an appearance of bewilderment on the D.C.I.'s face, so he could jump in and enlighten him. "Well, anyway, we were caught on the hop on the last case. Angela ended up facing a crazed man with a gun." He looked round at them all to make sure they were each paying attention. "This *will not* happen again." A general murmur of assent could be heard from all points around the room. "That could so easily have gone very, very wrong, and the ramifications would be with us still."

It suddenly struck Angela that the dramatic final scene in the Kirsty Manners case might have caused Stanway more sleepless nights that it did her.

Jim, rushing in, somewhat foolishly, it seemed to Angela,

spoke: "This isn't the same, though, is it, sir? The guns used in this show are all stage guns with blanks in."

Stanway glared at him. "Have you been following this case at all, Wainwright? Brendan Phelan and his bass guitarist, or whatever he is, might amuse themselves taking potshots at clay pigeons in the home counties, but they – and from what I gather, the majority of the people around them – are all very familiar with real firearms of all types; what's more, they're all crack shots. And do I have to remind you how the victim died? A real gun was in the theatre that night, and there could be one today."

Jim blushed and lowered his eyes. "Sorry, sir."

"I should think so too!" Stanway paused, and calmed down a little. "I know I might seem oversensitive about this, but you weren't in that room when Angela got shot at. I was. I can still go into a cold sweat at the memory. I'm not leaving anything to chance."

"Sir."

Stanway addressed the room again. "So there will be an Armed Response Unit in attendance. You will all wait for instructions from either Angela or me. Nobody is to even think an independent thought without the say-so of either one of us. Is that clear?" Another general murmur of assent travelled the room. "Are there any questions?"

"These ARU people, sir," asked Derek. "Where will they be stationed?"

"You won't see them but they'll be at strategic places around the auditorium. A staff meeting for all personnel, on some pretext or other, took place just a short while ago in the bar. This was to keep everybody out of the way while they were introduced into the place. As far as is possible, staff are to be given duties which will keep them away from the auditorium, but if any one of them should spot a man with a gun, the line is that police are in control of the situation and they must keep quiet on pain of immediate dismissal. But," he added, raising a finger, "you must act as if they're not present. All right, everyone. Let's get going."

The mood in the car on the way to the theatre was sombre. Stanway was obviously nervous and disinclined to speak. When they arrived they could see that a handful of fans had got news of who was rehearsing within. A barrier had already been erected to prevent them spilling across the entire pavement and obstructing passers-by. They cheerfully joked and gossiped, swapping "Brendan" stories among themselves. As the police moved into the theatre, Angela could hear the fans speculating who the newcomers might be.

Inside, a rather flushed Barry Grieves met them. "Good morning," began Angela. She indicated Stanway at her side. "This is Detective Chief Inspector Stanway."

Barry nodded at Stanway.

"Is everyone in place?" asked Stanway.

"Yes, the last of them got into position about five minutes ago," answered Barry.

"And nobody on your staff or any of the performers are aware of their presence?"

"Not apart from my immediate deputy, and I hope none of them have a reason to find out," Barry assured him. "But I must say, Inspector," he added, "I think this is all rather dramatic."

"I prefer to be accused of overdramatization before an event, than negligence afterwards," replied Stanway, unmoved. Barry had clearly been ready to further his protest, but he bit back whatever response he'd planned and merely nodded.

"All right," continued Stanway. "Let's just forget about the invisible company, shall we? We're a team of police officers who need to speak to those people currently rehearsing in this theatre. Lead on, please."

Barry led them through to the back of the auditorium.

The noise hit them immediately. They stopped and took in the scene. Among the few people sprawled in the front few rows, Angela recognized Jack Waring and Doug Travers, and she saw Carla move out from the wings to settle in the seat beside Jack. Don and his band sat close to each other, absorbed in the music. All the action, and the sound, came from the stage. Brendan, in his element, belted out a very lively song, a tale of love lost and found. He pranced about the stage, holding the microphone close to his lips, throwing it high and catching it again. He smiled with obvious pleasure, and the upbeat melody infected everyone on stage with him. Feet tapped, hands clapped, heads nodded in time with the music and a smile could be seen on everyone's faces.

"Looks like we're being treated to an impromptu concert," remarked Stanway, putting his mouth close to Angela's ear.

"Not so impromptu, sir," replied Angela. "This is a rehearsal, after all."

"What? Oh – oh, yes of course," he murmured. Angela looked and saw that his hands were jigging about in time to the beat. She looked to her other side and saw that Barry Grieves was caught up in the performance as well. Just at that moment he turned and saw her looking at him. He grinned.

"This is a new song," he said, leaning slightly over to her. "Jack told me this morning that Brendan hasn't written anything new for quite some time, but he's got his mojo back now. That's what he told me. I didn't realize it had gone. He's written a cracker here, though, hasn't he?" Angela nodded; she could only agree.

The song had none of Brendan's hallmark use of gunshots and whip cracks. Instead, an intricate and cheery riff cut across the melody at the end of a verse. They'd obviously already had a few teething problems with the timing because once the melody had been played right through, Angela and the others could see them smiling, nodding to one another and even heard a cry of: "Yay! Got it!" Brendan beamed round at them all, and threw the microphone up into the air again, gleefully giving them all a thumbs-up before catching it in the few seconds before the song continued and he started on the next verse.

Barry recognized the moment when the song began to wind down to its close. He moved down the centre aisle, half-turned and indicated with a gesture that the others should follow him. As the music came to a complete halt, his was the voice that could be heard in the silence. "Mr Phelan, Mr Waring, I'm sorry to interrupt this rehearsal, but the police have made a request to come and speak to you all."

Brendan put the microphone back into its stand and came to the edge of the stage. He peered out into the semi-darkness. "Inspector! How nice! And D.Cs Gary and Leanne – good to see you." He spoke into the microphone. "OK, let's take a break, everybody." He then leaned down as Angela and Gary reached him. "Have you got everything sorted?"

"We think so. We need to address those who were in the area of the stage door at the time Oliver was shot."

"OK, well Doug and Jack are already here." He looked round and saw Terry bending over the keyboard. "Terry," he called. Terry looked up and Brendan inclined his head towards Angela and Gary. "Police business, mate." Terry nodded, made his way to the front and jumped lightly down into the auditorium, followed by Brendan. Carla, looking wide-eyed and slightly apprehensive, made to rise from her seat beside Jack.

"Is this a private party?" asked Jack.

"Not especially," replied Angela. Carla smiled at Jack and sat down again.

Angela looked around. Apart from themselves and Barry Grieves, who'd placed himself a few rows back, the place seemed deserted. She found it difficult not to strain her head and try to search out at least the shape of a gunman hiding in the shadows.

With an effort she kept her eyes on the small gathering. "This has been a really tricky case," she began. She saw Brendan and Terry glance at each other and away again. Doug looked at Jack but the latter kept his eyes front, intent on Angela. Don sat just along the row from Terry and Brendan, and kept his head down. Carla gazed with undisguised longing at Brendan.

"It hasn't been a picnic for us, either," remarked Don.

Angela nodded. "I'm sure not. You were all in the vicinity of the stage door when Oliver Joplin was shot and you all, naturally, came into the frame for his murder. You, Don, have a history with Oliver. He nearly scuppered your band once before, didn't he?"

Several heads turned in Don's direction. Don looked up. "Yes. If I was the vengeful sort, I'd have a motive."

Brendan raised his eyebrows. "Even me? You surely can't ascribe a motive to me?"

"It's true you probably couldn't have fired the shot," she smiled. "We worked on that scenario. But you could have been involved in a conspiracy, Brendan."

This consideration clearly hadn't occurred to Brendan. He narrowed his eyes as he thought about it. "D'you know, you're right? I suppose I could have."

A horrified gasp escaped Carla. Jack laid a restraining hand on her knee and spoke. "Why on earth would Brendan want Olly dead?" he asked. "He wasn't *that* bad a techie." A ripple of nervous laughter ran through the group. Angela smiled to acknowledge the joke, inclined her head towards Brendan and raised her eyebrows.

Brendan nodded. "It's OK," he said. "I would have told them at some point anyway."

"Oliver Joplin had set Brendan up, several years ago. He and his sister arranged a situation that made it look as though Brendan had committed a crime. Brendan can give you the details later if he wants to. But suffice it to say, if this 'crime'" – Angela sketched quotation marks in the air – "had become known, he would have faced a severe penalty, his career would probably be in ruins and he would have been publicly disgraced."

Doug and Jack looked at her with almost identical shocked expressions. "Blackmail?" ventured Doug. Angela nodded. Doug turned and looked at Terry. "Did you know about this?" he asked. Terry nodded.

Jack gave a low whistle. "No wonder he had a guaranteed place on the crew."

"Not just that," said Brendan. "He was on a nice little kickback. He had me over a barrel."

"Happily," continued Angela, "the investigation exposed this lie and there's no possible danger to Brendan from this matter."

"Ah!" Doug slapped his forehead. "No wonder you've been so buoyant the last couple of days."

"And he's started writing songs again," added Terry, with a grin.

Doug thought for a moment. "Yes, I hadn't really thought... I hadn't; I mean you've got so much stuff you wrote years ago that you can use, I hadn't stopped to think." He ground to a halt and gave a shiver. "The bastard!"

"Yes. Sadly, Oliver doesn't leave any fond memories with most of those who knew him," said Angela. "His sister appears to be cut from the same cloth. This case really has turned the normal perception of 'victim' and 'abuser' on its head. If

Brendan decides to press charges, she's going to find herself in deep doo-doo."

"I probably won't in the end," said Brendan. "But I shall certainly leave her to sweat for a while."

An uncomfortable look appeared on Doug's face and he turned back to Brendan. "OK, so I can see why the police would think Olly's murder could have been a conspiracy, Bren, but... you didn't – did you?"

"No way! I'm strictly a clay pigeon man," Brendan assured him. Doug nodded and passed his gaze on to Terry.

Angela could almost see the thoughts going through his mind. "We had to consider all these options," she said. "Was Brendan involved? Did Terry fire the actual gun? As I said earlier, you were all there at the scene. We had to look at motives for all of you. Terry, you and Brendan go back a long way; you're like brothers. You could see the torment Brendan was in, and you knew it was getting worse."

Terry looked at her, his face solemn. "Don't think I didn't consider it once or twice."

"I don't know what motives the rest of us could have had," said Doug. "We didn't know anything about the blackmail."

"Ah, but blackmail wasn't Oliver's only sideline," answered Angela. "He'd started out on a brand-new venture; ticket fraud."

"Ticket fraud!" exclaimed Brendan. "No! Was he ripping off my fans?"

"Brendan really cares about his fans," murmured Carla. Brendan looked across at her.

"Yes, that's exactly right," affirmed Angela. "He might not have had much of a reputation among you all as a techie but he could definitely find his way round a computer when it suited him. He'd launched a two-pronged attack on your audience, Brendan. He'd developed a program which duped people into buying fraudulent tickets and then, on the relevant nights, knowing how many he'd sold, a friend of his, acting as a tout, approached the disappointed fans and offered them proper tickets at inflated prices. That little scam ran like a dream. My detective constable here watched it in action on the night of the murder. But, unfortunately for Oliver, this proved to be his undoing. He'd brought himself to the attention of a much bigger operation and they didn't want him getting in their way."

Brendan clicked his tongue. "I suppose it would be naive of me to pretend it doesn't happen."

Angela nodded at him and continued. "Oliver's computer contained enough information to give our IT people and our financial investigators plenty to keep them occupied. They're still at it, in fact, but we have enough to go on."

"Just a minute," interrupted Doug. "Are you saying the murder is linked to some ticketing scam?"

"Partly," replied Angela.

"Partly?" Doug looked puzzled, then shook his head as if to clear it. "But…" Doug looked all around at the assembled company. "We're a fairly tight-knit group so it's… it's one of us."

"That's the conclusion to which our enquiries have led us," answered Angela. *There you go, Angela,* she thought. *You've gone all formal.* Doug nodded and leaned back in his seat. He'd turned a little pale.

Angela continued. "It was a question of gathering everything we could to build up a picture. We had no way of knowing if the guilty party was jogging along in the centre of the pack, keeping his – or her – head under the radar; or pushing themselves well into the limelight so we'd be used to their presence and stop noticing it. Different things work for different people."

"Brendan's the only one in the spotlight around here," smiled Jack, "and, perhaps, Terry."

Angela turned her attention to him. "Actually, you're wrong, you know. Brendan's place in the spotlight is only on stage. As a character he's quite self-effacing. He's made it as a celebrity and he doesn't need to over-egg it." She moved towards Jack. "You're the one who looms large."

Jack smiled. "Come again?"

"You might think you're one of the backroom boys, unnoticeable, but we kept finding evidence of your influence everywhere. You probably got into the way of it in your magician days; being seen without being seen, if you get me."

Jack smiled and shook his head. "You're going to have to explain that to me."

"I think you know what I mean, but I'll indulge you. In the first place, my detective constable here got that tune stuck in his head. I had to put up with it every day for quite a while."

Jack laughed. "I know the one you mean. I'm always humming it. I don't even know I'm doing it."

"Possibly not, but I got stuck with it," she said. "It bugged me until my family reminded me it came from Walt Disney's film, *Fantasia*."

"Among other places," replied Jack.

"You're right. It's called 'The Sorcerer's Apprentice'. I've only just learned that Goethe wrote the original poem and Paul Dukas produced the music about a hundred years later. Walt Disney used several classical pieces in the making of that film." She paused. "It's barely a step from sorcerer's apprentice to magician's lad."

"What are you saying?"

"This melody wasn't the only way in which I sensed your influence. All the crew members can perform at least one card trick. I wouldn't be surprised if one or two of them can produce coins from behind the ears of anyone they're talking to, and I'm sure there's someone here who, if pushed, can get a rabbit out of a hat."

A small laugh could be heard among several of those present. Jack grinned. "Yes, well, it's no secret. They've been good pupils on the whole. It's how I started in the business; I like to keep my hand in."

"Yes. You used all the techniques, Jack – sleight of hand, diverting attention. But you pulled off the big one right under the eyes of my detective constable."

"Hey! I hope you're not accusing me of this murder."

"No, but you cleverly deflected our attention at the time. And you know what? You almost succeeded. You're quite a magician."

Jack frowned.

"You talked about every trick in the book, Jack, but after our first meeting you didn't once mention this one." Angela turned her head and looked pointedly at Carla. "The girl in the box."

Chapter Thirty

Slowly Angela moved her attention to Carla, sitting wide-eyed beside Jack, shrinking back as far as she could into her seat.

"Jack! What shall I do, Jack?" Jack moved an arm round Carla's shoulders as tears welled up in her eyes and her face crumpled.

"You did it, didn't you, Carla?" said Angela. "You finally realized Oliver would never be your ticket to getting together with Brendan. Did he promise you'd get your chance with him before the end of the tour? Was it like that, Carla?" He'd been stringing you along, hadn't he? Using you for sex himself and not giving you what you wanted. You thought he supplied Brendan with young women, didn't you?"

Out of the corner of her eye she saw Brendan jerk his head up and heard a gasp of amazement from him. She pressed on. "You wanted to punish him, Oliver, for his deception, didn't you?"

In a flash Carla leapt out of her seat. "He promised!" she shouted. "He said he could make Brendan do whatever he wanted. I knew he was blackmailing him and I hated him for it. He said he had him in his pocket!" Suddenly she stumbled her way to the edge of the seats and started up the side aisle. She had on a short denim jacket and as she raced away they all saw her put her hand into one of its pockets. Halfway up the auditorium she turned and stopped. The metal in her hand glinted into the overhead lights.

"She's got a gun. Everybody down!" Stanway's voice came sharp and authoritative. Even as she ducked down before the front row, Angela couldn't help registering the slight note of satisfied vindication in his voice.

"I did it for us, Brendan!" Carla sobbed. They could all hear the desperation and hysteria in her voice. Angela looked along the row to where Brendan was lying, saw him glance at Terry next to him, saw the look of hopeless pity in his face.

"Carla!" Stanway's voice rang out again from behind the safety of one of the speakers at the side of the stage. "There is an armed response unit in this theatre. I suggest you put the gun down and hand it over to one of the officers."

"What?" On that single word Carla sounded suddenly weak and vulnerable. Angela gingerly raised her head above the level of the back of the seat. The young woman stood halfway along the centre aisle. A sob escaped her, tears streamed down her face and she looked very much like the teenager she tried so hard to be. Three tall shapes stood at intervals along the back of the auditorium. Each of them held an automatic rifle pointing in her direction. Slowly, Carla turned and saw them. She gave another sob as she realized she was trapped.

She raised her gun high so they could all see it before she threw it away from her, among the rows of seats. Then she turned and raced down to the front towards Brendan.

"I did it for us, Bren!" she repeated. "I rescued you, so you would be grateful and fall in love with me. I knew how much he was getting to you. I had to do something so you and me could be together and be happy, like we're meant to be! I know I can make you happy. I just needed the chance to show you. Then you'd see. You'd know too. But he refused me that chance. He refused me my destiny. I saved you, Bren!" She crumpled in a heap at his feet and the sound of her sobbing was the only noise in the shocked, stunned silence.

Angela looked across at Leanne and nodded, but even as Leanne moved towards Carla, Brendan stood up and gently raised her up with him. A long procession of young women who thought they were the only ones who could make him happy had provided good training for this moment. "Carla, I had no idea how you felt. But what you did was wrong; very, very wrong. Come on," he soothed. "Nobody can make someone else love them. This can't be."

Carla continued to sob, but more quietly now. She leaned in towards Brendan and he put his arms round her. "Oh, Carla," he whispered, in a tone she'd probably longed to hear from him. "It's all over now. You're going to have to go with Leanne." He looked at Leanne over Carla's head and nodded. Leanne disengaged Carla and led her away.

Angela turned back to Jack. "You were very close to her, weren't you?"

Jack opened his eyes wide. "Yes. I'm friends with her dad. I look out for her. I… I don't know what to say."

"Spare me," replied Angela, with disdain. "We both know she didn't do this alone. You're an accessory, Jack, before, during and after the fact."

"You'll have trouble proving it."

"I don't think so. And I won't have any trouble proving who was behind the ticketing scam." She saw a momentary flicker of acknowledgment behind his eyes before his face hardened into impassivity. "Oh yes, we've got enough to go to court." She looked towards Barry Grieves, who'd risen from his seat and was approaching her down the centre aisle. "You and your partner," she said. "You had a prime position, didn't you, Mr Grieves, standing in the foyer night after night, looking out at all the punters arriving, watching the touts go into action, noticing a system that worked slightly differently from the others?"

A look of alarm crossed the manager's face. "I had nothing to do with the murder," he said.

"I'm sure not," she assured him. "That was something strictly between Carla and Jack. She, because – well, we all know her motive, don't we?" She glanced back to the production manager. "You played on that, didn't you, Jack? You played on her obsession with Brendan and ultimately used it to get rid of your business rival." A flash of anger appeared in his eyes. She nodded. "Yes, it should have worked like magic, shouldn't it? But at the end of the day, it's all trickery and you forgot that, didn't you? I worked out the final flourish, by the way. 'H' for Houdini." Angela looked over to Jim and Rick and nodded. "You arrest him," she said, turning away. "I've got a very nasty taste in my mouth."

Some days later, Angela and Patrick entered the secluded room of a restaurant a short distance from the Apollo. Like Leanne, she and her team had been given guest tickets for Brendan's charity concert and they'd decided to have dinner together first, as a way of celebrating a successful outcome to the case.

"Hey! It's the boss-lady," said Rick. He stood up and leaned over to the two empty places with a bottle of wine. "Red or white?"

"Red for me, please, Rick," answered Angela, relinquishing her coat into the waiter's care and making for one of the empty seats.

Once the order had been taken and everybody had a drink, Stanway stood up. "Before everyone gets a little merry," he said. "I would like to propose a toast. Actually, it's not a proper toast but I just want to say, 'Well done, all of you.' In following the trail of the murder you've uncovered two other very nasty crimes and I'm proud of you." They all raised their glasses and a general murmur of "Cheers" and "Thank you, sir" could be heard echoing around the table. Stanway turned towards Angela. "Sterling work, Angela; I have just one question."

"Sir?"

"When we were involved in the mopping-up operation, I asked you how you fixed on Jack Waring at the end."

"Yes, I remember."

"You said that young man, Alex Lindsey, had fingered him as the man he'd given the disc to. That tied up with the ticketing scam, but you also said some 'eureka' moment for Gary blew the case open for you, showing you he couldn't have done the actual deed. What was that all about?"

"Ah yes." Angela looked round at them all. "You've all seen the mock-up of the scene and the photographs, so picture this; the night of the murder, right?"

"Right," came the chorus.

"Gary hears the shot and goes rushing along to the stage door where he sees Brendan Phelan standing rigid and shocked and Oliver Joplin lying on the ground, dead. There's a van almost blocking the stage door and a flight case on the pavement, waiting to be loaded onto the van."

"It was full of equipment to be taken to the O2 for the charity gig," said Gary.

"Almost immediately it starts to get very confusing. Don Buckley comes out of the theatre and is quite helpful; then a small crowd of other people turn up, who aren't."

"Mucho confusion," murmured Rick.

"You're not kidding," added Gary, in a loud whisper.

"One of the other people turning up at that point is Jack Waring, pushing another flight case bound for the O2 and Gary, who's on the phone to me at this moment, breaks off in the middle of our conversation and tells him to take it away again as he's contaminating a murder scene. Gary then doesn't take a lot of notice, his attention comes back to our conversation and he also has to sort out a local CID officer who comes along to help secure the scene and then there's all the argy-bargy of the rest of us turning up and getting on with things."

"Quite a night, as I recall," said Gary.

"Absolutely. Well, here's where Jack was so cool. The original flight case was, in fact, empty. Carla, hidden under a couple of bin bags and a lighting gel on top of the van, killed Oliver and immediately jumped straight down into it, pulling the lid closed over her."

"That's the noise that I thought was the stage door banging to," said Gary.

"So, as she's hiding in there, all the kerfuffle starts and Jack turns up with the second flight case which he's ordered to remove."

"Ah!" said Patrick. "This is where the legerdemain comes into play."

"Yes, Paddy; you're right. In the few seconds Gary's attention was deflected, Jack moved the new flight case into position behind the van and pushed the original one away."

"So removing the murderer from the scene! Oh, how neat." Stanway nodded. "You can almost admire the man's colossal cheek, can't you?"

"Almost," agreed Angela.

"Why wouldn't Brendan have seen what was going on?" asked Derek.

"Carla knew how wound-up Brendan got whenever he had to have one of these meetings," replied Angela. "Oliver had told her – had boasted to her, probably – about how he'd got one of our biggest pop stars in the palm of his hand, and he'd become increasingly stressed by the whole blackmailing business. Well, we saw how shocked he was when we arrived, didn't we?" Angela turned to Gary, who nodded. "I don't think Brendan was up to noticing anything beyond his own emotions at that point. In any case, even if he saw the shot fired he wouldn't have been able to positively identify Carla. She would have just been a shape on top of the van that disappeared very quickly. And the noise he thought he might have heard he assumed to be the stage door banging shut as well."

"Yes," objected Stanway, "but you still haven't explained how you realized all this."

Angela looked at Gary. "Go on, Gary, you tell them."

"That's the 'eureka' moment. It was almost subliminal," said Gary. "I didn't realize I'd even seen anything until Derek and I did that mock-up and I just couldn't get hold of the memory until I saw Patrick wheeling the hostess trolley across his dining room floor, and then it hit me. When Jack Waring pushed that flight case over to the van he huffed and puffed a bit and it slewed about a bit because of its weight. They can be worse than supermarket trolleys to manoeuvre. He certainly had difficulty controlling it – not surprising when we looked later and saw it full of heavy-duty cables and stuff. I just caught the tail end of him pushing the 'same' case back into the theatre and this time it was gliding smoothly across the pavement."

"This one just contained a slip of a girl," said Angela. "Carla Paterson, five feet two inches and all of seven stone, if that."

"Of course... a girl in a box," said Patrick.

"Exactly," replied Angela. "And she obligingly left us quite a bit of DNA in that box for us to find."

"Including one of those false fingernails," said Gary.

"Even so," said Rick, "he took a risk."

"Yes, a fairly small one, though. As the production manager, he could probably assign everyone jobs that would keep them out of the area of the stage door."

"Yes, but people don't always do what they're supposed to, do they?" countered Rick. "He couldn't guarantee nobody wouldn't nip out for a crafty cigarette or a breath of air."

Gary nodded. "I expect he'd factored that in and could deal with something like that. But it was a sheer fluke that I was in the audience that night and just happened to be hovering around those gates at the relevant time. He had no way of knowing I'd be so distracted and turn away to try to block out the noise as he wheeled the flight case back inside. That's when it got very chancy."

"He certainly kept his cool," said Angela. "It's a shame about the criminal bent, because he's someone you'd want on your side in a difficult situation."

"And," Stanway beamed round at them all, "I was totally justified in calling in the Armed Response Unit." So pleased was he with himself, he didn't notice all his fellow diners were avoiding each other's eyes and trying not to laugh as the risible image of Alex Lindsey's arrest swam into view. They'd all got a great deal of mileage out of this episode, and the mere mention of guns or firearms set them off again. That briefly tense and dramatic moment at the back of the supermarket had become known as the "Loaded Banana Showdown", and after a very slight wrangle with her conscience, Angela had decided not to include this detail in the report of the incident.

It would remain their little secret.

Acknowledgments

Although the Apollo theatre at Hammersmith is a real place, I would like to make it clear that all characters in this novel are fictitious. Where I have depicted members of the staff they have no bearing on, or connection with, the actual personnel of the theatre.

I'm also very grateful to the team at the Eventim Apollo, Hammersmith, for allowing me to use the theatre as a backdrop to this story, and for the advice and help they gave me along the way.

Writing might be a solitary occupation but getting published is a group effort, and I can't let this opportunity to acknowledge the debt I owe to various people who've helped in the process slip.

Thanks to Tess for your support and helpful suggestions. I'm also very grateful to Tony Collins, Pen Wilcock, Jessica Tinker, Sheila Jacobs, the team at Lion Fiction, for their support and help.

I owe a continuing debt to Ann Murphy, Gordon Berry, and Dave Howard of the Brent and Harrow Coroner's office for their help and advice on police procedure – thanks, guys.

As this book is set in the pop world, I needed "insider" advice on how road crews work and for this I am indebted to Richard Bryce, a former roadie himself, who patiently answered all my questions.

Did you catch D.I. Costello's first case in
Game, Set and Murder?

ELIZABETH FLYNN

"A witty and intriguing whodunnit."
– Cindy Kent, broadcaster

"The aces keep coming chapter
by chapter."
– Tony Jasper, author

GAME, SET
and MURDER

A Mystery for
D.I. Costello

D.I. Costello returns in
Dead Gorgeous

*It's the first day of Wimbledon. And a dead body
is lying on Court 19.*

Newly-promoted detective inspector Angela Costello
recognizes the dead man as Croatian champion-turned-
coach, Petar Belic. A double grand-slam winner, Petar
was famous, and much loved.

However, Petar had an ex-wife who wanted him back;
a girlfriend who wouldn't let him go; a business partner
with secrets. Then there was the temperamental leading
Brit, Stewart Bickerstaff, whom Petar had been coaching.

"The aces keep coming chapter by chapter."
– *Tony Jasper*, author

"A witty and intriguing whodunnit."
– *Cindy Kent*, broadcaster

ISBN 978 1 78264 072 1 | e-ISBN 978 1 78264 073 8

D.I. Costello returns in
Dead Gorgeous

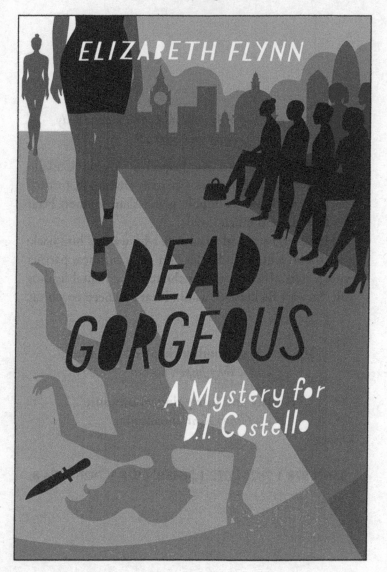

ELIZABETH FLYNN

DEAD
GORGEOUS

*A Mystery for
D.I. Costello*

Kirsty Manners is young, beautiful, and ambitious.
And dead.

Kirsty was trying to make it in the fashion world. As the in-house model for Ivano King and having dated the great designer himself, she believed she was well on her way.

But Kirsty is found dead in her flat one Sunday afternoon, and D.I. Angela Costello is called to the scene.

Kirsty has left behind a lovesick ex-boyfriend and a jealous flatmate. And what about King's new girlfriend, who openly admits she has a reason to wish Kirsty dead?

Behind the flawless make-up and gleaming catwalks, Angela's enquiries uncover theft, drug addiction, prostitution – and suddenly her own life could be in danger…

"Flynn creates an appealing detective in Angela Costello. She find solutions because she cares about people. Let's hope there's more of her to come."
– *Publishers Weekly*

ISBN 978 1 78264 131 5 | e-ISBN 978 1 78264 132 2

Also from Lion Fiction:
THE JAZZ FILES

THE
JAZZ FILES
POPPY DENBY
INVESTIGATES

Fiona Veitch Smith

"It stands for Jazz Files," said Rollo. "It's what we call any story that has a whiff of high society scandal but can't yet be proven... you never know when a skeleton in the closet might prove useful."

Set in 1920, *The Jazz Files* introduces aspiring journalist Poppy Denby, who arrives in London to look after her ailing Aunt Dot, an infamous suffragette. Dot encourages Poppy to apply for a job at *The Daily Globe*, but on her first day a senior reporter is killed and Poppy is tasked with finishing his story. It involves the mysterious death of a suffragette seven years earlier, about which some powerful people would prefer that nothing be said...

Through her friend Delilah Marconi, Poppy is introduced to the giddy world of London in the Roaring Twenties, with its flappers, jazz clubs, and romance. Will she make it as an investigative journalist, in this fast-paced new city? And will she be able to unearth the truth before more people die?

"What a delight to escape into the world of the irrepressible Poppy Denby in this cleverly-plotted debut."
– *Ruth Downie*, author of the *Medicus* series

ISBN 978 1 78264 175 9 | e-ISBN 978 1 78264 176 6